TWICEBORN

MARINA FINLAYSON

FINESSE SOLUTIONS

Cover design by Karri Klawiter
Formatting by Polgarus Studio

Published by Finesse Solutions Pty Ltd
2017/12

Author's note: This book was written and produced in Australia and uses British/Australian spelling conventions, such as "colour" instead of "color", and "-ise" endings instead of "-ize" on words like "realise"

National Library of Australia Cataloguing-in-Publication entry:

Finlayson, Marina, author.
Twiceborn / Marina Finlayson (author).
9780994239105 (paperback)
Finlayson, Marina. Proving; Book 1.
Paranormal fiction, Australian.
A823.4

For Mum and Dad.
Wish you could have been here to see this.

CHAPTER ONE

Glass is right up there with mankind's great inventions, like the wheel, penicillin and chocolate. Not only can you see *through* it, but you can look *into* it, and a shop window, even tinselled-up and sprayed with fake snow for the silly season, gives a great reflected view of what's behind you. In my case, that was Centre Court in all its Christmassy glory, and two guys showing way too much interest in a pregnant woman.

Giant baubles hung from the ceiling behind me, and a dozen white kangaroos hauled Santa's sleigh across the back of a temporary stage area, the only concession to the summery reality of Christmas in Australia. Santa himself had retired to the North Pole for another year, and his throne with its posse of photographers had been replaced by racks of bargain swimwear, much more suited to the season than snowmen and furs. The place was jumping with people, all out to find a great deal in the post-Christmas sales, as if they hadn't had enough of shopping before Christmas. Madness. Throw the word "bargain" around a few times, and people will swarm the tiredest old dreck like bees in search of a new hive. Or maybe locusts, ready to strip the place bare.

They even buzzed like swarming insects. Voices raised in conversation and laughter, plus the occasional shrieks of a tired child, formed a background roar that still failed to drown out the tired tinkle of Christmas music piped over the top. I'd only been here ten minutes and already I'd heard *White Christmas* twice. Two times too many in my book.

Without turning I scanned the reflected crowds heaving behind me, one hand on the small of my supposedly pregnant back. My two tails still followed.

One stood in front of a big touch-screen centre directory, pretending to be absorbed in locating the shop of his choice. Did they have a shop for spies here? Spooks "R" Us, maybe? He was a smallish guy, mid-thirties, receding brown hair. His mate was taller, a little younger, and too cool to take his sunnies off indoors. He was outside the jeans shop opposite me, pretending to talk on his mobile phone. Or perhaps he really was talking to someone.

Yeah, we've got her in sight. She's checking out the shops. Doesn't know we're watching her. Sure, Boss, I'll let you know as soon as she meets her contact.

Bet Boss wouldn't be pleased about the sunnies thing. Making yourself look like a tosser was a personal choice, of course, but it meant Sunnies Dude stood out from the crowd. Despite the heat and glare outside, no one else in here wore sunglasses. What did they teach these guys in spy school? Didn't he know he should be trying to blend in?

I meandered away, dragging my tails behind me. Beats me how I always managed to acquire them on these jobs. As if they had a sixth sense or something. You'd pick up the package with no one in sight, but before ten minutes had passed, hey presto! Someone would be following you.

Being stalked by strangers is an odd feeling. Guaranteed to get the adrenalin pumping, at least, so that's something. The old fight-or-flight instinct kicks in, bypassing the brain altogether, so for a while I remember what it's like to feel alive. Not that they ever do anything but watch. They only want to find out where the package is going.

It's my job to make sure they don't.

Don't ask me what's in the packages. Ben won't tell, though he promised me it's nothing illegal. I figure there's just some super-secretive people around. If it floats their boat to sneak secret messages around Sydney, well, good luck to them. As long as they pay me I really couldn't give a crap.

One time I peeked. I didn't mean to, but they're these thick beige envelopes, nice quality but kind of lacking in the glue department. They're always sealed with a blob of red wax. Fancy, but not terribly practical—sometimes the whole blob of wax comes right away from the envelope.

So I had a look, in case it was full of white powder, or hundred dollar bills, or something equally dodgy. I may not care about much any more but no money on earth would get me to deliver drugs. But I couldn't even tell what it was—a roughly disk-shaped piece of shiny hard something. It didn't look like any plastic I'd ever seen, and there was nothing written on it, nothing to explain why anyone would give a toss who received such a thing. But clearly someone did.

I threaded my way through the crowds. Some of them saw my enormous belly and gave way for me. The trick was remembering to walk like a pregnant woman instead of striding out in my usual fashion.

The food court lay ahead, tucked behind two monstrous escalators. The aroma of hot chips and deep-fried everything wafted toward me and my stomach growled, reminding me I'd forgotten lunch again.

"Mum!" a child's voice screeched.

Instinctively I turned toward the sound, and my heart clenched as I glimpsed a mop of light brown curls through the swirl of bodies. Only for a moment, but it was enough to set my pulse hammering in my throat. I stopped, and a woman bumped into me, apologising when she saw my pregnant belly, though it wasn't her fault.

When would I learn? I drew a deep, shaky breath. Lachie was gone. It would never again be his voice calling *Mum* in a crowd, never be his curly head I glimpsed from the corner of my eye, yet still I saw him everywhere. The turn of a head, a piping childish voice, even a T-shirt in his favourite blue and white stripes—anything could stop me with a hammer blow to the heart, even now, seven months after the accident.

I'd dreaded Christmas in my empty house. *It's not good to spend Christmas alone*, Ben had said. *You'll feel better if you come up and see the family, Katie*, Mum had said. Maybe they were right. I'd gotten as far as booking a flight, but in the end I couldn't do it. I couldn't watch my nephews and nieces opening their presents when this time last year Lachie had been with them, tearing the wrapping off yet another box of Lego with squeals of unholy delight. *Look, Mum, it's the Dark Fortress!* His bright curls had bounced with excitement, his mind already leaping forward to the thrill of the post-lunch construction even as he reached for the next present in the stack.

Turned out, Christmas was no worse than any other day. Pain was pain, regardless of the date on the calendar. I pushed away the memory of his glowing little face. Deep breaths. Okay, focus.

A sign beside the escalators pointed down a service corridor for toilets, phones and lifts. I threaded my way through rows of bright yellow tables filled with munching people and entered the corridor, pursued by the smell of Chinese takeaway. Skirting the crowd waiting for the lifts, I headed for the toilets. At the door I stopped for a woman coming out and threw a casual glance back the way I'd come. Sunnies Dude had stationed himself at the entrance to the corridor. His partner was coming my way.

I slipped inside, my heart stuttering a little. Surely he wouldn't follow me into the ladies' toilet? I waited in line—there was always a line when the sales were on—and watched the door.

I had nothing to use as a weapon, and a quick glance showed nothing useful in the gleaming white room either. The soap dispensers were secured to the sinks and the hand dryers to the wall, their roar muffling a saccharine rendition of *Silent*

Night. No respite from the Christmas schmaltz anywhere, not even in the bathroom.

Geez, what was my problem? These clowns never did anything. No need to be jumping at shadows. But when the door opened, I had my handbag ready to swing.

A tiny Indian woman entered, a little surprised to find me glaring at her. No sign of a marauding bald guy. I turned away, letting out a breath I hadn't even realised I'd been holding. He must have gone to guard the other end of the corridor, in case I went out that way.

As I reached the head of the line, one of those mother-and-child stalls with two toilets, one big and one small, opened up. It smelled strongly of pine air freshener and something much more toilet-y that the freshener couldn't quite cover up. Little people don't have such good aim and they tend to get distracted at critical moments. At home I still had a ping pong ball bobbing in my toilet, from the days when I'd been encouraging Lachie to focus on aiming properly.

I hung my bag on the hook on the back of the door and got to work.

First off was the curly black wig. Thank God for that. The shops were air-conditioned, but the wig was synthetic, and wearing it felt like walking around with a hot water bottle on my head. It had been hot as hell outside in the bright summer sun. I unpinned my sweaty hair and fanned it out, letting the air circulate.

Next came the dress, floral and tentlike. I wadded it up and shoved it into my handbag after the wig, then reached round to the straps that held the prosthetic belly on. The rip of velcro heralded sweet relief as I eased the heavy thing off.

In the hollow of the fake belly nestled a big roomy carry-all containing my new outfit, a short denim skirt and a black top that revealed my own flat stomach, the taut abs a new feature. Had to do something to help me sleep at night, and in the end Ben had convinced me that exercise was a better option than alcohol. Smart guy. I sat on the toilet seat to strap on the red stilettos that completed the outfit.

Maybe the shoes were a mistake. Ben had looked worried when I'd picked them out of our stock. But then, "worried about Kate" was a pretty common expression on Ben's face these days.

"What are you going to do if you have to run in those?"

I'd snorted. "There won't be any running."

I wasn't feeling so cocky now but it was too late for second-guessing. The black flats I'd worn as the pregnant woman would spoil the whole effect. I shrugged. What did it matter anyway? When the worst thing you could ever imagine has already happened to you, it puts everything else in perspective.

I buckled my shoes and gathered everything up. My original handbag and clothes went into the hollow of the fake belly, then I stuffed the lot into the carry-all and headed for the basins.

Like every other woman there, I checked my face as the cool water splashed over my hands, leaning in close for a good look. Mirrors are probably the best use ever of glass. How did we ever manage without them?

The concealer under my eyes was holding up despite the heat. Just as well. The dark circles were a permanent feature these days and they made me look more thirty-nine than my real age of twenty-nine. Weary green eyes stared back at me. Still, no man would be looking at my face in this outfit.

I glanced down in time to see a red swirl against the white basin as the water disappeared down the drain. Weird. I turned my hands over, curious. Palms clean. Backs clean. Hang on … I caught my breath, stomach knotting uneasily. I dug at the brown stuff under my nails, creating more red tinges in the water. What did *that* come from? I lifted one wet hand to my face and sniffed.

The unmistakeable iron scent of blood caused a wave of dizziness so strong I had to clutch at the basin to stay upright, swaying on my red stilettos. What the *hell*? A sudden vision of my hands, covered in blood, made my stomach heave in protest. I could see them so clearly, reaching … reaching for something. Bloody hell. Had I finally lost it? Was I having *visions* now? My sight blurred and prickled with darkness, the bathroom disappearing around me. No, not visions. Visions didn't come with bonus traces of blood under your fingernails. I clenched my hands on the cold enamel of the sink, holding myself up by sheer force of will while I waited in the spinning darkness. My whole body broke out in a hot sweat.

"Are you all right?" A hand on my arm. I turned my head toward the voice, vision returning in speckles of light. The Indian lady hung on to me, though she barely reached my shoulder. I don't know what she thought she'd do if I fell.

"Yeah," I lied. "Just a little dizzy."

"Maybe you're dehydrated. It's a very hot day, you know." Her tone was severe, as if I might not have noticed the heat, and what are the young people coming to these days? "You must drink plenty of water in this weather."

"You're right," I said, splashing my burning face. Summer in Sydney was always sweltering. Maybe I was coming down with something. *Sure, something that puts blood under your fingernails.* I felt ill. "Thanks."

I checked my reflection again. The concealer definitely needed some work now. My face was pale and sweaty, and mascara had oozed onto one cheek. My eyes had a haunted look, but that was nothing new. I dug my makeup out and got to work, ignoring the way my hands trembled. A slash of red lipstick. Mascara. *Come on, Kate, pull yourself together.* I scraped my hair back into a no-nonsense ponytail and clipped a fake fall of hair to it. It matched my own auburn colour and turned my modest ponytail into a luscious length that reached my waist.

Much better. The woman in the mirror looked maybe twenty-five. She was no supermodel, but dressed like this she was definitely a head-turner. Most importantly, she looked nothing like the dark-haired pregnant woman in the frumpy maternity dress who'd waddled into the bathroom five minutes ago.

Time to put it to the test. I had a job to do, and I could worry about mysterious blood later. With the heavy carry-all settled comfortably on my shoulder, I sashayed out of the bathroom and down the corridor, putting a little extra swing into my hips as those red stilettos tapped their way past the crowd at the lifts. I breezed past Sunnies Dude, still stationed at the opening of the corridor, on the look-out for a pregnant lady who would never leave that bathroom.

My swaying denim skirt and long legs had the desired effect. His head swivelled, checking me out as I went past. I concentrated on projecting a calm I didn't feel as my stomach roiled, but I doubt his gaze got as far as my face. I wondered how long they'd wait before one of them had to brave the ladies' bathroom in search of their missing woman. Wouldn't want to draw the short straw on that one.

I strode away to make the drop, ponytail swishing against my bare skin. As I left the centre the heat hit me like a furnace blast. Even down here in the canyons between Sydney's skyscrapers summer lay hot and heavy. A busker with a saxophone made a half-hearted attempt at jazz, looking like he'd rather be almost anywhere else. At least it wasn't Christmas carols.

Sweat sprang out on my face, under my armpits—even my feet soon felt sticky in their strappy red heels. Not the greatest choice for walking. The balls of my feet were burning already. Thank God I didn't have far to go.

I ducked into an arcade that led through to George Street. Where *was* I going? My steps faltered. Stopped. What in hell was wrong with me? How could I forget something like that? Shoppers and office workers sneaking home early streamed past as I scrabbled through my carry-all for the familiar beige envelope in a sudden panic. I couldn't even remember seeing it as I'd changed. Some courier I was.

But it was there, right down at the bottom under wigs and stomachs and all the rest of my gear. Maybe a little crumpled. If pristine condition was part of the deal I was screwed. I breathed a sigh of relief as I hauled it out, then stopped short at the address on the front.

Well, not even an address. Just a name.

Mine.

"What the hell?" I leaned back on the glass shopfront of the nearest boutique, feeling the thumping bass beat of their music vibrating against my back, and stared at the shaky handwriting. *Kate.* Nothing else. No address, not even a surname. Could it be some other Kate?

I turned it over and broke the thick wax seal. Who was I kidding? It had to be for me.

I drew out the single sheet of paper inside. No weird shiny disks this time.

You are in danger, it said. *Do not go home or try to contact anybody. Go straight to a hotel and wait for me.*

That was it. Frowning, I turned it over to be sure there was no more. No signature, or any explanation of how the writer meant to find me at some random hotel. And I was supposed to take this seriously?

I shoved it back in my bag. Yeah, right. Like *that* was going to happen.

CHAPTER TWO

By the time I got back to the The Dress-up Box, that sick feeling I'd had in the bathroom had come back big time. My stomach had been hesitating between diarrhoea and throwing up all the way back from town, but now it seemed pretty committed to the throwing up idea.

Ben had set up The Dress-up Box in an old warehouse space, cool and cavernous, with windows along the back wall too high to open and too dusty to let in much but the vaguest hint of daylight. Row after row of costumes packed the floor, leaving a warren of little pathways in between. Magic happened down those paths. Anything from a romantic velvet ball gown to a Cavalier's feathered hat could be waiting around the next corner. We stocked wigs, shoes, swords, hats and any other item of fancy dress you could imagine. Our neighbours were smash repairers and auto electricians, but being in an industrial area meant cheap rent, and the business didn't rely on passing trade anyway. No one experiences a sudden desire to dress up as Zorro or Cleopatra just because they see a costume shop.

I paid off the taxi and staggered in through the big roller door at the end of the drive. We left it open all day anyway, to let in some light and air, so most people ignored the front door.

Ben perched on his customary stool behind the counter, face stuck in another pulpy thriller. He wouldn't read a decent book if you paid him, but show him some third-rate Clive Cussler knock-off, and he was your man. He'd let his dark hair grow long enough that its natural curl gave him the look of a Greek god. All he needed was a laurel wreath and a white robe, though he cut a pretty fine figure just the same in jeans and a T-shirt.

He looked up at the sound of my heels on the concrete floor and laid the book down.

"How'd it go?"

I wobbled to a stop, one hand groping for something to lean on. The rough brick wall was all that held me up while I focused on not heaving my guts all over the floor. Dust motes spun lazily in the late-afternoon sunlight streaming in through the roller door, and my vision danced too. Ben's handsome face flickered as if I were watching him on a badly tuned TV station.

"Kate? You okay?"

He came round the counter in a smooth movement, long legs eating up the distance between us in three steps, hands reaching out to steady me. A familiar scenario. Ben had been holding me together for months now. Dark, worried eyes searched my face as I breathed in the familiar woodsy scent of his aftershave. He smelled of forests and bracing fresh air. His hands were warm on my bare arms as he half-carried me past racks of costumes to the tiny staff kitchen at the back.

He pushed me into a chair and felt my forehead, hand lingering almost in a caress. "What's the matter? You're all clammy."

My skin prickled with heat, as if a million tiny spiders crawled on me. I shut my eyes against a wave of nausea and lay my head back against the cool bricks behind me. "Feel sick."

"Getting-a-cold sick or throwing-up sick?"

"Throwing-up sick."

"Let's get you to the bathroom, then."

I felt his hands on my arms, ready to help me out of the chair, but I shook my head. Even that much movement hurt.

"Just let me sit here."

"Hang on. I'll get you a bucket."

He left and I heard him clattering around in the laundry room next to the kitchen. Thank God for Ben. Always so practical.

It wouldn't be the first time he'd held a bucket for me either. I'd given him plenty of practice in the first few weeks after the accident, trying to drink the pain away, or drink myself to death. I hadn't much cared which. What was the point of existence without Lachie? I'd been lost in those first agonising days, and only Ben's persistence had pulled me through.

My sister had tried to help, but she still had kids, and I didn't, and it formed an impossible barrier between us. Mum tried too but eventually she had to go home to Brisbane, which left me sitting alone in Lachie's room drinking till Ben had dragged me out of there with a job and a bracing, no-nonsense kind of friendship.

"Here." He shoved a bucket at me, and I had to open my eyes. My vision darkened in that same alarming fade-to-grey thing it had done in the bathroom at the shopping centre. I tried to focus on his face. His eyes were a deep, warm brown, now full of worry. He had lashes any girl would kill for—long and lusciously curled. Seemed a criminal waste. He steadied me as I swayed on the chair. "You're not going to pass out on me, are you?"

"Can't make any promises."

"What happened?" He tested my forehead with the back of his hand again, checking my temperature. I inhaled his comforting pine forest smell as he leaned close. "You were fine when you left here."

"I don't know. It came on all of a sudden, after I changed disguises."

"You had no trouble, then, with the outfit?" He grinned. "No running required?"

"Told you it'd work. You guys are so easily distracted."

"What about the pick-up? What was the big rush?"

The pick-up had been booked with less than an hour's notice. I'd barely had time to pull my outfit together and make it to the address—a house in The Rocks—in time. There'd been trees there. Lots of trees.

I frowned, letting my head fall back against the wall again as I thought. Yes, lots of trees, and … what else? I remembered a garden, I remembered arriving at the shopping centre afterwards; I even recalled when I'd first spotted the two guys tailing me. But in between? Nothing.

"Kate? You falling asleep on me?"

Why couldn't I remember? The image of my arms, red to the elbow, dripping blood—that was clear enough. As if I'd been bathing in gore. I shuddered. That couldn't have happened. Who forgets a thing like that? But then where had the blood under my nails come from?

"I can't remember."

"You can't remember what was so urgent?"

"No." My voice was very small. "Can't remember any of it."

I opened my eyes. Ben crouched beside me, lanky body crowding the tiny room, bucket at the ready. He leaned forward, urgency in his gaze.

"Have you still got the necklace I gave you?"

I blinked. "What's that got to do with anything?"

"Have you got it?"

"Geez, what's your problem?" The necklace sported a little silver man with a Robin Hood-style hat and tunic and tiny wings on the back of his sandals. The detail was pretty good for something so small—the figure was no bigger than the first joint of my little finger. I pulled the charm on its silver chain out of my singlet and he sat back, the urgency gone.

He'd given it to me when I'd first graduated from manning the shop counter to going on these odd little courier jobs of his. He had one too, on a leather thong round his tanned throat.

"Never take it off," he'd insisted. "Wear it the whole time you're on the job."

"What for?" I'd asked, watching it spin on the end of its silver chain.

"It's always been a good luck charm for me." His dark eyes had softened. "God knows you could use a bit of luck for a change."

Well, I couldn't argue with that, and if it made him happy it was no skin off my nose, though I couldn't see why he was bringing it up now.

"It's nothing." He frowned, lost in thought for a moment. "Tell me everything you can remember."

Well, that wouldn't take long. I strained after odd bits of memory that wouldn't stay still to be caught.

"I went to the address. There was a garden—a big garden." Big for The Rocks, anyway. Most of the houses there were well over a hundred years old and all crammed in cheek by jowl with their neighbours in neat little rows. "I remember lots of trees. Someone was waiting for me."

"Man or woman?"

"Don't know." I clenched my fists. What the hell was the matter with me? I tried to bring back a face, a voice, anything, but there was nothing but fog. "I guess they gave me the package, because I definitely had one when I got to the shopping centre. Oh, boy, did I have one."

His gaze was suddenly sharp, predatory. "What does that mean?"

"It was addressed to me. A note telling me not to go home, for God's sake."

"A note? On normal paper?"

"No, on the flayed skin of virgins. Of course on normal paper!"

He rose, clearly agitated. I was missing something here, but before I could ask, he thrust the bucket into my hands, looming over me. "Where is it now?"

The intensity of his expression was alarming.

"In my bag." I gestured vaguely out into the shop.

In a moment he was back with the bag, note in hand. He scanned the brief message. "Shit."

"What do you mean, 'shit'? Do you know who it's from? Why should I check into a random hotel on the orders of some lunatic who won't even sign their name?"

He said nothing, staring down at the note as if he could read a whole novel in its scant lines.

"Don't give me that poker face, buddy. If you know what's going on you'd better tell me."

He looked up, forehead creased in a frown. "Makes no sense to me."

Liar. I could tell, the way his eyes didn't quite meet mine. All those years of practice being married to Jason had well and truly fine-tuned my personal lie detector.

"Don't bullshit me, Ben." I put the bucket down and surged to my feet. Marvellous how a little rush of righteous anger could make me forget my heaving stomach and pounding head. I glared at him, nose to nose in the tiny kitchen.

Or nose to collarbone, at least. He towered over me, which meant I always ended up looking like a Chihuahua yapping at a Great Dane when I had a go at him.

"A person I don't remember gives me a cryptic note saying I'm in danger. How is that possible? A good half-hour of my life has simply disappeared into a black hole. Gone. Have I been drugged? What am I supposed to do now? Go to the police and accuse someone I don't know of doing something I don't remember? They'd lock me up."

"You can stay at my place." His deep voice had the soothing tone I'd heard so many times before when I'd cried on his shoulder. Now it just made me mad.

"So you think I *am* in danger? Why?"

"Look—"

The bell on the counter dinged. "Yoo-hoo! Anyone there?"

"I'll get it," said Ben. "You stay here. I'll be right back."

I glared at his back as he escaped into the shop. Talk about saved by the bell. He was my closest friend—one of my only friends, since the accident—but how much did I really know about his past? Only that he'd been Jason's best friend till Jason had dumped us both, and that he ran a costume shop and occasionally a rather peculiar courier service. Like me, he had one sister and a couple of nieces, and he kept pretty much to himself. No girlfriend, despite looking like Eric Bana's sexier twin.

And that was about it. He was a pretty private guy. I'd trust him with my life, but I knew I couldn't trust him on this. He knew something he wasn't telling.

In the shop the customer asked for Elizabethan costume ideas and their voices receded as Ben led him through the racks to the English historical section. There were a lot of choices on that rack. They could be lost in Elizabethan England for a while.

I massaged my aching temples. I could wait here, but if I didn't get a headache tablet soon my head would explode, and the kitchen cupboards held nothing but a couple of chipped mugs and some teabags and biscuits. Was I really going to let some nutjob keep me from my own comfy bed and well-stocked medicine cabinet?

I grabbed my bag and headed out the back door. If Ben wanted me to stay at his place, at least I'd get a chance to worm the truth out of him—but I'd need to collect some clothes first. Surely it wouldn't hurt to duck home for a few minutes. I could grab a couple of Panadol for my head at the same time.

My little car beeped a welcome as I unlocked it. I wouldn't be long—and maybe if I could get this headache under control I'd be able to figure out what had leaked out the hole in my brain.

***

I drove home with one eye squinted shut against the pain. My head felt like someone in heavy boots was trying to kick their way out of my skull. When I finally pulled into my driveway and cut the engine, I dropped my pounding head on to the steering wheel, trying to work up the energy to open the door. Maybe I'd sit in the car for the rest of my life instead.

Only the siren call of Panadol got me to open my eyes again.

I shrieked. A thick coating of blood dripped from my fingers. I slammed them against the wheel and the blood disappeared, leaving me shaking. Enough with the crazy! I jack-knifed out of the car and stood panting, leaning against its sun-baked metal.

It was still hot. The cicadas were going for their lives, screeching up a storm in the trees. There'd be no relief till it got dark, which at this time of year wasn't till after eight. Daylight saving was a great idea, but it had its downsides. I'd certainly had my issues with it when Lachie was alive. Trying to get him to go to sleep on summer nights was always a battle.

"But Muuum! it's not night-time yet!" No kid wants to go to bed when the sun's still shining through his window.

"I'll make it night-time," I'd say, pulling the blind down with a flourish. As a single mum, I was always desperate for some child-free time back then. Ironic, isn't it? I'd give anything now to have that time over again. "Abracadabra! See? Night-time! Now go to sleep."

He'd lie down again, his bright curly head sweaty on the pillow, and try some other strategy to keep me there. A drink of water, another story—or a sudden compelling need to tell me every last detail of his latest Lego construction. The kid could talk underwater and he was never chattier than five minutes after bedtime.

"Goodnight, Monster."

"'Night, Mum."

I sighed and pushed myself upright. Panadol, here I come.

Tanya was watering her roses next door. "Hi, Kate!"

I gave her a little wave and kept walking, but she came over to the fence, dark hair bouncing with the force of her strides and her fierce tugs on the hose to make it stretch the distance. She was tiny, with all the energy of a Jack Russell and just as exhausting.

"I haven't seen you in weeks," she said. "How are you?"

Tanya was the only person besides Ben still trying to be my friend. Everyone else had taken the hint and drifted out of my life, but Tanya didn't do hints. She threw herself one-hundred-and-ten per cent into any project, including her current favourite: rehabilitating me. We'd been close once, with her oldest starting school at the same time as Lachie. The kids had been in and out of our houses all the time, treating both like home. I didn't need the reminder of her happy family in my face, but admitting defeat was another thing Tanya didn't do.

"Oh, you know," I said, trying to keep it vague. My pounding head wasn't up for one of Tanya's long chats. "Been busy at work."

"You still working at the costume shop? With that good-looking fella?"

"Ben. Yeah, he's great." Except when he kept secrets from me.

"How are things going? Any chemistry there?" Tanya played the hose over her azalea bushes, pretending it was a casual question, but I knew her better. "He's pretty hot."

"You think so?" I knew if I agreed with her she'd be planning our wedding before she'd finished the watering. Hey, I had eyes, didn't I? I could see the man was gorgeous, with his black curls and chocolate brown eyes.

Since Jason and I broke up Ben had been the glue that held my shattered world together. Even more so after the accident. But did people truly think it was that easy? *Sure, my husband dumped me, then killed our child with his lousy driving, but I'll just jump into bed with the next hot guy who happens along.* Romance wasn't exactly top of my priorities. Love was a country I wasn't planning on travelling to again. If other people wanted to go there, well, good luck to them. They could send me a postcard.

As for Ben, he hadn't had a steady girl in a while, but I'm pretty sure he'd held a bucket for me a few too many times to be interested. Maybe if I'd met him before Jason, things might have been different. Sometimes I wondered. But it was too late now.

Besides, he had such crap taste in novels. It would never work.

"We're just friends," I said, pinching the bridge of my nose between thumb and forefinger. My sinuses were about ready to explode. Even the gentle patter of water on the leaves sounded like thunder to my aching head.

"Rubbish. I've seen the way he looks at you—like he could eat you up with ice cream on top."

"He does not. Truly, we're friends, that's all."

"Shame." Tanya grinned. "He could fit my costume any old time."

"I'm sure Roy would be thrilled to hear you say that." There was no getting away from Tanya when she wanted to talk. I sighed and gave in. A couple of minutes wouldn't kill me. Probably. "Your roses look great."

Her whole garden looked fabulous, in fact, in complete contrast to the scorched-earth vibe going on in mine. Tanya had a green thumb for sure. All her plants were the vivid green of blooming health.

Water from the hose dripped through the leaves and soaked into the rich loamy soil, releasing an earthy scent that teased at my memory. I'd walked down a shaded path past garden beds bursting with colour and breathed in that same smell just recently. Today? A woman had waited under a tree in dappled sunlight. She'd had her back to me, but as she turned the image froze, like a DVD on pause, and try as I might I couldn't find the play button.

Had she given me the envelope? And maybe a spiked drink? Did that mean the blood was hers?

Tanya chattered away, smiling at her garden like a proud mother. It took me a minute to realise she'd asked me a question.

"Well?" she prompted. "Would you like to come in and have dinner with us one night this week?"

Dinner with Tanya and Roy and their two adorable little girls? I'd rather chew my own arm off.

"Oh, that'd be nice." I'm sure she knew I was lying, but even after seven months I wasn't ready. Time for another lame excuse. "It's just—I'm kind of busy at the moment, with work and everything. Maybe some other time."

Sometimes I thought it would be easier if I moved away, somewhere people didn't know me. But then I'd lose my last connection to Lachie. He'd lived here his whole short life.

I'd brought Lachie home here from hospital, a red, squalling newborn, and watched him sleep with the exhausted wonder common to new mothers everywhere. He'd fallen down those front steps when he first started toddling around, all pudgy legs and fat inquisitive fingers, and he'd carried a scar on his chin for the rest of his life.

It had been a fine house once, and it still had good bones if you looked beyond the peeling paint and sagging gutters. I loved the old-fashioned walled veranda, its high ceilings and roomy bedrooms. I loved its dark hardwood floors and the cheerful green exterior it showed the street. But I loved it most for the memories it held.

So many memories: story times and bath times; meal time battles—what *is* it with kids and broccoli?—tears shed and kissed away; homework at the kitchen table with the afternoon sun streaming in the window. Every room echoed with his non-stop chatter and the clatter of small impatient feet.

I could no more leave this place than fly.

But one day soon I'd have to tackle the garden. More grass rioted through the garden beds than on the patchy lawn, and the only time any of it got watered was when it rained. Summer in Sydney had scorched the whole thing to a brown and desiccated crisp. That this pile of neglect festered next door to the best garden in the street—maybe in the whole suburb—was just the icing on the cake. I definitely didn't share Tanya's green thumb.

The smell of her roses was overpowering. If I could remember the damn roses from this afternoon, why couldn't I remember anything else? Except the blood, of course, but that could hardly have been real, surely. My head pounded with effort, and a wave of nausea hit me. My stomach gurgled, loud enough for Tanya to hear.

She frowned. "I hope you're feeding yourself properly." Like a terrier, she refused to give up. "We're going away on Monday for a few weeks. How about we make a date for when we get back, the last week of January?"

Damn. My brain was so fried. I was still struggling for an excuse when my mouth abruptly started filling with saliva. Oh, shit. I was going to chuck.

"Sorry, ate some bad sushi!"

I clapped a hand to my mouth and rushed up the path to the front door, leaving Tanya gaping after me.

Swallowing hard, I fumbled with the key in the lock. Sweat broke out on my forehead as I staggered inside, kicking the door shut behind me. Oh, God. The bathroom was too far.

I fell to my knees and chucked my guts up all over the tiled floor of the foyer.

When I was done I sat back on my heels, dazed and panting, and surveyed the mess. Why are there always carrots? I didn't remember eating any carrots. And what the hell was *that*?

A black stone, the size of my thumbnail and covered with silver tracery, lay amid the rest of it. I *definitely* didn't remember eating that.

CHAPTER THREE

I'm wearing long red evening gloves of shiny satin and holding a knife. Not a harmless knife for peeling apples, either, nor even a domestic "let's cut up the veggies for our home-cooked dinner" kind of knife. It looks more like a hunting knife, with a wide lethal blade and a slight curve to its glinting edge.

Wait. That's not satin. It's blood; blood that gleams and drips in the sunlight. Blood coating both arms to the elbow, thick and viscous. It glues my hand to the knife's hilt. The iron tang of it is in my nostrils—as is the heady scent of roses in full bloom. I'm kneeling on the ground, surrounded by flowers, grass prickling my bare knees.

Yes, that's it, says the voice, panting, trembling with the effort of forming words. That's it. Now reach in.

I lay the knife down, not thinking, compelled to obey. The voice fills my head as my vision narrows to the blood. So much of it—and I see my hand reaching, reaching ...

I came back to myself with a gasp, the floor tiles of my own foyer smooth and cool beneath my cheek. I didn't remember blacking out.

Stretched out beside a pile of vomit—that was a new low. Could have been worse, I guess—I might have been lying *in* the vomit.

Head still spinning, I sat up. Movement made me retch again, but there was nothing left to bring up. After a moment I staggered to my feet and made it all the way down the hall to the kitchen. I wrenched open the medicine cupboard, knocking bottles over as I scrabbled for the Panadol. A shower of small boxes cascaded on to the floor. *Come on, come on.* Any minute my brain would explode right out of my head. I'd had bad headaches before but this was something else. Where the hell was the Panadol? I swept the lot out on to the bench with a crash. Nothing. Damn it, how could I be out?

Maybe I'd left the box in my room. God, that was all the way at the front of the house.

It was only a small house, with two bedrooms and a bathroom opening off one side of the central hall and a lounge and dining room off the other. The kitchen and laundry were at the back. Nowhere was more than a few steps from anywhere else in the house, but at the moment that bedroom felt impossibly distant. Back in the hall, I found I couldn't even walk straight. Pain lanced through my head with every step. I lurched sideways against the closed door to Lachie's room, knocking his door hanger to the floor. He'd made it himself in preschool. *Keep Out unless I say your alloud to com in!!!* it shouted in his best five-year-old printing.

I steadied myself on the handle, leaning my head against the door for a moment. Cool wood soothed my burning forehead. I kept the blinds closed during the day to keep out the heat, and it was dark in the hallway. *I'm not coming in, Monster. Mummy's just resting here for a sec.*

I hadn't been inside for nearly four months. Tanya said it was unhealthy to leave it as if Lachie might walk back in any day, and I should let her box up all his things and put them away. Tanya didn't know what she was talking about.

As if out of sight was out of mind. As if I couldn't picture the whole room without even opening the damn door—his bed under the window with its Minecraft quilt cover, the ranks of Lego castles, spaceships and vehicles arrayed on the bookshelf, the comfy chair by the wardrobe where we'd sometimes snuggled up to read together but which mostly held more clothes than the wardrobe itself.

My days of lying on his bed sobbing might be over, but I wasn't ready to let go yet. Keeping the door shut was the best I could do. Knowing it was all still there was a weird kind of comfort, and if that was psychologically unhealthy, too bad.

After a moment, I felt capable of movement again and staggered down the shadowy hall, hands out for balance. My trailing fingers felt every bubble in the wallpaper, my whole body acutely sensitive, as if someone had turned up the volume on reality. When I reached my own room I sagged gratefully onto the bed and yanked the drawer of my bedside table open so hard the bedside lamp rocked.

The drawer bulged with junk—tangles of jewellery jumbled in together, bits and pieces of paperwork, old keys—but no headache tablets. Dammit. I flopped back on to the bed and wrapped the pillow round my pounding head. Now what?

I could go next door and ask Tanya, but then I'd have to face Tanya's manic cheerfulness again. Probably wouldn't get out of there without having to admire all the girls' latest artworks and certificates either—or even stay for dinner. The thought made me groan. I didn't have the energy. I'd have to walk down to the corner shop.

The delightful aroma of vomit drifted into the room as I debated. Ah, yes, that pile of sick still waited at the front door. If I turned my head I could see the edge of it from where I lay. Awesome.

Gritting my teeth, I heaved myself off the bed and down the hall again to the laundry for cleaning supplies. Back in the foyer, the black stone still lay there, defying reality with its impossible presence. How could I even have swallowed something that size in one piece?

Gingerly I picked it out of the mess, and a shock of static burned up my arm. I dropped it with a yelp. The damn thing zapped me!

When I'd finished the clean-up I took it to the bathroom to give it a scrub. This time I felt nothing when I picked it up. The silver lines winked at me, glittering under the bright bathroom lights. Embedded in the stone, they looked like tiny silver veins coursing through the black. The effect was quite pretty. I turned it over in my hand. It was warm to the touch, and very smooth. It would make a striking pendant—if I fancied decorating myself with things I'd chucked up, of course.

Something tickled at my memory, as if I should recognise this little piece of rock. I closed my fist around it, feeling its warmth. Holding it felt … comfortable, somehow. Right. I didn't want to leave it behind, so after I'd got myself changed and cleaned up I slipped it into my handbag and headed out to the corner store.

Going outside felt like stepping into a warm bath, and not in a good way. Hot and sticky, the air hung heavy with moisture. Summers in Sydney were always humid, unless you were rich enough to live right on the coast and catch the sea breezes. My neighbourhood was definitely not coastal. On a bad day it felt like living in a sauna, every breath drawing in almost as much water as air. The temperature had hit the high thirties earlier in the day, and it took a while to come down.

By the time I reached the corner of the street I was damp with sweat. Across the road I ducked through a small reserve, where my shadow stretched long across the rough ground in front of me. It would be dark soon. Bark crunched underfoot and cicadas screeched from the trees, the sound throbbing through the streets. They'd quieten down after dark but then the mosquitoes would come out to replace them. At least it would be cooler.

At the little row of shops in Curtin Road I headed straight for the tiny supermarket and bought Panadol. Outside I cracked open the packet straight away and dry-swallowed a couple. Relief couldn't come soon enough.

My phone rang as I stood there. Ben's number.

"Where did you get to? I thought you were going to wait for me. Suddenly every man and his dog wanted to hire a costume—it's been non-stop for the last hour—and I finally got rid of the last one and came to check on you and you were gone."

Ben's one of those people who expects others to do as they say. Not because he's controlling; it's just the way his mind works. If he always has the best ideas, it only seems logical to him that everyone else should fall in with his suggestions.

"I've got a shocking headache, so I headed home."

"But you're not home now. I just rang you there."

"What are you, my mother?"

"Don't be so prickly. I was worried, that's all. You didn't seem yourself. Where are you?"

"Down at the local shops, picking up some Panadol. I'd run out."

Shadows lengthened as the light leached from the sky. Might as well head home. The supermarket closed at eight; soon only the bottle shop and the takeaway joint would be open, and I wasn't interested in either. Nor were many others, judging by the handful of cars in the little parking strip outside the shops. I passed the darkened newsagent, then stepped aside abruptly to avoid a guy coming out of the Chinese takeaway. He muttered an apology.

"No worries." Then I did a double take. Ben said something, but I missed it in my shock. "Uh, Ben?" I lowered my voice, watching as the guy went into the bottle shop. "There's a guy here who's *glowing*."

"Glowing? What do you mean?"

Maybe I had a migraine. I'd never had one before, but I'd heard some sufferers saw flashing lights. Glowing guy was average height, probably early thirties, dark hair, kind of chunky. He wore jeans and a nondescript dark T-shirt. He looked like any regular guy picking up takeaway—except regular guys don't have a faint orange nimbus around them.

"Glowing. I don't know how else to describe it. He's got a—like an *aura* around him. Very faint."

In fact, I had to squint to see it against the lights in the shop. If it hadn't been nearly dark I probably wouldn't have noticed it in the first place. I lurked outside, pretending to be fascinated by the specials in the window while sneaking glances at the strange man. Yellowglen champagne for only $9.99 a bottle! A slab of Tooheys for $33.95! Imagine my excitement.

"What colour is it?"

What *colour*? That was unexpected. Better than *okay, I'm sending the nice men with the straitjacket*, but unexpected all the same.

"What does the colour matter? I'm seeing glowing people!"

"People?" His voice was urgent. Well, at least he was taking me seriously. "I thought you said one guy?"

I glanced around. A couple of teenage boys lounged against their car's bonnet outside the newsagent. They weren't glowing. Neither was the lady coming out of the bottle shop, or any of the people I could see inside. An uneasy feeling began to grow inside me. Guess I couldn't blame it on the headache, then. I'd never heard of a migraine *that* selective.

"Just the one. He's orange, if it makes any difference."

"What's he doing?"

"Buying a bottle of wine."

The guy on the checkout put the bottle into a paper bag, a bored look on his face. Guess *he* couldn't see any weird auras. Glowing guy pulled a twenty out of his wallet.

"Is he looking at you? Paying any special attention to you?"

"No."

I watched him put his wallet away and pick up the bag. As he came out of the shop I turned aside. His aura intensified the further he got from the lights of the bottle shop.

"Are there plenty of people around?"

"Yeah, I guess." The two teenagers on the bonnet of their car, a woman getting out of another one; the bottle shop with a handful of customers, plus the lady behind the counter in the supermarket. "A few."

"What's he doing now?"

"Getting into his car."

An ordinary guy, picking up Chinese and a bottle of wine for dinner. His aura, or nimbus, or whatever you want to call it, was more obvious in the darkened car. I could see he didn't actually glow; it was more like being outlined in light.

I watched him drive away. His blinker flick-flick-flicked as he turned the corner, then the sound of the engine receded into the distance.

"Okay. He's gone." I sucked in a deep breath, trying to calm my racing heart. "Mind telling me what that was all about?"

"Maybe you've got a touch of food poisoning. Did you eat anything unusual today?"

I laughed. *You mean besides a black stone? No, nothing strange at all.* "Ben, it's not food poisoning. Don't jerk me around. Something's going on and you know what it is. Just tell me."

There was a long pause. So long I thought the mobile had dropped out.

Finally he sighed. "Not while you stand around in the dark on your own. I'll meet you at your place in ten; I'm already on the way. Go straight home and lock yourself in, okay?"

"O-kaay. Should I be scared?" The vision of my hands dripping blood popped back into my throbbing head. Any *more* scared, that is.

"Just go home. I'll be there soon."

He hung up. Damn. I'd never realised before how good Ben was at speaking without actually saying anything. With that kind of skill he could run for parliament.

All the way home I watched for glowing people, jumping at every shadow, but saw nothing unusual. Just suburban streets full of ordinary houses, lit up against the gathering dusk. In some windows I saw the flickering lights of TVs. Others were still dark, their owners not yet home from work, or perhaps lucky enough to be holidaying on a beach somewhere instead.

Every time a car passed I shrank away from its headlights like a spooked cat. It was a relief to turn into my own driveway at last. The porch light was out, though I could have sworn I'd turned it on before I left. Did I even have another forty-watt globe? Might have to pick one up on the way to work tomorrow.

I unlocked the door and fumbled for the hall light switch. It clicked, but nothing happened. Damn. Must have blown a fuse. I groped my way down the hall, the house with its drawn blinds pitch black compared to the streetlit night outside. I'd need the flashlight from the kitchen drawer to check the fuse box.

As I entered the kitchen, someone grabbed me and slammed me against the wall.

CHAPTER FOUR

I was too winded to scream. All I managed was a yelp as I fell heavily against the kitchen dresser. It rocked, sending plates smashing to the floor. I landed on broken china, arms flailing. *Hope Grandma's willow plate is still in one piece.* Strange how you can think such things in the middle of a crisis.

My wild landing caused another shower of objects to fall from the dresser. Groping in the dark for a weapon, my hand closed on a pepper grinder. Not the most effective weapon, but I was in no position to be choosy. I clenched its smooth wood in my fist, my heart pounding somewhere up in my throat, but before I could use it my assailant grabbed me by the upper arm and hauled me off the floor.

I screamed. My shoulder burned like fire. I struggled, tripping and sliding on the debris at our feet, as he dragged me back against his body. He was taller than me and strong—he'd yanked me to my feet as if I weighed nothing at all—and his arm felt like a steel band across my chest. Somehow I managed not to drop the pepper grinder.

I gulped in panicked breaths, still struggling, but there was no shifting him. Unseen objects skittered and clanged across the floor as I kicked out, desperate to escape. Then I felt the prick of steel at my throat and fell still.

"Who are you working for?"

His voice was low and raspy. I could feel his breath on the side of my face, and from the corner of my eye I caught the glint of light on the knife blade. My eyes had adjusted to the dark now, enough to see the back door standing wide open and half the contents of the dresser scattered broken across the floor.

I licked dry lips and drew in a shaky breath. "I—I work for a costume shop. What do you want?"

He shook me, the knife pressing closer. It felt like a line of cold fire across my throat.

"There's no money in the house, if that's what you're after!"

"Don't play dumb," he growled. "Who are you working for? Alicia or Valeria?"

What the hell was he talking about? The guy must have the wrong house.

"I don't know any Alicia or Valeria." *Please believe me, crazy man, and get the hell out of my kitchen.*

He growled, really growled, just like a dog, and the sound was so inhuman it raised all the hairs on my arms and sent tickles of fear down my spine. Somewhere deep in my monkey brain a long-dormant instinct came to life—an instinct which told me that wasn't a sound I wanted to hear all alone in the dark.

"Do you think I won't use this?" he whispered, pressing on the knife till it cut me. I swallowed convulsively, feeling a trickle of warm blood on my neck. "I can smell your fear, you know." He could probably hear my heart, too, trying to pound its way out of my body in terror. He lowered his face to my neck and breathed in as if he were savouring a fine perfume. "You're right to be afraid."

I started to tremble. To think, six months ago I might have welcomed this—the chance to give in to forces beyond my control, and let it all end. No more struggling to get through the empty days. Now, with death breathing down my neck, I realised that somehow, without my noticing, things had changed. I wanted to live.

My therapist would be thrilled, if I had one. The closest I had was Ben … Ben, who was on his way here right now.

Okay, now I had a plan. I just had to keep this guy talking till the cavalry arrived.

"Why do you care whether it's Alicia or Valeria?" I didn't have the faintest clue what any of it meant, but I had to say something. My voice shook.

"Well, sweet pea, I need to know who to go after next. After I've killed you."

Oh, God. Sweat ran down my back. The pepper grinder in my hand was slippery with it. I tightened my grip. Looked like I needed a Plan B. I might not last till Ben arrived.

"What if …" Thinking on my feet wasn't normally my strong suit, but it's marvellous how having a knife at your throat sharpens your concentration. "What if I told you it was neither of them?" And please *God* let that be the right thing to say.

"I'd say you were lying."

Through the kitchen window I could see the lights of Tanya's house, a beacon of normality in a world gone crazy. Maybe I should cut the mind games and just scream my lungs out and hope somebody came running. It could work. On the other hand, crazy knife-wielding guy might decide to slit my throat before he bolted.

"Can you afford to take that chance? Surely you can think of someone else who might have hired me?" Hell on a stick, maybe someone *had* hired me to do whatever Crazy Guy thought I'd done. After all, I couldn't remember what I'd been up to this afternoon.

I felt his tautness relax, his body ease away from mine a little, as if I'd distracted him.

"Elizabeth?" he said, as if to himself. "No. Impossible."

I seized on this, improvising like mad.

"I can prove it." Suddenly the plan was back. God, this had better work. "I have the documents in that drawer over there." I gestured to the side with my chin.

His head started to turn and I brought the pepper grinder up lightning fast and slammed it as hard as I could into the hand holding the knife. He yelped, and I tore out of his grasp and scrambled for the open door.

He barrelled into me. I skidded across the floor, spraying broken china everywhere. He growled again and got between me and the door. He was so fast. My heart hammered in my throat, and time seemed to slow down.

He lunged for me but lost his footing on the uneven surface. His hand caught at my leg, but I managed to kick him off and half-hurdled, half-fell across the kitchen bench.

I turned to face him, breathing hard, the bench a flimsy barrier between us. Never had I wished so hard for a bigger kitchen. His muscular shape was silhouetted against the open door, haloed in light. He looked like someone who worked out a lot. His neck was almost as wide as his head, and I could see the bulge of his biceps from here. My measly sixty kilos plus pepper grinder didn't stand much chance against that.

"I'm going to enjoy killing you," he said, in the way a normal person says they enjoy ice cream. "I'm going to rip out your heart and eat it."

Now that was just going too far. So much adrenalin raced through my veins that I'd gone beyond fear to a strangely calm place. I drew in a shuddering breath and squared my shoulders. I refused to be eaten by some gym junkie in the grip of roid rage.

I reached behind me to the knife block and pulled out the biggest knife, a wicked number with a blade near as long as my forearm.

"Come any closer and it might be *your* heart getting cut out, sunshine." How dare he break into my house, wreck my kitchen—and probably my Grandma's best willow-pattern plate—and then threaten to *eat my heart*? "If you don't get out of here right now I'm going to scream the place down and all my neighbours will come running."

"Then they'll only have themselves to blame for what happens to them," he said, all low and menacing, like a villain in a B-grade movie.

He didn't move, and for a moment I thought we had a stand-off, until there was a distinct and nauseating crunch, like a dozen people all cracking their knuckles at once. I stared at him, standing there in the doorway outlined against the light, and it hit me that some of the light came from him—oh Lord, please no more glowing people—just as the shape of his silhouette changed. He seemed to melt and fold forward.

He groaned as if in pain and stepped into the square of light from the window, hunched and horribly misshapen. Something popped, and I screamed as hair sprouted on his rapidly deforming face, faster than the time-lapse photography in a David Attenborough film. I swear I heard the hissing as it grew.

I kept on screaming as he took another step, on all fours now, his mad eyes never leaving my face. And then, oh God, the man was gone and a wolf stood in my kitchen, growling fit to shake the rest of the plates down out of the dresser.

Its lips skinned back from its teeth and my heart hammered so hard it could probably hear the panicked rhythm from where it stood. My monkey brain screeched at me to run, almost gibbering with fear, but there was nowhere to go but back down the hallway, and he would be on me before I'd taken two steps. I had no hope of outrunning the death that stared me in the face. I shrank back against the stove, knife held out in one wavering hand.

With a snarl the creature leapt. It cleared the bench as if it wasn't even there. I slashed wildly with the knife but went down under a ton of fur and muscle, rolling frantically as its jaws snapped in my face. Claws ripped at my bare shoulders, but I scrambled away. I scooted back till I felt the kitchen cupboards behind me. Nowhere else to go. I was caught in the little U-shape formed by the cupboards, the sink and the bench.

Its yellow eyes gleamed in the moonlight from the window over the sink, almost as if it were laughing at me. I had the impression it was toying with me, that it had let me escape to enjoy my terror for longer.

It took a step forward, ignoring the knife. I stared into the nightmare's eyes, long-ago taekwondo lessons returning. *Watch the eyes, not the hands or feet.* I groped beside me as its weight shifted.

It sprang and I whipped a cupboard door open in its face. Its weight jammed me painfully half into the cupboard, the door between my throat and its snapping jaws. Its claws raked me again and I screamed.

A bang like a car backfiring shook the room. The monster collapsed on top of me, a dead weight.

Ben stood in the doorway to the hall.

"Are you hurt?"

He lowered his arm, then crunched across broken china and laid something on the bench. I caught a whiff of gunpowder as he dropped to his knees. It took my overtaxed mind a moment to put things together.

"You shot it?" I hadn't even known he owned a gun.

He heaved the creature off me—not an easy job, given the size of the thing—and caught me in his arms. "You're bleeding!"

"A few scratches." My right shoulder throbbed with the promise of agony. The scratches there were long and deep. Blood ran freely down my arm. Looking at it made me queasy, and I started to shake again.

But looking at the creature was worse. My mind couldn't accept that such a thing could be, though I could feel its fur against my bare leg. The fact that it was so dark I couldn't see it properly made it seem all the more menacing. I blurted the first thing that popped into my head. "My kitchen wasn't built for this kind of thing. Too small."

The battered cupboard door hung crazily from one hinge.

"I don't think many kitchens are designed to repel werewolves." He pulled me to my feet—a lot more gently than the last guy. Even so, my shoulder screamed in protest.

I looked down at the impossible creature. "Is it dead?"

"Unfortunately not. I didn't have the gun loaded with silver. The body will heal itself soon."

It took a minute before the implications of that statement hit me. "Bloody hell. You *knew*?"

That werewolves existed. That I really was in danger.

Ben wouldn't meet my eyes. "Come on, let's get out of here."

As he spoke I realised I could hear Tanya's voice next door shouting for Roy. The whole thing felt as if it had taken forever, but in fact only moments had passed since I'd started screaming.

"But what about—?" I gestured at the monstrosity on the floor. A paw twitched, and I was sure its fur had been longer a second ago. Was it turning human again? "We can't just run away! What if it attacks them?"

The creature spasmed, its wolf face starting to slide.

Ben grabbed my hand and pulled me to the open back door. I tripped on a pile of rags that must have been the remnants of its clothing, then ducked aside to snatch up my fallen handbag.

"It's not interested in anyone but you. And if we don't get out of here *right now* it'll be after you again."

That was a damned persuasive argument. I followed him to his car and we roared up the street as if all the hounds of hell were after us.

For all I knew, they were.

CHAPTER FIVE

I sagged back against the soft leather car seat and burst into tears. I'm not usually a waterworks kind of girl, but if you can't cry when a guy promises to eat your heart out, then turns into a wolf and attempts it, I don't know when you can. On top of losing my memory and the other weird crap that had gone down, it was enough to send anyone into shock.

Ben drove like a madman. We were around the corner before I even had my seatbelt on.

He reached back and dug under my seat, producing a huge first aid kit.

"Bandages in there," he said. "Get that bleeding under control. I'll have a look as soon as I get some distance between us."

With shaky fingers I folded a bandage and pressed it against my shoulder, which was bleeding the worst. Ben took us north along Pennant Hills Road. We passed the car dealerships and the driving range, now dark. Trucks thundered past in a swirl of fumes. The normal grime of a busy main road was outside my window, the houses and shops along this stretch a familiar sight, but suddenly I didn't recognise the world I lived in. The clock on the dash read 8:39—a lot had happened in the last few hours.

Traffic was reasonably light—as light as it ever gets on Pennant Hills Road, anyway—but every time we stopped at a red light I found myself looking around, checking over my shoulder, as if I expected to see a wolf come charging out of the dark.

"It's all right." Ben read my mind. "We're not being followed."

How did he know? And how come he knew so much about this stuff, anyway?

"Okaaay. Would you mind telling me what the *hell* is going on? That was a—a werewolf, wasn't it?" I held the wadded-up bandage against my burning shoulder. I'd been attacked by a *werewolf.* "I feel stupid even saying it. Werewolves are *real*? What is this—the Twilight Zone?"

"I know it's a shock."

The calm in his deep voice irritated me. "Shock? No, this is not a shock. A shock is what you get when you hear your favourite TV show is being axed. A shock is looking at your watch and realising you're ten minutes late for an important meeting. Being attacked by a werewolf in your own kitchen is not a *shock.* I don't think they've even *invented* a word to describe that particular feeling."

He glanced across at me but said nothing. The glow from the dashboard lent a greenish tinge to his skin, making him look a little supernatural himself.

"So now I have to believe in werewolves? What else? Are vampires real too? Witches? Geez—the abominable snowman?"

He snorted, which only inflamed me further.

"And what about this?" I popped the glove box and let it dangle open, revealing the gun he'd thrown inside. It had a silencer fitted to its gleaming barrel. A silencer! Clearly there were sides of Mr Stevens' personality I'd never seen. My voice was getting shriller, and I made an effort to wrench it back down out of the stratosphere, though I wasn't ready to let go of the accusing tone. "By the way, I think your silencer's broken. My ears are still ringing."

He leaned across and shut the glove box. "This isn't Hollywood. In real life silencers can only do so much. They can disguise the source of a gunshot, not make it sound like a water pistol. Keep pressing on that bandage."

"What in God's name are you doing with a gun? This is Sydney, not America." I'd never even seen a gun in real life before, only in movies and TV shows. "The only people who own guns here are policemen—and Ben Stevens, apparently. Do you even have a licence for that thing? Cause if you do I think you just broke half the rules."

"Would you rather I didn't have it?"

I glared at him. "Oh no, I'm grateful you got there when you did, with your silencer too, so prepared—except, whoops! You forgot to bring the silver bullets." And there was the crux of the matter. I stopped yelling. "You *knew*. You knew all this crazy shit existed. You knew werewolves were real, and God knows what else—and you never told me. Somehow you got me mixed up in all this." I couldn't imagine how, but he wasn't getting out of this car till I found out. "That thing could have *killed* me, Ben. A little heads-up would have been nice."

The car turned on to the M1, the main northern highway, as a strained silence fell. It was a six-lane divided road with a speed limit of 110 kilometres per hour. We sped up, the big diesel engine purring as we swooped around the first bend, leaving the streetlights and houses behind.

"I know," he said at last, eyes firmly on the dark road ahead. "I'm sorry. But you should have been *safer* working for me—I don't understand what's going on. Besides, would you have believed me if I'd told you?"

I considered his profile, lit by the soft green glow from the dashboard. Of course I wouldn't have believed him. Who would? But that didn't make me feel any better.

"I don't like being lied to," I said stiffly. Especially not by him. Hadn't I had enough of that with Jason? Ben was different: reliable, practical, blunt. He'd never make the diplomatic service, but you always knew where you stood with him.

At least, I thought I had.

"So when I said I could see glowing people, and you said *what colour*—what was that about? Can you see them too?"

"No. And you shouldn't be able to either."

Well, add that to the list of things which shouldn't be happening, then. It was getting scary long. Werewolves, memory loss, the black stone ...

My phone shrilled by my feet, and I nearly leapt out of my seat. I'd forgotten my handbag was there.

I should have been expecting the name on the screen. "It's Tanya. What do I tell her?"

"Stay calm," said Ben. "Let her do the talking."

"Oh, thank God!" Tanya screamed as soon as I answered. "You're alive! I was so worried."

I held the phone between us so Ben could hear too, though it was hardly necessary. Tanya had no volume control when she was worked up.

"Um … of course I'm alive." Playing dumb seemed the best option.

"Ohmygod, that wasn't you screaming? I thought you were dead for sure!"

"Why? What's going on? Where are you?"

"I'm at your place, hon. The police are here too. I called them as soon as I heard the screaming—oh, it was terrible. It sounded like someone was being murdered. I sent Ron over with the cricket bat, but he couldn't see anything, so then we waited for the cops—and your power was off at the board, it looked really suspicious, you know? and your back door was wide open—my goodness, you should see the mess they made of your kitchen! and the police asked us if anything had been taken, but really, how would we know, and anyway I was more worried about what had happened to you—there was blood on the floor—"

"Does she ever take a breath?" Ben muttered.

"—so I thought I'd try your mobile, even though your car's still here, and hope to God you answered. But where are you?"

"With Ben."

"You'd better get home real quick then; see if anything's missing. The police say it looks like the thieves were interrupted, because it's only the kitchen that's been touched. Thank God that blood's not yours. God knows what they were doing."

I threw Ben a panicked look.

"Tell her your mum's sick and I'm taking you to visit her."

Obediently I relayed the lie. "I can't. Mum's in hospital and Ben's driving me to the airport. I've got a plane to catch."

"Oh, no! What's wrong?"

Good question. It had to be something serious, with a sudden onset. I hated gifting my mother with a fake disease; it felt like tempting fate.

"It's her heart." *Sorry, Mum.* "They're running some tests, but I don't know much yet."

"Poor thing. How scary for her! Do you think you'll be gone long? The police want you to let them know if anything's been stolen."

"Don't know yet. I'll have to play it by ear—tell them I'll get in contact when I get home. Is the back door busted?"

"No, not a scratch. They must have picked the lock."

"That's something, at least. Could you lock up for me, and keep an eye on the place till I get back? You know where the spare key is, right?"

"Yes, of course. Don't you worry about a thing. We'll take care of it. You just look after your poor mum, okay?"

"Thanks, Tanya."

"No worries, hon."

I ended the call and looked at Ben. "Okay, where are we really going?"

Maybe I should have asked before, but I'd been a little distracted. At least the bleeding had slowed, and I'd stopped shaking.

"One of my mates has a holiday house at Avoca. Nothing fancy, but I know where the key is and he won't mind if we borrow it for a few days. Better lie low till we find out what's going on. How are those scratches looking?"

Cautiously I peeled the wad of bandage away from my arm. "Red. Kind of puffy." Were my tetanus shots up to date? "Hurts like hell."

What kind of infection could you get from a werewolf's claws? I patted at a slow ooze of fresh blood, then blinked.

"Shit. I'm not going to turn into a werewolf, am I?"

"Don't think so."

"You don't *think* so? Geez, that's reassuring." A hollow opened in the pit of my stomach. To lose control of my own body, to become a monster …

Ben pulled off the road and switched on the interior light. A cliff loomed above us, honey-gold in the light from the headlights, its straight edge showing its manmade origins. When they'd built the road they'd cut right through many of the sandstone bluffs. "Let me look at you."

He pulled out pads and tape and rigged a proper dressing for my arm and the big scratch below my ribs, his hands warm and sure. "He didn't bite you, did he?"

"No-o." Had he? It was hard to be sure now. The snap of his jaws in my face was an instant of pure terror seared on my memory forever, but after that the details were hazy.

"You should be okay, then." His voice was soothing, but he wouldn't meet my eyes. I wasn't reassured. "Although we'll have to clean those scratches out."

He picked up his phone.

"Who are you calling?"

"A friend. He can tell us for sure. He's an expert."

"Why, is he a werewolf too?"

Ben shushed me as the phone answered. "Damn, message bank … Hi Trev, it's Ben Stevens. Please call me back. It's urgent."

He hung up and glared out the windscreen for a moment, lost in thought. We were a little island of light in the darkness, with only the occasional whooshing roar as another pair of headlights swooped past us. I felt exposed, vulnerable. I switched off the interior light, making us less of a target.

Ben put the car into gear and pulled onto the motorway again. Being on the move felt safer. Cliffs were replaced by trees, blurring past as the car picked up speed.

"Trev'll know why you were targeted. He's usually got his finger on the pulse."

"Isn't there anyone else you could ask?" Personally, I was more interested in the answer to the original question—whether I was likely to start sprouting teeth and fangs—and I didn't want to wait to find out. My heart raced. I took a deep breath. Hysterics wouldn't do either of us any good.

He gave me a level stare. "I trust Trevor. Anyone else I rang might be the guy who attacked you."

Right. Good point.

"Unless you can tell me what he looked like?"

"I didn't see much. It was too dark." I rubbed at my temples. The rush of adrenalin had banished the headache for a while, but now it was back with a vengeance. There'd be a worldwide shortage of paracetamol if it didn't let up soon. And I was so tired. Thank God Avoca wasn't much further.

"He looked like a gym junkie—big guy, all neck and shoulders. He was already in the house when I came home. Must have turned off the power at the mains. No lights. I thought I'd blown a fuse. Anyway, it was dark, and he jumped me when I came into the kitchen. He asked who I was working for—Alicia or Valeria. Do those names mean anything to you?"

He nodded, looking grim. "People you don't want to cross."

"People? Or werewolf people?"

"Neither. The wolves aren't the only shifters."

I shut my eyes. They were gritty with exhaustion. "Of course they're not. What else? Vampires? Don't make me play twenty questions."

He sighed. "A lot of the old stories are true, or at least based in truth—all those ones about people changing into something else. Turns out there's a surprising number of creatures passing themselves off as human—things like vampires and werewolves, plus lots of others you might not have heard of. Even mermaids, though I've never met one of those."

Which implied he had met the others? Holy supernatural freak show, Batman.

"Considering how many different types there are, it's a wonder there's not more trouble, but they mostly keep to their own kind. I guess it's in their own interests to lay low. No one wants to be the one who starts the humans off with the pitchforks and the burnings again."

"That guy in my kitchen didn't seem to care about laying low." I couldn't stop replaying the horrible images over and over in my mind. Hot meaty breath in my face, yellow soulless eyes, hulking body bristling with shaggy fur. And my *God* the teeth. I would *not* turn into that. I'd rather die. I realised my hands were shaking and tucked them into my armpits to hide them.

"No." He chewed his lip for a moment. "It's out of character. Something's going on. Did he say anything else?"

I thought back. "We exchanged threats. He said he was going to eat my heart."

"You exchanged threats with a werewolf?" He sounded amused.

"Well, I didn't know he was a werewolf at the time. I just said 'not if I cut yours out first, buddy', or something like that. Oh, and I pretended I was working for someone else, to try and stall him. He asked if it was Elizabeth, but he didn't seem to like the idea."

"Lord, I hope she's not involved," said Ben.

"Who's Elizabeth?"

Fierce blue eyes regarded me from a face beginning to show its great age. Her white hair was impeccably styled in a sleek bob, the ends coming to a sharp point on either side of her jaw. On the wall behind her head hung a famous Renoir, and it was no print. Only the best for Elizabeth. She had more money than Midas, more power than God—yet she still wasn't happy.

At the moment her unhappiness seemed largely my fault, judging by the sour expression on her face every time she forced herself to look at me.

She pushed the deeds across the desk and I glanced at the paper. The address was in the heart of The Rocks and I had no doubt it would be impressive. There was money too, in shares and cash— enough zeroes to satisfy anyone. But who was she trying to impress?

Not me. Dragon queens rarely showed much interest in their progeny, but I had the distinct impression that in my case she'd gone beyond lack of interest to active dislike.

Not her other daughters, who would all be receiving similar largesse. She could afford to be generous, since only one of us would live through the proving, and she would get it all back from those who didn't survive. She seemed to be going through the motions, as if this were a book she'd read before.

Or a trial with a foregone conclusion.

"Is there any hope for the rest of us?"

She raised one perfectly arched eyebrow at my hostile tone. The queen wasn't used to attitude from her subjects.

"What do you mean?"

"Is there any point going through the motions of a proving when you've already decided Valeria should succeed you?"

Her spymaster stirred from his position by the window. "Don't address your mother like that, Leandra."

Odious little man. How dare he chide me? He was probably sleeping with her again.

"Watch your own tongue. I'm not a child any more."

Elizabeth waved us both to silence with an impatient hand. "No queen 'decides' on her heir. Your hostility would be better directed at your sisters. I have given you each enough money to get you started. You are free to seek any alliances you wish within the domain, except among the members of my own household."

Her tone made it clear she thought the possibility of anyone allying with me unlikely. She might be in for a shock there. Not everyone considered her precious Valeria the obvious candidate.

"Aren't you going to wish me luck, mother?" My whole life had been leading to this moment. Finally I could seize my fate with both hands. Luck had little to do with it. Who was better prepared? Who had the wits—and the right alliances—to outscheme and outlive the other four?

Her lip curled into a sneer. "The true queen doesn't need luck. And the rest of you will find that no amount of luck will save you."

"Kate? Kate!" Ben sounded urgent.

"Don't yell. I've got a headache."

I squinted at Ben, barely able to focus on his worried face. The pressure in my skull was unbelievable. If someone stuck a pin in my head it would explode into little pieces like a popped balloon. My mind whirled with fragments that dissolved as I tried to grasp at them: a cold face; a feeling of anger …

"I'm not yelling. You just kind of sagged in your seat as if you'd blacked out."

"Did I?" It seemed to me we'd just been talking when he suddenly started yelling my name. Guess I'd have to take his word for it. With an effort, I turned my throbbing head to face forward again and watched the headlights sweep along the road. The dark trees whizzed by at a phenomenal rate. "Are you speeding?"

"I need to get you somewhere safe. Don't go to sleep. Keep talking to me."

"Fine. You were telling me about … Elizabeth?"

The name started bells ringing. A flash of cruel blue eyes. But I didn't know her, did I? Why did I feel as if I should?

"Well, that's the other reason the shifters don't like publicity. At the top of the shifter food chain are the dragons. They're determined to stay hidden, and dragons generally get what they want."

I nodded. Yes, that was right. No, wait … What the hell?

"Their queens carved up the world between them centuries ago and keep their own kingdoms under tight control. Or domains, as they call them, since there are no kings."

"Is that who Valeria and Alicia are? Dragon queens?"

"No, but their mother is. Elizabeth has been around a very long time. I've heard she was actually Queen Elizabeth the First, though I don't know if it's true."

"As in, the daughter of Henry the Eighth? The Virgin Queen? *That* Queen Elizabeth?" The strongest sense of déjà vu gripped me. Surely we'd already had this conversation?

He nodded.

"But she died! It's in the historical record—how could it be the same person?"

"If you have a lifespan of a thousand years, you need to move on every so often to avoid suspicion. Dragons get a lot of practice at staging realistic deaths and re-establishing themselves with a new identity." He shrugged. "Anyway, as I said, it could just be a rumour. The point is, she's old and powerful, and if she's involved we're in deep trouble."

Great. Well, at least he said "we". Silence fell as the car swooped down the long hill to the Mooney Mooney bridge. The yellow windsocks hung limp on their poles, mocking the signs that warned "High Wind Area". Beneath the bridge the river gleamed in the dark like satin, flat and still.

I was hot and headachy and my arm burned like hellfire. In fact I was hot all over. Anxiously I scanned the backs of my hands for any sign of fur. I wished I could pretend this was all some crazy fairy story of Ben's, but I'd seen the creature, felt its weight, smelled the meaty stink of its breath. And had the scars to prove it. Please God scars was the end of it.

Neither of us spoke for a long time. I had a lot to think about.

He took the Gosford exit and we cruised down quiet streets. Gosford was the hub of a loose collection of beachside towns known as the Central Coast, prized for their proximity to Sydney as much as their prettiness. But even the "big smoke" of Gosford was pretty dead at night. Still, Ben kept closer to the speed limit here. The last thing we needed was having to explain my blood-soaked appearance to a curious highway patrolman.

After about ten minutes we turned off the main road, following the signs to Avoca. Once a seaside tourist haven, it was now increasingly settled by commuters who had to work in Sydney but didn't like the big-city lifestyle. Despite the encroachment of apartment blocks, it still kept a lot of its old-style charm, with old beach shacks nestled among the newer developments. Lachie and I had visited its grand old cinema once on holidays and paddled canoes on the lagoon behind the beach. Or rather, I'd paddled and he'd yelled excited commands as the captain of our little vessel.

No one moved on the streets now as Avoca lived up to its sleepy reputation.

Ben turned left and slowed the car to a crawl. "It's along here somewhere. Ah—there."

He pulled up in the carport of a tiny little box of a house, with a front door in the middle and a window each side, like something a child might draw. I got out and gulped big lungfuls of the salty air as Ben disappeared around the back. I could hear the faint shush of the surf; the beach must be close—probably at the end of the street—but it was too dark now to see.

Ben came back brandishing the key and let us in. The door opened straight into the main room, with lounge and dining table at the front and a primitive kitchen along the back wall. Inside was hot and stuffy; Ben went around opening windows while I yawned fit to crack my jaw, barely able to keep my eyelids open.

"Come on, Sleeping Beauty, let's get you cleaned up and into bed."

I followed him into the tiny bathroom, forcing myself to hold it together. "Best offer I've had all day."

CHAPTER SIX

The little bathroom was too cramped to fit a chair, so Ben boosted me on to the small sink, where I perched with my feet resting on the edge of the bath. It was an ugly shade of pink that matched the pink and caramel wall tiles. Probably the height of fashion in whatever long-ago decade the house had been built. I wondered how long Ben's friend had been coming here. Maybe the house had been built by his dad, or even his grandfather. Bet they'd never had any werewolf victims here before.

Today was turning out to be a real day for firsts.

The house seemed like the kind of basic, homey place a family would come to year after year. On one side of the main living area two doors opened into the bathroom and a bedroom boasting a lumpy double bed. On the other was a small bedroom with two double bunks for the kids. Nothing flashy, but what kid would care? They probably spent their days at the beach, sunburnt and carefree, while mum and dad enjoyed the quiet. In the evenings dad would cook a barbeque, and after dinner they'd sit around playing cards or some noisy board game. Dad would probably cheat or pretend to be hilariously bad at it.

I sighed as Ben peeled the bandage from my arm. Why torture myself imagining happy families? Didn't I have enough to worry about?

Red and inflamed, the wound looked nasty. The skin all around it felt hot and itchy. Was that a sign I was turning into a werewolf? Anxiety opened a pit in my stomach.

Gently Ben cleaned away the dried blood. He pressed against me in the small space, warm and solid and reassuring.

When he'd finished he produced a bottle of Dettol from the first aid kit. Right. Disinfectant—for werewolf germs. Bet the manufacturers hadn't planned for that one.

"This might sting a bit."

I snorted. "Yeah, I used to say that to Lachie. He didn't believe me either."

In fact he usually made more of a fuss about the Dettol than he did over the original scrape. I sucked in a breath at the bite of the disinfectant. Poor kid. No wonder he'd cried.

"Sorry." Ben's hands were gentle. I studied his face, so close to mine. Stubble shadowed his cheeks. It had been a long day. A single vertical line down the middle of his forehead spoke of concentration as he bent to his task. Or maybe worry. I had the feeling there was a lot Mr Stevens wasn't telling me about our current situation. It was typical of him to try to shield me, but it only made my imaginings worse. And right now *worse* was pretty bad. The idea of being taken over by a monster, of changing into that nightmare thing in my kitchen, was doing my head in. I was barely holding it together. When would this guy Trevor ring back?

"So, tell me more about these dragons the werewolf mentioned." Anything for a distraction. I winced as Ben dabbed carefully down the length of my arm. "Elizabeth's what? Queen of Australia? And who are Alicia and Valeria?"

"Elizabeth's queen of Oceania, which covers most of the south Pacific. She's been queen a long time, and she's old even by dragon standards. About twenty-five years ago she laid a queen clutch, which is a sign she knows she doesn't have a lot of time left."

"What's a queen clutch?" I wriggled a little and steadied myself with a hand on Ben's shoulder. The tiny pink sink didn't make the most comfortable seat.

"Dragon queens are the only fertile females, and for most of their lives they lay only male eggs, with a few infertile females thrown in. Apparently when they get to an advanced age it triggers their reproductive system to produce a queen clutch—anything from three to a dozen eggs, all fertile females."

"So how come dragons haven't died out? Seems a dodgy way of doing things. How many queens are there?"

"Eight usually, depending on territory wars and inheritance fights."

"Ouch! Careful!"

"Sorry." He began rebandaging my shoulder with practised movements. The antiseptic reek of Dettol filled the little bathroom.

"Eight fertile females doesn't seem much."

He grimaced. "Trust me, that's plenty. With their long lifespans, the world would be overrun with dragons otherwise. Not a world I'd like to live in."

"But what happens to the poor males who don't get to do the deed with one of the queens?"

"You wouldn't want to let a dragon hear you say it, but it's certainly been suggested they're all crazy because they're so inbred. But you needn't worry about their sex lives. Dragons have very healthy appetites, and if there aren't enough females to go around, they'll settle for something else. Human playthings, mostly."

"Okay, so Elizabeth lays some queen eggs. That's Valeria and Alicia?"

"Among others."

"And then what?"

"They fight to see who gets to be queen after Elizabeth dies. It's called the proving. Not a good time to be a shifter. Lift your shirt and let me see that scratch on your belly."

I held the shirt with my good arm and tried to sit straighter so he could see what he was doing. Everything hurt. I was a mass of stings and throbs and aches. I laid my injured arm across his shoulders, grateful for somewhere to rest it.

"Hope you've got some painkillers in that little box of tricks." I inhaled the smell of him, warm and woodsy. I had to get close to make it out over the sharp scent of Dettol. He smelled like home. I could easily lay my head on his shoulder and drift off to sleep. The edges of the room were starting to blur.

A massive ballroom, with French doors all down one side, opening on to an even larger terrace. The golden sands of Palm Beach curving away just below. Daylight fading, the sky shot with pinks and oranges as the sun nears the horizon.

Pretty as a picture. On this night, even the weather didn't dare interfere with the plans of Her Most Mighty Majesty, Elizabeth of Oceania.

I stood in the doorway, posing between the huge double doors. My first time in the palace. My first time anywhere other than the estate where I'd been raised, sequestered from my sisters.

"The fourth candidate," the herald boomed. "The Lady Leandra."

I stalked down the aisle, the chiffon clouds of my dress whispering about my legs. Other whispers followed my progress too. Some were hostile, others thoughtful. The whole shifter community of Sydney was here tonight for the Presentation of the Candidates, as well as many from around Australia and other parts of Oceania.

The crowd shimmered on the edges of my vision, a rainbow of colour. A huge range of shifters were here tonight, their auras glowing in every imaginable hue. Werewolf orange was well represented—Sydney had a large and thriving pack—though most looked uncomfortable in their tuxedos. Dragon red featured heavily too, of course, along with a large goblin contingent, though not all who glowed brown were goblins. Several taller shifters were clearly leshies. All watched me, but I kept my gaze fixed straight ahead.

My three older sisters already waited at the dais, one step below our mother the queen, having walked the red carpet before me. As the oldest, Valeria stood closest to the throne, with Alicia in stark black and white beside her, looking as though she'd just stepped off the catwalk. Ingrid, next in line, was not so chic, her makeup a little overdone, but she filled out her green ball gown so well that most would be prepared to forgive her.

We had never met, my sisters and I. The queen's heirs were raised separately, ostensibly to protect them from each other till they were all of an age for the proving to begin. In reality I suspected it was to keep them safe from the manoeuvrings of the court.

We had never met, but already I knew them more intimately than anyone else in the world. They were more real to me than my teachers and all the servants who'd raised me. These last few weeks, since the date of the Presentation had been announced, I'd studied every scrap of information I could get my hands on, pored over every photo. I knew what Ingrid ate for breakfast, I knew Alicia's fondness for designer fashions and Monique's small cruelties to her servants. And I knew that Valeria, the oldest, considered the proving a mere formality standing between her and our mother's crown.

Tonight she was channelling her inner ice maiden in a pale blue satin the exact colour of her eyes, blonde hair piled atop her head to give her extra height. The expression in those eyes was frosty.

I'd already decided Valeria was my chief rival, but I was surprised at the fury I felt as those eyes raked me up and down, then turned away to watch the entrance of our last sister as if I was of no more interest. Clearly she'd dismissed me as a threat. I *had to force my hands not to clench into fists at my side as the herald called out again.*

"The fifth and final candidate, the Lady Monique."

I took my place next to Ingrid and watched Monique approach. She was a delicate little thing, with dark hair and big brown eyes. Her dress boasted a very grown-up plunging neckline, but those eyes, coupled with her tiny size, made her look more like a hopeful puppy than a potential dragon queen.

I let my attention wander across the crowd, searching out possible allies, noting any who refused to meet my gaze or returned it with animosity. Tonight would see the tentative beginnings of alliances that would make or break fortunes. For the lucky few who threw their support behind the successful candidate, riches and privileged positions at the court of a grateful dragon queen awaited. For the rest, the picture was not so rosy.

Many shifters lacked the necessary appetite for risk. Those were the ones who looked away, hoping to stay out of the whole bloody business. I didn't like their chances. It was fortunate provings were so rare, because once one got started, it threw the whole shifter world into turmoil.

I jumped when his phone rang. My headache had started to fade, thank God, but it had left me so muddle-headed I hardly knew where I was. The pink wall tiles had begun a flickering dance unless I stared directly at them.

"Ben Stevens. Oh, hi, Trevor."

The werewolf guy. I tried to focus on the conversation, but I felt strangely detached, as if I hovered near the bathroom ceiling watching a battered auburn-haired girl lean back against an old-fashioned mirror. Wow, she looked tired. A gorgeous guy on a phone crowded up against her bare legs in the tiny room, sandwiched between the bath and the toilet.

"Shit," said Ben. "This afternoon? What time?"

That caught my attention for a moment, then I lost the thread again as I stared at his eyelashes. They really were preposterous. He was looking at the floor, and they lay so thick against his tanned cheek I wanted to touch them, to see if they felt as velvety as they looked.

His lips moved, but somehow the words that came out didn't connect to my brain. I watched his mouth as if I'd never seen it before.

"… attacked … don't know … at a friend's place …"

He laid a warm hand on my leg, starting an unexpected tingle in my skin. His brown eyes were distant, preoccupied with other things. This close, I could see every pore in his tanned skin. He had a tiny scar on his chin I'd never noticed before. It made him look even sexier, if that were possible.

"Kate? Kate!"

It took me a moment to realise he was off the phone. How long had he been talking to me?

He frowned. "How are you feeling? Everything okay?"

"Why? Am I turning into a werewolf?" Fear jolted me back to alertness. That's right, he'd been talking to the werewolf guy.

"No. You're fine. Trevor says there's nothing to worry about."

"Thank God." In a rush of relief, I seized his face with my good hand and planted a kiss right on his lips.

He blinked, the strangest look on his face—almost *guilty*. "What was that for?"

"Just celebrating." The hard knot of terror in my gut unwound. Suddenly all the rest of it felt manageable. "What's wrong? If there's nothing to worry about, why do you look so worried?"

He took me by the arms, careful of my injuries. "Kate, this is important. Are you sure you can't remember anything from the pick-up today?"

I shook my head. I'd almost forgotten that whole mess in my werewolf panic. Losing a little piece of memory just didn't rate against the possibility of turning into a vicious beast and howling at the full moon every month.

"I remember a woman with blonde hair, but I don't recall her face or anything else about her. There's just ..." I broke off, some of my relief dissipating. Maybe I already was a vicious beast. "There is one thing. I had a—I don't know what you'd call it—a vision? I can't tell if it's something that actually happened, but I can see my hands covered in blood."

He didn't move, didn't even blink, but I sensed the tension in him.

"That's not good, is it?"

"No. That's not good." He scrubbed a weary hand over his face. I wanted to reach out and smooth the worried lines away. His lips had been soft and warm. I could still taste him on mine. "Trevor said someone died at that address, at about the time you were there. Her name was Leandra, and she was one of Elizabeth's queen daughters."

I sucked in a shocked breath. "And you think I killed her?"

"No! No, of course not." His hands reached for mine, enclosing them in a warm comforting grip. "But I'm guessing other people do. Like that werewolf who attacked you. Must have been one of hers."

In a way that werewolf had done me a favour. Forget letting life just happen to me, as if I were a piece of flotsam being swept along a storm-filled gutter. I looked back at the person I'd been only a few months ago and marvelled at the change. I'd thought I wanted to die. And maybe, if death had come then, I wouldn't have struggled.

I gazed into his eyes, their dark brown rich as liquid chocolate. Be careful what you wish for, they say. Death, once longed for, looked different when you were staring it in the face. People—at least, things that looked like people—wanted me dead, because of something they thought I'd done. Maybe I'd even done it. It made no difference. Guess what? I'd decided to live.

Somehow, without my even realising it, life had become valuable to me again.

Perhaps the reason stood before me, brown eyes full of worry. I looked down at our joined hands, then at his mouth, wanting to taste it again. A rush of emotion—and something even more basic—filled me. It had been a long time since I'd kissed anyone.

"Ben. I'm alive. We're safe. And I'm not going to turn into a werewolf. You can't imagine how good that makes me feel." I leaned in till our foreheads touched. Whatever that guilty look had been about, he didn't draw away now. Sudden heat flared in the little bathroom. My hands tightened on the muscles of his shoulders. Now or never, before I lost my nerve. "Really, *really* good. Let's celebrate some more."

He froze as my lips found his, asking a silent question.

"Kate ..." I trailed one hand across his shoulder to the smooth column of his throat. His pulse hammered under my fingertips. "This isn't a good idea. I don't think—"

"That's right," I breathed into his mouth, "don't think. Just feel."

He gathered me against him. For once he didn't argue.

CHAPTER SEVEN

My empty champagne flute clinked against the stone balustrade of the terrace as I set it down and looked out over the dark scene below. There was no moon tonight, but the white dots of streetlights cascaded down the hill below us. Their light showed the rest of the world lay dreaming beneath the summer stars; the only signs of life were up here at the party of the century.

My mother was desperately old-fashioned: the strains of a waltz floated out the open French doors from the ballroom. Of course the dragons knew how to waltz—most of them had been around since before the waltz was invented—but some of the lesser shifters looked nonplussed, eyeing the members of the formally clad orchestra as if they were aliens.

"Better?" asked Luce.

She leaned back against the stone beside me, but she wasn't relaxed. She hadn't wanted me out here in the open, but the ballroom was stuffy and I refused to be pawed any longer by lesser creatures looking to hitch their wagons to my star. Her dark eyes were never still, darting from one person to another, constantly assessing possible threats to my person.

No one was armed tonight, of course, in the presence of the queen, not even my security chief, but Luce was a weapon all by herself. Perhaps, like others before her, my mother underestimated Luce because of her slight stature. She had the look of a pretty Chinese doll with her flawless skin and hair like a river of black satin. But Luce had a wiry strength and agility that had to be seen to be believed. Many who'd seen it hadn't survived the experience.

More likely my mother overlooked Luce because she was only a wyvern. Her aura, the soft blue common to the lesser winged shifters, glowed with a purity that spoke of her vitality and strength, but there was no denying a wyvern was lower down the social scale than a griffin. Valeria, favoured in this as in everything else, had been given a griffin as her security chief. I'd been assigned Luce, and I thanked my mother's prejudices for it every day.

"The evening seems to be going as expected," I said, ignoring the question.

"I'd be happier if Valeria didn't have quite such a crowd around her all the time." A sour expression marred the prettiness of her wide face with its dark almond-shaped eyes as she glared at my sister. Valeria stood just inside the doors, surrounded by sycophants and opportunists. Her back was turned to us, but I had no doubt she knew where every one of her sisters were, including me.

A flicker in Luce's aura betrayed the strength of her feelings. She certainly took her job seriously. In fact she was the only woman here tonight not wearing a gown, having opted for a tux instead as being more practical. The fall of her long dark hair was confined in a bun, instead of her usual business-like ponytail. It revealed the elegant curve of her neck, but I couldn't help thinking she'd chosen the style more for the vicious-looking hairpin that secured it than any consideration of attractiveness. I was sure that hairpin could prove lethal in Luce's hands.

"Ever the pessimist, aren't you? The werewolf pack leader seems receptive."

I was more interested in other dragons than werewolves. Dragons were where the real power lay, but no doubt I could find a use for a pack of the beasts. But it amused me to bait Luce. Predictably, she rose to the bait.

"It's not pessimism. I'm being realistic. One dragon is worth more than Trevor and his whole werewolf pack."

We both contemplated Valeria again. Three men jostled for positions at her elbow; I could tell they were dragons from the red glow of their auras. In fact a veritable rainbow of auras surrounded her, with shifters of every type clamouring for her attention. My mouth quirked with distaste. I probably looked as sour as Luce.

The waltz finished to polite clapping, and one of the dragons broke away from Valeria's little gathering. He stepped out onto the terrace. The lights from the ballroom cast his face into shadow as he approached.

"Is that Jason Hepburn?" I murmured to Luce. She'd been around so long she knew nearly every shifter in the whole domain.

She nodded, her dark eyes dismissive. "A minor player."

"You wanted a dragon," I reminded her, choosing to overlook her impudence. She was not paid to have opinions on her betters.

His bow was carefully calculated to gratify without seeming too subservient. "I see you're drinking champagne." His deep voice *promised a warmth that was reflected in his twinkling blue gaze. "May I get you another?"*

"No, thank you. I find the occasion calls for a clear head."

"Very wise, my lady. Or may I call you Leandra?"

He could call me whatever he liked if he chose to take my side in the coming war. He was a tall man, handsome in a slightly unconventional way—his nose was a little too big, but his generous mouth and bright blue eyes distracted from that fact. His eyes had the predatory gleam so common to our kind. I could probably have guessed he was a dragon even without the tell-tale colour of his aura.

"That depends if we're going to be friends or not," I said.

He wore his blonde hair long, grazing the shoulders of his tux. And what broad shoulders they were.

He leaned closer and my pulse quickened. I wasn't yet used to my body's instinctive reaction to the presence of a male dragon. The only one I'd had any dealings with up till now was my mother's odious little spymaster, and he was hardly the type to make my libido sit up and take notice.

"Why don't we try a friendly dance and see where it takes us?"

He made it sound as if he were offering sex and my body thrilled in response. I took his proffered hand and let him lead me back into the light-filled ballroom. Crystal chandeliers sparkled overhead and the hum of conversation filled the large room. He shouldered his way through the crowd to the open space in front of the orchestra, my hand clasped firmly in his. Luce trailed us at a discreet distance, but I was hardly aware of her any more.

He twirled me into his arms as another waltz began, the full skirts of my gown flaring out around us in a cloud of deep blue chiffon, the colour chosen to bring out the gold flecks in my brown eyes. My stomach clenched as his leg thrust between mine and we began to move. I'd waltzed many times before, but never with another dragon. Flushed with heat, I was acutely conscious of his body pressed against mine.

He bent his head close, a small smile playing round those full lips. "Luce is watching like a hen with only one chick. Does she think I'm a threat to you?"

His breath against my ear ignited a fire deep inside. Perhaps dancing was a mistake. I needed my wits about me, tonight more than ever.

"Are you a threat to me? You seemed very friendly with Valeria earlier."

He shrugged, as if Valeria were of little importance. "Did you know there used to be quite a lot of interest in the science of auras?"

He hadn't answered my question, but I let that pass, curious to see where he was leading. Auras were not something we usually spoke of, since the ability to see them was peculiar to dragons. No need to give away even a hint of the edge it gave us to the lesser shifters.

"I didn't."

"Well, this was a couple of centuries back. Before your time."

Everything was before my time. I was twenty-five, barely mature even by human standards, but considered little more than a hatchling by other dragons, most of whom counted their age by decades, if not centuries. Other dancers whirled by in a riot of colour—both dresses and auras—as I gazed up into his face.

"*The proper reading of an aura can tell us many things.*" I watched his lips, fascinated. That husky voice made everything he said sound suggestive. We swayed to the music, our bodies moving as one. "*Not just a shifter's type, but their emotional state, their general health—even something of their character. For instance, I can see that your bodyguard is fiercely loyal to you ... and that she doesn't like me much at all. I wonder what either of us has done to provoke such feelings?*"

As we circled the glittering room Luce came into view over his shoulder. I checked her aura, but it told me nothing I didn't already know.

"*Don't take it personally,*" I said. "*Luce doesn't like most people.*"

He threw back his head and laughed, exposing the strong tanned column of his throat. Heads turned to look at us, but I was too busy fighting the urge to bite his neck to pay any attention.

"*Do you know what I see when I look at your aura?*"

Hopefully not the height of my arousal. I struggled to focus on the conversation. "*What?*"

"*Bloody-minded determination.*" He smiled down at me. "*I think perhaps I am the first dragon to dance with the next Queen of Oceania.*"

"*I'm flattered. Does that mean you'd be willing to consider an alliance?*" The lights seemed somehow brighter as the violins swelled to a crescendo.

Before he could answer, Luce appeared out of the eddying crowd.

"*Let's dance this way, people,*" she hissed, shoving us both back toward the terrace.

I staggered, but Jason held me up, his arm curled protectively around my waist.

My temper flared. How dared she interrupt? "What's the matter with you?"

She looked like a small black crow, shifting anxiously from foot to foot in the middle of the colourful swirl of dancers.

"Recognise that woman over by the flowers?"

"Which woman?" There were several in a clump by a huge floral display on the far side of the room.

"The one in red."

The woman in question stood slightly behind the others, not part of their group, and seemed to be doing nothing more sinister than watching the dancers glide past.

"I can't be expected to recognise everyone here. What of her?"

"She's a griffin," Jason said.

I could see that. Her aura was the right pale blue shade. She had light brown hair and wore more jewellery than was perhaps tasteful, but I could see nothing to give Luce the jitters.

"But which one?" Luce asked him, ignoring me.

"Ah ..." He frowned. "I don't know her."

That started alarm bells ringing. Jason had been around the court for a long time, long enough to know everyone here tonight. I let him tug me closer to the doors out on to the terrace, though the press of people made progress through the crowd slow.

The woman took a huge bouquet of roses from the arrangement beside her. It had been tucked into the larger arrangement as if it were part of it, but it was wrapped in delicate paper and tied with a gold ribbon. Carrying the bouquet, she worked her way through the crowd toward us.

"I don't know her either." Luce eyed the oncoming woman and began to push more forcefully, jostling people out of our way. "But I've seen that big gold bracelet before. On Nada Kusic."

It was a distinctive bracelet, with chunky square links and set with rubies. I'd only seen Nada Kusic in photos. She was Valeria's head of security, and I'd studied her as I'd studied everyone connected with my sisters. This woman looked nothing like her, but if Luce's nose for danger had sniffed something out, I would be a fool not to listen. It could be a coincidence, but we all knew that for the right price, there were goblin spells that could temporarily change a person's appearance.

We were almost to the doors when the woman stopped, and I realised her target was Monique, who stood nearby watching the dancers with a tall leshy at her side. A sharp breeze from the dark terrace cooled my overheated skin, bringing with it the faint scent of jasmine. I tugged Jason to a halt as the woman smiled and laid a hand on Monique's arm.

They stood so close I could have covered the space between us in three strides, but the room was too noisy to hear what she said. A dozen people stood between us, chatting and laughing. The bouquet quickly changed hands. Monique dipped her head like a queen accepting tribute and the woman disappeared back into the crowd. The exchange took only a moment.

I looked around to see where the woman had gone and found Valeria not far away, watching both of us with a look of hunger. I flicked my gaze back to Monique, who had her face buried in the bouquet, delighting in the scent of the roses.

Luce had seen Valeria too, and that peculiar look on her face. "Out!"

She shoved me in the back, hard, so that I all but fell through the door, Jason right behind me. People had just begun to whisper at our undignified exit when a massive explosion shook the ballroom. Broken glass from the French doors sprayed us as we rolled across the stone terrace.

Screams erupted as the fire alarms began to shrill. My cheek burned where the rough stone flagging had scraped the skin off. I lifted my head, ears ringing from the blast, and caught sight of Valeria's blood-spattered face through billowing smoke. I had no doubt the blood was Monique's. Judging from her look of frustration, mine was supposed to be mingled with it.

My oldest sister was going to have to learn to deal with disappointment.

***

I snuggled into Ben, my head in the crook of his shoulder. Couldn't really do anything else, given the size and age of the mattress. It was small—I was used to having a queen-sized bed to myself—and so bowed in the middle I couldn't have moved away from him even if I'd wanted to. Which I didn't, luckily. Being together like this felt strange after so long on my own, but comfortable too, as if we were always meant to end up this way.

Was it wrong to feel like this? I couldn't help a nagging sense of guilt. How could I be happy when Lachie was dead? What sort of mother forgot her baby so easily?

But I hadn't forgotten him. His eyes, his smile, the sound of his piping voice, the feel of his scrawny little arms around me—they were all burned into my soul forever. I would never forget, no matter how long I lived or what happened to me. I would never stop missing him, every day of my life.

Did that mean I could never feel joy again? It had been so long since I'd felt … well, anything. Grief had turned me to stone. In my head I knew life went on. Hadn't I been eating, sleeping, going through the motions all these months—even occasionally laughing at a joke? In theory I could accept that one day some kind of happiness might be possible. But my shattered heart had never believed.

Only now warmth seeped back into it. The possibility of joy lay beside me, the hairs on his chest tickling my nose, his skin sweaty against mine.

He lay on his back, breathing evenly, but he wasn't asleep. His eyes glinted in the moonlight from the open window as he stared up at the ceiling.

I peered into the darkness too, but saw nothing but the bare light bulb hanging from the ceiling and a suspicious darker patch in one corner which might have been mould. "Something interesting up there?"

"Just thinking." One hand absentmindedly stroked my bare shoulder. I shifted to make the bandaged one more comfortable. It felt surprisingly good. Marvellous what a good orgasm can do for your sense of wellbeing. My body sang, regardless of the guilt that told me I had no right to feel this way. Stupid guilt. I could have been a werewolf by now. Didn't I deserve a little celebration?

Ben hadn't said much.

"Still think this was a bad idea?"

"You've got to admit the timing's not great," he said.

"Rubbish." In the end sheer happiness at still being alive emerged triumphant from the welter of emotions inside me. "You've got to seize the day. We could both be eaten by werewolves tomorrow. Speaking of which ..." I clambered over him and gave him a shove. "Swap sides."

"Why? Do you normally sleep on this side?"

Ah, the awkward getting-to-know-you stage. "No. But if you insist on sleeping with the window open, you can damn well have that side. Then if the wolves come in the window they get to eat you first."

The bedroom door was open too, in an effort to get a cross-breeze going, but so far no luck. I was covered in sweat, and it wasn't just from the sex. The heat in the little house was stifling.

He laughed. "Nice. Glad to know you care. You seem to be taking the whole shifter thing much more calmly than you were a couple of hours ago."

"Must be your magic hands," I said. "Among other things. Or maybe I'm too tired to get worked up about it any more. It's been a hell of a day. How do you stand living like this?"

I felt him shrug, his naked body warm against mine. "It's not usually quite so ... eventful. It's just a job. A very well-paying job, but fairly routine. The Dress-up Box doesn't bring in that much on its own. The real money comes from the courier side of the business."

I shut my eyes, determined to enjoy the feel of his arm draped over me. Lachie had always loved Ben. He would have been thrilled to see us together. "And all the courier jobs we do are for shifters, right? That's why all the crap with disguises and people following us?"

"Uh-huh."

"Gee, thanks for joining me up to magical Fed Ex without even telling me."

"I meant it for the best," he said. "It should have made you safer, and given you some easy money on the side."

"Instead of which I ended up with a werewolf in my kitchen. But before that—nothing. Why did they always follow and never do anything?"

"It's the proving—it makes everybody jumpy. The amount of plotting and backstabbing that goes on is unbelievable. Sometimes knowing who's talking to who can mean the difference between life and death."

"Why don't they just ring each other up? Haven't these people ever heard of email? Texting?" I yawned. I'd been so cranky with him for keeping this from me before. Now I could hardly stay awake to hear it. Good sex beat a sleeping pill hands down. Tomorrow. I'd deal with it tomorrow.

"Did I mention dragon paranoia?" I could hear the smile in his voice. "They have their own way of ensuring messages can't be read by anyone except the person they're meant for. And they have us to deliver them."

"Us?"

"The heralds. We're go-betweens. No one will let in messengers from other camps in case they're spies, or worse. But heralds are protected so they know their enemies can't use us to send them any nasty magic surprises, and no one messes with the heralds because everyone needs them. Think of us as magical Switzerland. Neutral territory."

"Uh-huh."

"You're nearly asleep, aren't you?"

The man was a genius. "Uh-huh."

He leaned over and brushed his lips against my cheek. "Goodnight, beautiful."

Ben thought I was beautiful. I smiled into the pillow and went out like a light.

CHAPTER EIGHT

My long red fingernails tapped the glass of mineral water in an impatient rhythm. I'd give him five more minutes and then I was leaving. I'd suggested this restaurant for its history—we'd been here many times, he and I, and I hoped to unsettle him with memories of better times. Perhaps his reaction when he walked in would give me some clue as to whether he was genuine or not.

In a moment he appeared in the doorway and surveyed the room. Every eye in the room turned to him, the women—and some of the men too—with looks of pure greed, drinking him in. For a moment the low buzz of conversation stilled. Then he moved and the spell shattered; people turned back to their companions and the noise levels rose again, though some still followed him with their eyes.

Those who saw him drop a lazy kiss on my cheek turned away, disappointment on their faces. Damn, he's with her. *If only they knew how my skin prickled with apprehension at the touch of his lips, once so familiar. Was I insane, to even consider trusting him again?*

He sat down and flashed me a brilliant smile, unfazed by the choice of location. "You're lovely as ever, Leandra."

"*And you're still turning heads wherever you go.*" *I didn't return the smile. He was the supplicant, not me. Let him work for it.*

"*What can I say?*" *He spread his arms wide, displaying their powerful muscles. His white shirt, open at the neck, showed taut tanned flesh beneath.* "*I can't help being beautiful.*"

Perhaps, but he certainly didn't dislike the attention either. I made no comment.

"*What are you drinking? Mineral water? That's not like you, my dear. Let me get you something stronger.*" *He clicked his fingers at the waitress, who hurried over. Jason always got good service.* "*I'll have a scotch, and the lady——*"

"*Nothing for me.*"

"*Something to eat? No? You don't mind if I do? I'm starving. I'll have the linguine.*" *He dismissed the waitress with a careless flick of his hand.* "*You should eat something, precious. No need to watch that perfect figure.*"

"*I had a horse yesterday,*" *I said, and was rewarded with a flinch.*

He was much older than me. I was one of the few who'd actually been born in Australia. He, on the other hand, had been born before Captain Cook had even discovered the place and had lived so long in his present form he seemed to have forgotten the joys of trueshape. The old ones considered the hunt rather low class.

"*Let's get down to business,*" *I said, another lamentable lapse of form, but I saw no reason to indulge him under the circumstances.* "*You said you had a proposition for me.*"

"Of course. By all means let's cut to the chase if it pleases you." He smiled, the hunting metaphor a gentle mockery. "I've been feeling a certain … nostalgia for our time together recently. I thought we might negotiate my return."

I snorted. "You want to make a deal? The fact that I haven't struck you down where you sit for your flagrant betrayal is the only concession you're likely to get from me. And why you would imagine I'd ever trust you again is beyond me."

And yet, here I was. Desperate times call for desperate measures, as they say, and the times could hardly be more desperate, with most of my thralls destroyed in the strike on Ingrid, and the wolves off licking their wounds. Trevor, the pack leader, wouldn't even take my calls, an insult he would never have dared when I was at full strength.

In hindsight, it had been a foolish move. I should have waited and let Valeria take her down, but I'd been afraid to let Valeria grow too strong. The more successful she'd seemed, the more allies had flocked to her aid. And Ingrid had given the impression—wrongly, as it turned out—of being an easy target. Instead I'd weakened myself, perhaps fatally.

Jason's drink arrived and he took an appreciative sip, considering me over the rim of the glass. "What if I told you that business with Luce and the bomb was all part of the plan? That I wanted Valeria to believe I'd betrayed you so I could spy on her for you? A double agent, as it were."

I sipped my own drink, equally cool. "I'd say you were the worst double agent in history. Not a single piece of information from you in over six months? Spying's clearly not your forte."

He threw his head back in a familiar gesture and laughed, showing even white teeth. "Exactly. You know me too well. And that's why we work so well together. I made a choice, and it was a bad one."

"So now you want to unmake it." I spun my glass in damp circles on its coaster, ignoring his earnest look. "I'm afraid it doesn't work like that."

"Be realistic, Lee. Getting rid of Ingrid all but wiped you out. You know you need help. Don't let injured pride stand in the way. I have a lot to offer. Valeria is planning an attack on Alicia even as we speak. With me on your side we could set it up so Valeria bought it as well. You'd be home free."

A pretty picture. My sisters dead, the proving over and me the last one standing—he knew the way to my heart. Imagining Valeria dead, in particular, was one of my favourite pastimes. My other sisters were mere obstacles on the path to success, but with Valeria it was personal. It was her smugness I couldn't stand, as if being the eldest automatically granted her superiority. The way she wore her hair up, braided around her head in a not-so-subtle attempt to give herself a crown she hadn't yet earned, made me grind my teeth every time I saw her.

Fortunately that wasn't often. The last time had been at Ingrid's house; before that, not since she'd killed Monique, our youngest sister. I'd barely made it out of that ballroom alive. Valeria's ball gown had been sprayed with scarlet; even her perfectly braided hair dripped gore.

"You're next," she'd mouthed as I'd stared through the smoke, my own face bloodied in escaping Monique's fate. She revelled in

the proving. To the rest of us it was a bitter necessity, but to her it was a cause for sheer delight.

Jason still waited for my answer, watching me with a lazy glint of amusement in his eye as I checked the room. It was three-quarters full, mostly of businessmen lunching on the company account. My thralls were at a table by the door, one watching us, the other with his eyes on the street. The one watching nodded when I caught his eye. Nothing to report.

My cool act probably wasn't fooling Jason. Finishing off Ingrid had cost a lot, both in money and in lives. Add to that the blow of Jason's defection and his almost-successful attempt at killing me, and my situation remained dire even though months had passed. Continual harrying by Valeria hadn't helped. Here a thrall would go missing, there a deal would fall through or another shifter defect, till I hardly knew who to trust. Always I was playing catch-up, always a few steps behind her. If Jason was genuine in his desire to change sides again, it could make a huge difference.

But that was a big if.

The fawning waitress brought Jason's meal, but he hardly noticed her. His gaze rested on me as he ate.

"Valeria doesn't trust me, you know," he said round a mouthful of linguine. "I'm sure the only reason she wanted me was to deprive you. Nada's always in her ear, trying to turn her against me. I'm walking a tightrope every day. Believe me, I want out."

My phone buzzed. Luce. "Yes?"

"Are you with him?" she demanded. "Why didn't you wait for me? I'm your head of security—it's my job to protect you. Are you crazy?"

"You forget yourself," I snapped. Jason busied himself with his pasta, trying to look as though he wasn't listening. I turned away, cupping the phone with my other hand for at least the illusion of privacy, and lowered my voice. "This unreasoning hatred is exactly why you're not here. You're not yourself where he's concerned."

"Not myself? I'm not the one making small talk with the man who damn near killed me a few months ago."

Jason beckoned the waitress and murmured something I didn't catch.

"Not to mention what he did to me. Or doesn't damage to a mere wyvern count?"

"Lucinda." My voice hardened. Her petty grudges could not be allowed to take precedence over my best interests.

"Sorry," she said at last, though her tone held little of apology. "But you can't afford to take a stupid risk like this."

"You're wrong," I said. "I can't afford not to."

"I take it that was Luce?" said Jason when I'd hung up. "Does she still hate me?"

"With a passion."

He grinned. "She'll get over it."

If he thought so, he didn't know Luce as well as he imagined.

"Finish your drink." He indicated the last sip of mineral water in my glass. "I've ordered champagne. We should celebrate our new partnership."

I arched one eyebrow. "That's a trifle presumptuous. I haven't agreed to anything yet."

He laid one long-fingered hand over mine. "Don't get huffy, Lee. You know you're going to. Let's skip over the part where you object and I try to persuade you with my brilliant arguments and get to the good part where we're a team again."

His hand was warm on mine and his blue, blue eyes sparked with amusement. I didn't trust him for one minute, but I felt myself weakening regardless. I stared down at our hands on the snowy white tablecloth.

"Suppose I did agree—what then? I assume you'd have to lie low for a while, though Valeria's not stupid. She'd guess where you were. I'd have to get Luce to beef up security on the house. You'd have to stay with me; I don't have the manpower to protect more than one site."

He grinned. "That should be no hardship."

"That wasn't an invitation."

"Of course. Strictly business. I understand."

I finished my water as the waitress arrived with a bottle of French champagne. The older ones were such snobs about wine— wouldn't drink anything made in Australia. They didn't know what they were missing.

"Let's have a toast," he said, raising his fizzing glass. "To the future!"

I took a sip and set the glass down, while he drained his and refilled it. I'd never cared much for champagne, so I toyed with my glass while he drank and chatted. His talk centred on complaints about Nada, Valeria's lieutenant, and happy thoughts on how she might be brought down, and how Valeria had never appreciated him and therefore deserved everything that was coming to her.

"Not like you, Leandra, my sweet. You always knew how to make a man feel wanted."

True. But I could learn from my mistakes. I wasn't going down that particular path again, however attractive I found him, no matter how hard he flirted. Luce would be proud. She treated everyone with a fierce suspicion and wanted me to do the same.

One of my thralls approached our table. "Mistress, Steve reports two of Valeria's servants three blocks away, moving in this direction."

Anger stirred inside me as I turned to Jason. "Know anything about this?"

He grimaced. "I told you she didn't trust me. She's sent her lackeys out searching, to see what I'm doing." He pulled out his wallet and placed a handful of fifties on the table. "I hate to eat and run, but I'd rather she didn't find out yet."

I watched him leave, wondering how far I could trust him.

"Mistress? We should leave too, just in case ..."

In case it was all a lie and he'd just sprung a trap on us. Indeed.

I picked up my handbag, but it wasn't till I stood that I realised something was wrong. The room spun so dizzily I fell heavily against my thrall. Taken by surprise, he couldn't catch me before I careened into the neighbouring table, sending glassware crashing. Red wine spread like a bloodstain across the white tablecloth. The couple there drew back in shock, and suddenly the whole restaurant was staring.

My man showed great presence of mind. "It's all right, folks. A little too much champagne, that's all."

He helped me across the room to his partner. Good work, Steve. I'd have to give him a raise. No, Steve was the other one. I gasped and stumbled again as my stomach clenched with a vicious griping pain.

Champagne? But I'd hardly touched it, and Jason had drunk half the bottle. They hustled me outside, one of them phoning the driver to bring the car around. The colours on the street were all wrong, and the people passing by seemed stretched and deformed. A woman on the other side of the street stared at me. I blinked, and she was gone. Was it only my imagination, or had her blonde hair been braided into a crown around her head?

The pain slashed its terrible claws through my abdomen again and I moaned. The bastard had poisoned me. How? The car oozed up to the curb. Its open door gaped like a mouth and swallowed me up.

Must have been just before the champagne came, when the conversation with Luce had distracted me. Was she in on it? "Finish your drink," he'd said. That one last gulp of mineral water. I tried to laugh but only a whimper came out as I broke out in sweat all over. "Can't you drive any faster?" someone demanded.

Poison. How very old-fashioned. How stupid was I, to fall for his lies again?

"Mistress? I'll call a doctor. Just hang on till we get home."

My mind raced as my body rode the waves of pain. "No. No doctor." We were immune to most poisons, so there were only a couple of possibilities here, and no doctor could do anything for me in either case. I had an hour or two, three if I was lucky. I clenched my fists, anger coursing through me. No! I refused to admit defeat. Not like this.

"I'll call Luce, then." Not-Steve, whatever his name was, clearly didn't want to take responsibility for a rapidly disintegrating situation. But I didn't want Luce either. The timing of that phone call was suspiciously convenient.

I could trust no one. If there was a way out I had to find it on my own. Another spasm racked me. And soon. I fell against my panicking thrall as the car rocketed around a corner.

My mouth was so dry I could hardly speak. The only thing I could think of was so desperate it seemed hopeless.

"Don't call Luce," I croaked into his shoulder. "Just get me home. Have a herald meet us there. Make sure it's the same one as last time, do you understand? The girl."

If the alternative was to lie down and die, I had no choice.

I had to try.

***

I opened my eyes on an unfamiliar ceiling. Moonlight lay across the sheets, and the breeze from the open window carried a faint hint of salt and the sound of waves, like a great animal breathing. It took a moment to figure out where I was. A jumble of images filled my head, the fading shards of a dream.

Jason had been in it, smug as ever, but it wasn't Jason lying beside me. Why the hell was I wasting good brain cells dreaming about *him* when Ben lay here, snoring gently in my ear? If I never saw him again it would be too soon.

I'd lost the thread of the dream. It had made perfect sense at the time, as dreams did, but now all I recalled was something about poison and a deep feeling of distrust.

The red numbers on the clock said 3:05. Halfway through a luxurious stretch, my bandaged shoulder twinged. It hardly hurt at all. Seemed odd, but I wasn't about to look a gift horse in the mouth. Maybe the scratches hadn't been as deep as they'd looked with blood everywhere.

Thinking of blood recalled the hideous image of my bloody hands. I shifted restlessly, glaring into the dark. Through the bedroom door I could see the black shapes of unfamiliar furniture in the tiny house's main room. Ben stopped snoring and rolled over, his arm curving protectively round me. Why couldn't I remember what had happened?

I could see the garden, hear the faint tap of my shoes on the paving stones as I walked the tree-lined path. Red roses bloomed on my left, their perfume rich and heady. The path curved around an ornamental fishpond where fat carp slipped lazily under a Japanese-style bridge.

Again I saw the woman waiting beneath the trees, her back to me. She looked like she'd stepped out of an office on her lunch break: slim grey skirt with a matching tailored jacket, long blonde hair caught back in an elegant tortoiseshell clasp at her nape. Then she turned, but this time I saw her face, corpse-pale and beaded with sweat. Her huge brown eyes were desperate.

Help me, Kate.

I jumped, heart pounding, and Ben muttered a sleepy protest. Was this Leandra? Had I helped her or killed her?

"You okay?" Ben's breath tickled my ear. He sounded only half awake.

"Fine." I was turning into such an accomplished liar. "Go back to sleep."

He knew me too well to be taken in. "You're not still worried about becoming a werewolf, are you?"

"No."

"Are you in pain?" He propped himself up on one elbow, trying to get a good look at my face in the dim light. "Do you want some more painkillers?"

"No. Really, Ben, it hardly even hurts. Stop fussing." I stroked his stubbly face to soften my words. I'd never admit it, but I kind of liked the fussing. "I was trying to remember what happened today. It drives me mad that I can't."

I told him what I'd recalled.

He pressed a thoughtful kiss into the palm of my hand. "Could be Leandra. She's—she *was*—blonde."

"But it could be anyone, couldn't it?" She certainly didn't have a monopoly on blonde hair. My skin tingled everywhere his lips touched.

"True. Is that all? You didn't see anyone else? Nothing out of the ordinary?"

"Not that I can *remember*." Frustration filled my voice. "Ben, what if it's true? What if I did kill her?"

"Don't be ridiculous. Why would you?"

"I don't know. Maybe she attacked me. And why can't I remember? It seems suspicious—something weird's going on. And then there's the stone, and the glowing guy—"

"Whoa, back up there. What stone?" Suddenly he sounded wide awake.

With all the other excitement, I'd forgotten to tell him. "Wait here."

I padded across the cool floorboards, back through the main room to the tiny pink bathroom. My handbag was there, tossed into a corner.

"You won't believe this." I offered him the black stone as I came back into the bedroom. "I threw this up when I got home from work."

The bed creaked as he sat up and took it, holding it up to the light from the window. The silver tracery sparkled even in the dark room. "You threw this *up*? What the hell is it?"

Deflated, I sat on the lumpy bed. The sheets still held the warmth of my body. "I was hoping you'd know."

"Nope." He shook his head. "Never seen one before."

I took it back, turning it over as he had done, as if the answer would suddenly appear in glowing letters on the dark surface. It felt warm in my hand. Sighing, I thrust it back into my bag and stared out the window at the black silhouettes of gum trees against the sky.

Outside a patch of darkness broke from the shadowy trees and flowed across the yard. I froze.

"Ben. There's something out there."

He followed my gaze to the window, but nothing moved outside now.

"Get dressed." He pulled on his jeans in two quick moves. I hunted for my T-shirt on the floor, painfully conscious of the open window looming behind me.

"What is it? Can you see anything?" I whispered, struggling into my shorts. I had a bad feeling about this. My fingers shook as I tried to do up the button of my fly.

"Could be nothing. A cat, maybe." The shape I'd seen had been much bigger than a cat. "Just get—"

The front door burst open and slammed back against the wall with a crash that shook the floor beneath my feet. I screamed and whirled to face the noise. Ben dived for the bedside drawer where he'd left his gun.

Too late. In two seconds our visitors had crossed the main room and stood in the bedroom doorway.

"I wouldn't reach for that gun if I were you, Mr Stevens," a woman said. Someone flicked on the light. I blinked at the sudden brightness, still frozen to the spot. "Keep your hands where I can see them."

A woman stood there, wearing a black dress more suited to a cocktail party than breaking and entering. Her dark hair was pulled back into an elegant chignon, her makeup flawless. Good God. Who wore makeup to break into someone's house at three o'clock in the morning? And all that jewellery? Her bare arms were weighed down with gold bracelets.

Then a large grey wolf pushed past her into the room and I completely lost interest in her.

The wolf bared its teeth, a blood-curdling growl rumbling in its chest. And not a knife block in sight. Ben stepped in front of me, facing the monster with apparent calm.

"What do you think you're doing, Nada?" He spoke to the woman as if the wolf wasn't even there. He *knew* her? I looked at her more closely. Was it my imagination or was there a faint blue glow around her?

"The queen's justice," she replied without inflection, inspecting her nails in a show of boredom. Nice touch. Pity the smirk she couldn't quite keep from her face spoiled the effect.

A guy with a gun joined her. Quite a crowd for the small bedroom. He gestured the wolf back. I kept my eyes on the wolf; I figured a gun could only kill me.

Ben laughed. "What do *you* know about justice? You're nothing more than a gun for hire. We're heralds, under the queen's protection."

Nada's eyes narrowed. Easy there, Ben. Making her mad didn't seem like a great game plan. There was obviously some history between these two. I swallowed, trying to look as calm as Ben, but the wolf could probably smell my fear.

"And *you're* nothing but glorified couriers," she sneered. "Micah, get their charms."

The guy with the gun gestured me out of the way and took my necklace with the little Robin Hood guy from the bedside table. He was so close I could smell the garlic on his breath. I could have knocked him down—or through the window. Instead I backed up against the wall and let him squeeze past. Having a werewolf in the room certainly dampened my enthusiasm for heroics. Ben still wore his necklace. Wordlessly the gunman held out his free hand until Ben handed it over.

"Does Valeria know you're here?" Ben sounded remarkably cool for a man with a gun in his face. Maybe he was used to it. I was coming to realise there was a lot I didn't know about him. "She's a fool if she thinks the queen won't punish both of you for this. Elizabeth doesn't like having her peace broken."

"Her Majesty doesn't like having her daughters killed by the meat either," she snapped. I didn't like the way she looked at me as she said it.

"We had nothing to do with Leandra's death."

I wished I could be so sure.

"Really. Word on the street says otherwise." Her gaze flicked over me briefly. "Come and tell Valeria all about it; I'm sure she'll be fascinated."

"Why should Valeria care who killed Leandra, as long as she's dead? She would have done it herself if she could. And we don't answer to Valeria."

Nada laughed. "Maybe not this week, little man. But how long do you think it will be before Valeria's queen? Is it wise to disobey your future sovereign?"

She waved one languid hand at the werewolf, who trotted obediently from the room. Her perfect manicure suggested she usually gave the orders and left the actual work to others.

"Bring everything," she said to the one called Micah. "I don't want any sign left that they've been here. Tell the other two to follow in the herald's car."

Micah nodded and pulled a cable tie from his pocket, which he used to cuff my hands firmly in front of me. Remarkably dexterous for a man still holding a gun. Must have had a lot of practice. Then he did the same for Ben, who glared at him.

"You cross this line, you can never go back."

"Shut up," Micah growled, shoving Ben toward the door.

Nada strode out. Another gunman waited in the main room, and he and Micah hustled us after her, one gun on each of us. There was no sign of the wolf.

A black four-wheel drive sat in the driveway behind Ben's car, motor already running, headlights off. The only light came from the moon and what little spilled from the open front door. No chance of anyone seeing us and calling the police; every house on the street stood dark and quiet. Micah forced us into the back seat with the other gunman, then went around to the driver's side. Two others brought my bag and Ben's first aid kit out and got into Ben's car. Maybe one of them was the werewolf? It was impossible to tell now.

Nada spoke to them then got in beside Micah. I glared at the back of her sleek head all the way to the motorway.

CHAPTER NINE

I woke to find Jason leaning over our bed, fully dressed.

"What are you doing?" According to my brand-new alarm clock, we didn't have to get up for another half-hour. It was still dark, but light from the hallway illuminated the mantelpiece where the clock sat, its ticking loud in the quiet house.

"Luce is worried."

"So?" I stretched like a cat, enjoying the slide of satin sheets against my skin. His eyes lingered on my curves. "Luce is always worried. That's her job."

"One of the boys coming in this morning saw Nada down in the village," Luce said from the doorway.

"Nada?" I frowned at my security chief. Dressed in jeans and boots, her dark hair pulled back in a no-nonsense ponytail, she stared back with her usual impassivity. You could never tell what Luce was thinking—unless she wanted you to know. "Nada Kusic?"

Valeria's second was a griffin with a mean streak a mile wide—perfect for Valeria, in fact—and a burning desire to prove herself as good as a dragon. Not a person to be taken lightly, despite her laughable ambitions. She'd killed my sister Monique at the Presentation ball and come close to taking me out at the same time.

Luce nodded. "So he said. With a couple of thralls."

"What's she hanging around for?"

Jason shrugged and grinned at Luce. "That's what Luce wants to know. I said I'd go with her."

I pouted. "Send Garth instead and come back to bed. It's still practically my birthday."

He laughed and kissed the tip of my nose. "It was your birthday yesterday, and I already gave you a present." My new alarm clock, modelled on a clock owned by Marie Antoinette, gold-plated and studded with diamonds. It was a beautiful piece, and supposedly the alarm was something special. My favourite song? A recorded message from him, maybe? He wouldn't say. "Stay in bed and wait for the surprise."

"I hate surprises," I grumbled. "Why don't you just tell me?"

He wagged a finger at me. "That would spoil all the fun. Now go back to sleep. This shouldn't take long."

He strode out. Luce lingered in the doorway, her gaze roaming the room as if she expected to find an assailant lurking beneath the four-poster bed or hiding in the shadows of the walk-in wardrobe.

"I'll take Dean and Charlie," she said, "and leave you Garth and the others."

"Really? Only ten men to keep me safe?" Luce took her job as head of security very seriously. "Are you sure that's enough?"

"Maybe I should be worried about keeping them safe from you," she muttered as she followed Jason out.

Fancy that—a joke from Luce. She mustn't be feeling well.

"*Are you coming, Luce?*" *Jason roared from downstairs as I snuggled down into the blankets. It was good to see him taking an interest again. He'd been jumpy and difficult lately. I suppose it was to be expected—his child had been dead mere weeks. Though it had only been half dragon Jason had taken its loss hard.*

At least it meant he no longer had to see its mother. Not that I was jealous, of course. Dragons weren't monogamous and I didn't spend too many lonely nights. But Jason was one of my favourites.

I rolled over, trying to find sleep again, but the sheets were cool without Jason. Damn it! Thralls couldn't lie, but the magic that enthralled them made them dull-witted. The thrall was probably mistaken, and Jason and Luce off on a wild goose chase.

If it was true, however … Nada's being so close practically constituted a declaration of war. Valeria usually liked to work more subtly than that. Poor Monique had died without even knowing what had hit her: one minute waltzing, big puppy-dog eyes laughing up at her partner, the next smeared in little tiny pieces all over the ballroom. If not for Luce's quick mind, I would have been right behind her.

Why would Nada risk coming this far into my territory? Was it some scheme of Valeria's, or was she working on her own?

Thoroughly awake now, I gave up on the idea of more sleep. My beautiful clock, standing proud on the mantelpiece, said I had five minutes before the alarm went off. Enough time to duck downstairs for coffee. I could start my day with coffee in bed, listening to my birthday surprise. Maybe I'd get one of the thralls to get the fire going in the hearth, too. Naked flame was so much more satisfying than air-conditioning.

Sunrise was peeking through the big kitchen windows as I entered, the clear pink sky promising another fine day. Moving out here had been a good decision. Apart from the stables and the garage, I could see nothing but fields and trees. The property was so big, and the neighbours so far away, I had room to breathe. Security was easier too than in the city.

Three of the thralls were gathered round the coffee machine with Garth, gossiping like old grandmothers. The word must have spread about Nada. They fell silent when I came in, except for Garth, who offered me coffee. The thralls were just interchangeable bodies. They watched my every move with single-minded devotion, but I didn't take enough notice of them to be able to tell one from the other. Garth, on the other hand, was a wolf, an outcast from Trevor's pack. There'd been some trouble over a woman, as there so often was with wolves. Passionate creatures, but not always the brightest. Still, it worked out well for me. I gained a follower so grateful to find a place that his loyalty was as fierce as if I'd enthralled him—but with the bonus that he could still think for himself, unlike the thralls. He was Luce's right-hand man these days.

He made a mean coffee, too. Though the rest of them were drinking out of mugs, he got out the fine china for me. A thoughtful touch.

"Sugar? Milk?"

"Just make it strong." Like my men.

He nodded and passed the coffee across, his big hands careful with the delicate china. I eyed him as he checked his watch and sent the thralls off to their duty. He could have been mistaken for a soldier, with his short greying buzz cut and well-muscled body.

He was taller than me, and powerfully built, with a fine pair of shoulders. I did like a man with strong shoulders. It might be worth getting to know him better.

He leaned back against the gleaming steel of the kitchen bench, arms folded. The fingers of one hand drummed an impatient rhythm on an impressive bicep. When he checked his watch again I laughed.

"Stop fretting, Garth."

"They've been gone nearly half an hour. What's keeping them?"

"Don't worry so much. That's what I pay Luce for. They can take care of themselves."

Luce was the most competent person I knew, and Jason was old and cunning, a lethal combination in a dragon. Still, it took me a few moments to settle Garth, and time was ticking away. I hurried back upstairs, spilling hot coffee into the saucer, hoping I hadn't missed the alarm.

I realised I had when, halfway up, an explosion rocked the house and my bedroom door blew into the hallway.

I hurled the cup and saucer aside and took the stairs two at a time. Garth and two thralls pelted up the stairs after me. Debris lay scattered across the upper steps. I coughed, waving a hand in a vain attempt to clear the clouds of dust billowing from my room. Rubble had blasted from the door in a wide semicircle. Beneath my bare feet the carpet felt gritty with pieces of brick and plasterboard.

Garth held me back with one arm. "Get away. There might be another bomb."

That would be clever, wouldn't it? One explosion to draw a crowd, another to finish them off. But I didn't think that was the intent here. One bomb, one victim.

I stood in the doorway and surveyed the gaping hole in the side of the building that used to be my bedroom. There wasn't much left. The four-poster bed had been obliterated. The chairs, the dressing table, the window with its heavy brocade drapes—all gone. No sign remained of the mantelpiece or the beautiful clock which had stood there—in fact, the fireplace no longer needed a chimney, as half the roof had blown off. Early morning light streamed through the hole and lit the swirling dust and smoke, incongruously cheerful. A few scraps of carpet clung to the scorched floor by the door. I stared at the place where the bed had been. Where I should have been lying, waiting for my birthday surprise.

I was surprised, all right—surprised how much it hurt.

Garth, with singular presence of mind, already had his phone out. "Luce isn't answering," he said after a moment. "Or Jason either."

"No, I imagine not." I felt listless but stirred myself to instruct the thralls to stamp out the fires starting in the wreckage and secure the building. Garth gave orders too, sending others out to check the grounds and one to review the security tapes.

But I knew the tapes would show nothing. I'd been betrayed. It happened to us all in time. Dragons were a backstabbing race by nature. But this was my first time, and though I'd expected the rage, the pain truly surprised me. I hadn't realised how fond I'd grown of Jason.

And Luce too. Was she a willing participant in this, or had Jason betrayed her as well? If he had she was likely dead by now. I clenched my fists so hard my nails cut into my palms. The pain helped me hold back shameful tears.

"It's lucky for him his child is already dead," I said when I had mastered myself. "Otherwise I'd wring its neck with my bare hands."

Then I remembered the female. "But there's still the wife ..."

Garth's face was white with shock and something that looked like fear, but he drew me back downstairs and urged me into a chair in the sunlit kitchen. I stared at my bare feet, cold on the tiled floor, and didn't realise I was shaking till he pressed a fresh cup of coffee into my hands. Little ripples trembled on its surface, its delicious aroma strangely out of place in this new, darker world.

"They split a while ago—before the kid died," he said. "They hate each other now. You might be doing him a favour if you got rid of her."

Well, that would never do. I drew in deep shuddering breaths, trying to think. The steel benches gleamed in the first light of the day; the cheery red appliances looked the same as they had five minutes ago, but everything had changed. "Call Trevor. Get the pack out here to hunt him down. Find out where he's gone, and if Luce is involved."

Garth recoiled. Clearly he believed her innocent, but I could rule nothing out.

"I'll kill him myself if he's hurt her," he said, his grey eyes fierce.

I nodded, barely listening, dreaming already of vengeance for my battered heart. When I was queen, Jason would pay.

CHAPTER TEN

Déjà vu. Another night journey on the M1, this time heading south. A tense silence filled the car. Ben's body pressed against mine, but his warmth did little to reassure me.

The smell of smoke filtered in from outside. Fires in the national park again, most likely. Summer was peak bushfire season. At this point a bushfire almost seemed preferable to whatever Nada had in store.

No one spoke. The road unrolled before us, the steady drone of the engine the only sound. The lights of passing cars whooshed past like little beacons of normalcy in the darkness. I edged a little closer to Ben.

After a time I realised I could see other lights. In the tense darkness of the car, the nimbus around each of our kidnappers glowed softly. All three were different colours. Damn. I wished I'd had more time to find out what Ben knew about this.

Micah shone with a faint orange tint, like the man I'd seen at the shops in Curtin Road. Was that really only yesterday? So much had happened since then. The werewolf who'd attacked me had also carried that same faint orange aura. Were they all werewolves? Or were the colours random? Another question to add to the list.

Nada's aura was blue, a pale arctic shade. Suited the cold bitch. Maybe she was a were-polar bear.

I frowned, something struggling to the surface of my mind. As if a bubble popped, the knowledge suddenly appeared. She was a griffin, blue as all the lesser creatures of air were. And I'd seen her before.

What the hell? I shivered, my skin crawling. Where had that come from?

I sneaked a glance out of the corner of my eye at the man next to me. His aura shone a dull muddy brown. No miraculous bubble-popping this time. He could be anything. Or maybe his soul was just dirty. Not surprising, if he made a habit of kidnapping people at gunpoint.

He'd put the gun away now, but I daresay he could draw it fast enough if he needed to. Not that either of us were much threat with our hands tied in a car travelling at 110 kilometres an hour. What were we going to do? Open the door and jump out? It'd be certain death.

Where the hell were they taking us? Sydney, or further south? The cable tie was already cutting into my wrists. Sydney was an hour away. That would be bad enough. What if we were headed for Melbourne? Ten hours in the car with these clowns and jumping out might start looking a whole lot more attractive.

I glanced at the door. If they had any sense they probably had the child-safe lock on anyway. I went back to staring out the window and reading road signs as they loomed out of the dark. Anything to avoid seeing those strange coloured auras around my fellow passengers. I tried not to think about what might happen when we got wherever we were going. I tried not to think at all.

After nearly an hour of this my wrists had passed through agony into blessed numbness, and at last we turned off on to the Pacific Highway. In a couple of hours the city would start to stir, and this road would be choked with traffic, funnelling toward the Harbour Bridge and the central business district, but for now it was quiet. As the skyscrapers of the CBD appeared glittering out of the night we turned off down Military Road, whizzing past silent shops and restaurants.

I hadn't been this way since last time I took Lachie to the zoo. We did our animals proud in Sydney—Taronga Zoo had a prime piece of real estate right on the northern shore of the harbour, with million-dollar views across to the Opera House and the city. Funny how tame even the most exotic of Taronga's residents looked now compared to the creatures in the car with me.

We joined the right-turn lane down towards Taronga. Wherever we were going must be close; much further and we'd end up in the harbour.

At the big roundabout before the zoo we turned off and purred through the dark side streets. The closer we got to the water, the bigger the houses grew. This was Mosman, enclave of the offensively wealthy. You wouldn't get much change out of three or four million for any of these places, with their city views and their "architect-designed" structures. Some of the oldest ones sat on huge blocks and looked more like small country estates than suburban houses. The land alone probably cost more than I'd earn in my lifetime. Old money.

At last we turned into a driveway barred by high iron gates. The sandstone wall on either side looked so old it might have been built by the convicts. The gates slid open and the car crunched across gravel into a huge courtyard featuring a fountain to rival the Trevi in Rome. Behind it loomed a house that looked as if it had come straight off the set for *Gone With the Wind*, complete with huge portico and massive Corinthian columns.

No grand entrance for us, though. We followed the drive around to a separate garage the size of a small barn. From the back the house was no less huge, though not as imposing, and it tickled at my memory. Micah and his mate hustled us out of the car and we crunched across more gravel—there would be no sneaking up on this place—to a side door of ordinary size, and suddenly I had it. I'd been here before, dropping off one of those mysterious envelopes.

"Valeria's house," Ben whispered as Micah shoved us inside. "Don't tell them anything."

Well, that should be easy. I couldn't tell what I didn't know.

We entered a huge kitchen/eating area, all gleaming steel and granite. Utensils hung from ordered racks and two outsized ovens stood side by side. Jamie Oliver would have been proud to call it home. At least twenty chairs were spaced along a long table. How many people lived here?

Our captors marched us down a carpeted hall till we arrived at a large lounge room. One long wall made entirely of glass offered a stunning view of the Opera House and Bridge across the water, with the lights of the city behind them.

A man rose from a chair by the windows. The short hair threw me for a minute, but then he turned, and the shock of seeing that face again felt like a kick to the gut.

This just got better and better. What in hell was my ex doing here?

Jason looked as shocked to see me as I was to see him. We stared at each other for a long, horrified moment, then he whirled on Nada.

"What's *she* doing here?"

Ben moved closer. Funny, though; he didn't look a bit surprised. I glared at him, and he looked away, abashed. Clearly, if this relationship was going to last, we had to work on his communication skills.

Nada looked like the cat that ate the cream. She stalked forward in her designer heels, all fluid and smug and ready to pounce.

"Why don't you tell me?" she purred.

"What are you talking about? I haven't seen her in months."

I stared at him. The last time we'd met had been at Lachie's funeral, when I'd still been so angry with him I couldn't even bear to look at him. With that new haircut he looked as he had in my dream. And with the dark glass behind him—what the *hell?*—I could plainly see the faint red glow pulsing off him. *You have* got *to be kidding me.* What next? If someone had told me my mother was an alien I couldn't have been more surprised.

"And yet here she is, turning up in such unexpected places, with that low-life friend of yours. Very suspicious."

Jason glanced at Ben, as if he'd just realised he was there too. Emotion flashed across his face, too fleeting to identify. Fear? Anger?

"He's a herald, Nada. What do you think you're doing? Why are they tied up?"

"Kate's a herald too," said Ben.

I doubt Nada even heard him. She was too busy giving Jason the death stare. I felt like joining her. It was hard to believe I'd ever loved this piece of scum. Was there no end to his betrayals?

"Very convincing." Her voice dripped with sarcasm. "You play the innocent so well. I hope Valeria finds your act as entertaining. You told her you poisoned Leandra. You were the golden boy then, weren't you? But word on the street is that this thrall of yours stabbed her to death. What game are you playing at, Jason?"

Ben leapt to my defence. "She hasn't stabbed anyone!"

"You're out of your mind. If she's anyone's thrall, it's not mine. She hates me. There's a reason we're divorced, you know."

He shoved his hands in his pockets and stared out over the harbour as if the conversation held no further interest for him.

Nada clenched her fists. "We'll let Valeria be the judge, shall we?"

His glance was contemptuous. "I'm sure Valeria will be simply *thrilled* at your assault on two heralds. Do what you like. It's your funeral."

We seemed to have reached an impasse.

"Jason, this is insane. You know the penalties for interfering with heralds," said Ben. "We have nothing to do with this. Tell her to let us go. The queen's peace—"

"Shut up, messenger boy," Nada cut in. "Micah, take these two away. Put them in separate rooms."

"And cut off those ridiculous cuffs," Jason added. "Are we afraid of humans now?"

Micah obeyed. As I rubbed the circulation back into my wrists a familiar ringtone, slightly muffled, broke the tense silence. My phone, in my handbag, which Micah had brought in from the car along with Ben's first aid kit.

"Get it," Jason told the gunman.

Without comment Micah passed the bag to Jason, who dug out the phone and checked the display. For a moment I thought he was going to let me take the call, as if we were partners again and answering my phone was something he did all the time.

"Oh, for God's sake," said Nada. "Give me that!"

She snatched the phone from his hand and ripped the battery out of the back, cutting the sound off mid-ring.

"Get them out of here," she snapped.

Behind her, Jason still held my bag. Horror flashed across his face as he reached into it again, but by the time he looked up he'd got himself under control. He slipped something into the pocket of his jeans and dropped the bag on the nearest couch.

His eyes met mine as Micah took my elbow to lead me away. Only one thing in there could cause such consternation. The mysterious black stone.

He still watched me as I left the room, his expression unreadable.

CHAPTER ELEVEN

The pack had tracked Luce to a dingy warehouse near the airport. Rain hammered the car roof as Garth drove through the industrial area. At this time of night the streets were deserted. Ugly grey buildings loomed out of the downpour as we passed, locked behind their steel mesh fences. Fast food wrappers and other junk swirled in the water running down the gutters. Lovely neighbourhood.

I checked my watch as a jet roared overhead. Probably one of the last; it was nearly eleven, which meant the airport would soon close for the night. Though if the thunder rumbling in the distance got much closer the point would be moot.

A couple of blocks from our destination Garth pulled in next to a heavily graffitied bus shelter. A man waited there, coat collar turned up against the weather, cap jammed down on his head: Trevor, the pack leader. The rain pelted down so hard he got drenched just getting into the car.

"What a night." He wiped his face; a pointless exercise. Water dripped off him all over the Merc's leather seats.

"The storm seems very localised." I had to raise my voice to be heard over the rain and the rhythmic thud of the wipers.

The clouds had gathered the closer we got to the airport. Thunder rumbled ominously, like a beast prowling closer.

"That's because she has an ala in there." Trevor's expression was sour.

Ah. That made sense. The ale were demons of bad weather, often appearing as a black wind or a storm. We didn't get many in Australia; they preferred their climate a little cooler, and getting them to forsake the ice and snow of the northern hemisphere took some doing, though they'd make an exception for a good cyclone now and then. I wondered where my sister had managed to find this one—or what she'd promised it to work for her.

They liked to eat children, and our royal mother would not be impressed if that had been the inducement. She'd become ever more conservative as she aged, and didn't like anything in her kingdom that might set the humans aflutter. She was paranoid about the shifter world being discovered, which in this internet age of mobile phones with their ever-present cameras seemed inevitable. A modern queen should have a disaster plan already in place. Modern technology was not some passing fad. We'd had a few close calls already. Fortunately the preference of most humans to dismiss as hoaxes anything they didn't understand or wish to believe in worked in our favour.

"I don't know how we're going to get around it," Trevor said. "It's perched up on the roof in raven form, above the doors. It can see the whole forecourt from there. There's no way to sneak past."

Damn it. Trevor was not one to panic or give up easily—he would never have made pack leader if he were. His slight stature made him look weak, but challengers soon discovered the will of iron lurking beneath the mild exterior. Still, I had to find a way.

If I couldn't get Luce back I'd be the one looking weak. Quite apart from the embarrassment, the loss of my security chief would be a heavy blow.

Damn Jason! Rage swept through me again. She'd trusted him—we both had—and had never suspected a trap. Why would we? He was supposed to be on our side.

And now he was on Valeria's, and this was his farewell present to me. How he must be laughing now, the bastard. He'd always said I was too trusting.

"Any other doors?"

The rain sheeted down the fogged-over car windows and drummed loudly on the roof. I watched it slice through the headlights' beams and bounce back off the road as I considered my options.

"There's an office door, but it's on the same side as the main door."

"What about windows?"

He shook his head. "They're all too high. Some broken ones around the back, but we'd need a ladder."

And the ala wouldn't sit still while we climbed ladders.

Garth twisted to join the conversation from the driver's seat. "You know they'll be expecting us."

"Of course."

Valeria wasn't obvious enough to send a ransom note or a demand for a meeting, but she hadn't made it hard for the wolves to find this place. It was all part of the proving, this game we played with our lives. I dare you, *she said with her abandoned warehouse and her pet ala.* Come and show me what you've got.

Valeria had most of the local goblins on the payroll, so there could be golems in there, or just plain old mundane firepower. Goblins loved a good assault rifle. Or, considering the ala, there might be other surprises. Valeria must be feeling pretty smug right now. I wondered if she watched somewhere, waiting for the show to start.

So I'd give her one.

The problem was how. Wolves against guns, no doubt loaded with silver, was not a winning combination. This would be so much easier if I could take trueshape. Longing rippled through me at the thought of tearing goblins apart and feeding on their flesh. But shifters who defied the queen's interdiction against taking trueshape where humans might see them had a nasty habit of turning up dead. Life was complicated enough without painting a target like that on my back. I needed a surprise.

I eyed the soggy pack leader, who waited patiently for orders. A good man in a crisis. He was slim, about my height. He'd even worn a baseball cap to keep his hair dry.

"Take off your clothes."

He shot me a startled look. "Sorry?"

"Swap clothes with me. We're about the same size." I wore jeans and a dark green T-shirt, nothing overtly feminine, but his horrified expression suggested I'd asked him to put on a pink dress. "If anyone's watching us—and we have to assume they are—they saw a man dressed like you get in the car. If that man gets out again, but the car drives to the warehouse, they'll assume I'm still in it."

"Right." He unbuttoned his shirt, still reluctant. Did he think he'd lose face with the pack? "And what will you really be doing?"

I pulled off my T-shirt and started wriggling out of my jeans. Now I was glad for the ala's storm and the foggy windows it produced. No one could see what we were up to. The confined space made the mechanics challenging, and we bumped heads a couple of times, but shifters are used to getting naked. His clothes smelled of wet dog.

"I'll be dealing with the ala. Give me twenty minutes, then get the pack to show themselves out front. Make it look as if you're preparing to rush the place. That should hold its attention."

I twisted my ponytail into a coil and stuffed it under the cap, then clambered across my cross-dressing pack leader and opened the door. "You should wear green more often. It suits you."

His shirt clung to me, clammy and cold. I shivered as I stepped out into the rain. The car pulled away in a spray of water, its tyres swishing on the wet road.

I strode off into the downpour away from the warehouse, shoulders hunched against the rain. It trickled down my neck and pelted against my back.

Once I'd covered half a dozen blocks the rain eased. The streets were deserted—who'd venture out on such a night? No sign of anyone following. Perhaps switching clothes had done the trick.

At a small overgrown park—little more than a vacant lot that boasted a rusty swing set—I pushed my way into the dripping bushes and hunkered down to wait, watching the street I'd just left. Best to be sure.

Five minutes ticked by, then ten. Nothing moved. I scanned the sky, but saw nothing but rain. The clouds hung so low they touched the tops of the buildings. After twenty minutes I felt secure enough and peeled off Trevor's wet clothes with relief. Drops of water plopped on to my bare skin and ran like cold fingers down my spine.

Time to pull a rabbit out of the hat.

As far as I knew, no one had ever attempted this before. Minor detail. No reason to be nervous. I drew a deep breath. No reason except that I had no fall-back plan, and time was ticking away for Luce, if she was even still alive.

In theory it made perfect sense. Dragons were so much bigger than humans that when we took human form all that mass had to go somewhere else. Dragon-sized humans would find blending in something of a challenge. Fortunately we had the ability to channel the extra mass elsewhere. In theory there should be no reason that it all had to come back when we took trueshape. In theory, if I channelled even more of my human-sized mass away at the same time I sought trueshape, the result should be a miniature dragon.

In practice? Time to find out.

It had never been done before since no self-respecting dragon would choose to be the size of a cat. Massive size was part of the joy of trueshape. No other shifter approached it, and it served as a physical reminder of dragon superiority. But for Luce's sake, I was prepared to throw self-respect out the window. Though perhaps huddling naked in the rain while a werewolf wore my clothes meant I'd already done that.

If I was lucky, my small size and the ala's convenient storm meant there would be no crazy photos appearing on the internet. I did not *want to get into my mother's bad books. If she decided to punish me by throwing her weight behind Valeria—or even Alicia, though that seemed unlikely—I wouldn't stand a chance.*

I blew out a deep breath and opened myself to otherwhere. The wholeness of union beckoned; it felt like coming home. The urge to pull my essence back together and take trueshape was immense. My body trembled with the strain as I started pushing instead. It was harder than I'd expected: trueshape and human form were like moulds I poured myself between, firm and unchanging. Now I had to break the mould, if I could.

I pushed harder and felt a trickle begin, reluctant at first, then gaining momentum. My self rushed away like a river in flood. What if I accidentally sent my whole essence through the void? I clamped the connection shut in a sudden panic.

When I opened my eyes the bushes loomed over me, grown huge and black. I was tiny, perhaps the size of a three-year-old, but still fully human. I clenched my pathetic little fists in frustration. The ala might die laughing when it saw me, but that was the best I could hope for.

Doubt assailed me. Was I truly the first dragon in millennia to conceive of such an idea, or was that my pride talking? What if it had never been done before because it simply wasn't possible?

I stood—plenty of room under the bushes now! Trevor and the pack were waiting, and Luce needed me. No time for doubt. I began to channel again, more cautiously this time, holding the form of trueshape in my head all the while. This was where I needed to go. Here, and here, and yes! Like that! Gradually the warmth of change crept over me as my limbs found their new shapes, sinking into familiar forms. It was much slower than usual, but at last it felt right. I knew I'd done it before I opened my eyes.

Success! I was a dragon, but no bigger than a cat. Tiny, perfect scales covered my body. I emerged from the bushes, which now towered over me, and extended my wings. How delicate they were. No thunderclap sounded as I leapt skyward; the leaves barely stirred in the tiny puff of air I displaced. Still, everything seemed to be working, though being so small made me uneasy. I wasn't used to feeling vulnerable. Best get this over with. It was not a feeling I wished to prolong.

Level with the rooftops, my form wavered. This size felt unnatural, and I had to fight to stop myself swelling to something more dignified. Being airborne called to the rest of my essence, which ached to join me in trueshape. Buffeted by gusts I wouldn't even have noticed at full size, I circled a while, till I had myself under control again.

I climbed into the clouds, grateful for the ala's concealing storm, though I had to fight against the wind to gain height. The storm centred on the warehouse, and the blasts of wind grew stronger as I approached. If I were only a little larger this would be easier, but I didn't dare try adjusting my size in mid-air. I barely had myself under control as it was. A full-size dragon suddenly appearing in the sky would be hard to miss, even on a night like this. At my current size, no one would think me anything but a bat.

I spiralled down warily, my straining wings glad for the respite, and scanned the rooftop for the small black shape of the ala.

There—right above the doors, as Trevor had said. Still in raven shape, though its feathers remained curiously unruffled by the wind that tore at me. Its beady eyes were fixed on the wolves prowling up and down outside the chain-link fence. The Merc was parked across the street, its windows dark.

I folded my wings and dropped out of the storm like an avenging god. The raven looked up at the last minute, but too late for more than a squawk before I had it in my claws. I dug in deep and pulled. *With a satisfying crunch, audible even over the pounding rain, the bird shape came apart. Feathers flew as the ala dissolved into mist.*

Too easy. I'd missed something.

That something slammed into me a heartbeat later, and I went skidding across roof panels slick with rain. A second ala, an amorphous dark shape of roiling cloud, hurled lightning at me. I leapt from the roof with a yelp, hearing the sizzle of electricity behind me.

Twisting in mid-air, I aimed a blast of fire at the ala. At this range the creature would be incinerated.

Except I'd forgotten my tiny size. The pitiful lick of flame I produced made a cigarette lighter look good. I twisted out of the way as the ala lunged after me, morphing into a new shape: cloud warrior, complete with sword.

The figure was wispy and indistinct, but the sword looked sharp. Would my tiny scales armour me as well as they did at full size? At least my size made me agile. I dodged a sweep of the sword and snapped at the creature's head. Best not to put it to the test.

The sword darted out again. Sparks flew as it scraped down my shoulder. I tumbled away from the blow, numbness spreading from shoulder to wing. The air thrummed with power; the scent of ozone strong on the wind. The ala surged after me as I struggled to regain height, narrowly avoiding another stinging blow.

I darted away into the complex, dropping below roof level as I dodged between buildings. A chill of fear stole through me. At this size I was no match for the storm creature.

It roared after me, buffeting me with its icy wind. Squalls of rain spattered the buildings like gunshots. My right wing throbbed, but I was still faster, careering desperately between the dark buildings. Trueshape screamed for release, but I clamped down on it. Just a little longer.

I slammed around the corner of the last building in the complex, tucked away at the back of the lot, and turned to face my pursuer. The ground trembled as I reached at last for my essence. Trailing streamers of ice, the ala rounded the corner, sword upraised in triumph—and found a full-sized dragon waiting in the dark.

It hardly had time to register the shock before I blasted it with fire. The sword tumbled to the ground as the night lit up with flame. It lay there, the blade glowing softly red, as the storm abruptly disintegrated and tiny flecks of ash drifted down.

God, but that felt good.

With a sigh I forced my essence away and felt my body dwindling again. Cat-sized once more, I launched myself into the air and flew back to the front warehouse the two ala had been guarding. From its roof I checked the forecourt. Nothing moved among the parked trucks and forklifts. The only movement came from the wolves, still pacing the fence line, being careful not to look at me. I wondered if they'd seen the burst of flame light up the night. Hopefully no hostile eyes had noted the death of the warehouse's guardians.

Satisfied nothing had changed, I darted from the roof. The back of the warehouse was covered in scrawls of graffiti—bright looping tags and a black skull and crossbones. The windows were high off the ground, too high for the graffiti artists to reach, and a couple were broken, as Trevor had said, their edges like jagged teeth. I chose the one with the biggest hole and landed on the window ledge.

Inside was dark, but low light was no problem for dragon eyes, and I could see Luce slumped against one wall in chains. Down at the other end of the vast empty space, a phalanx of goblins faced the big warehouse doors. They stirred uneasily and muttered in the sibilant goblin tongue, probably alarmed by the sudden cessation of the storm. Between them they had enough assault rifles to mow down a small army.

The set-up could hardly suit me better. If only Jason were with the goblins, it would be perfect. A fierce joy rose inside me as I crouched on the ledge and contemplated my next move.

I launched myself through the window and pulled. *Releasing my tight self-control felt like a dam breaking: truesize rushed back to me so fast my tail smashed half the windows from their frames. Glass rained down on the astonished goblins as a full-sized dragon materialised inside the warehouse with them, but they would never inform on me. I belched forth flame and incinerated the lot of them where they stood. The screaming had hardly even started.*

With little room to manoeuvre, my landing was graceless. I stomped toward the glass-walled office space at the end of the building, ready for anything, but no one else was there. Just Luce and I and a pile of fried goblins. The smell made my mouth water.

So much for Valeria's big ambush. Clearly she'd put too much faith in her ale.

Feeling mighty pleased with myself, I took human form again and opened the door, signalling to the wolves. But my pleasure faded when I saw what they'd done to Luce.

They had her chained in silver, manacled at wrist and ankle. Not only couldn't she shift, the silver impeded her usual supernatural healing. By the look of her they'd taken full advantage of the situation. The area reeked of blood, and patches of rust red stained the concrete floor. Hideous burns covered her bare arms, as if someone had tried writing on her flesh with a soldering iron. Her face was so bruised and swollen she was unrecognisable as my dainty Chinese wyvern.

For one awful moment I thought she was dead. Then her eyes cracked open and she fixed me with a true Luce glare.

"What kept you?" she croaked.

CHAPTER TWELVE

Micah and the guy who'd driven Ben's car back from the Central Coast marched us upstairs. Our feet made no sound on the plush grey carpet. The wide hallways were still, the panelled doors all closed, as if most of the residents were tucked up in bed, as any normal person would be at this ungodly hour of the morning. My eyes felt gritty from lack of sleep.

The whole place screamed money, but in an impersonal way. Tasteful paintings hung on tasteful grey walls. Bland. It looked more like something out of a home decorating magazine than an actual home.

They locked us in separate rooms.

"Don't worry," Ben said over his shoulder as Micah led him away. "I'll think of something."

Right. Don't worry.

Locked in, back against the door, I checked out my room. Not bad for a prison. More like a high-class hotel. The queen-sized bed groaned under such a mountain of pillows it looked like it had been styled for a magazine shoot.

The room was bigger than my combined lounge/dining room at home, and through a door I glimpsed a corner spa in the en suite. Sliding glass doors led on to a small balcony. Locked, of course. Still, if you have to be imprisoned, a soft bed and a private bathroom beats rats and dungeons every time.

I yawned and rubbed my burning eyeballs. Past five. The sun would be up soon and I'd hardly slept.

My lips curved in spite of everything. The main reason for my tiredness was somewhere down the hall, and he'd been well worth losing a little sleep. A thrill of warmth shot through me at the memory. Gorgeous Ben.

Gorgeous, stupid Ben. *Don't worry?* Seriously? Who did he think he was fooling?

I explored both rooms, looking for some kind of weapon. The pepper grinder had taught me not to discount anything, but Nada's people hadn't left anything useful. Not even a soap dish in the bathroom. Nothing in the bedside drawers, no table lamps or vases. Nothing. If they stood still long enough I might be able to suffocate someone with one of the three dozen cushions from the bed, but that was it.

I clenched my fists. Wouldn't I love to drive them into Micah's face and feel his nose crunch under the impact, see the blood spray. I'd lay into him, pummelling his face to a pulp, feeling his eyeballs burst, hearing his agonised screams.

Good God. I drew a shaky breath. I wasn't usually so bloodthirsty. Stress did funny things to people.

Disquieted, I tried the balcony door again, as if repetition was the magic key to unlocking it. My room was on the first floor, at the back of the house. No harbour views for me, just a high stone wall and glimpses of the neighbouring houses across the laneway, still slumbering under the streetlights. I sank on to the bed, shoulders slumped. My bandaged one throbbed in time with my heartbeat.

What were they going to do with me? Nothing good, I supposed. I tried to ignore the frightened knot in my stomach. No use thinking about it.

At least I needn't worry about developing Stockholm syndrome with Jason here. I'd rot in hell before I fell in with any cause of his, and as for falling in love! I snorted. Been there, done that. I may be a slow learner but he'd betrayed me twice now, the filthy bastard. Lied to my face even as he poisoned me!

No, wait. That had been a dream. I scrubbed at my tired face with both hands. This was all so crazy—no wonder my thoughts were all jumbled up. Last time I'd seen Jason he'd been at Lachie's funeral, sombre in a black suit, dry-eyed and tight-lipped.

As always my mind shied away from the memories of that day: the mourners gathered around the grave, the smell of freshly turned earth and rose petals assaulting my nostrils. The priest's voice an incomprehensible drone. My sister's arm around me, my mother pressed close on the other side. But still I was alone, lost in agony as that small white coffin was lowered into the grave. How could the sky still be blue? Only my sister's grip had stopped me throwing myself in after it.

How could he stand there and not even shed a tear?

I hurled an overstuffed cushion at the locked door. I'd wanted to kill him then, and nothing had changed. And now I discovered he was a *dragon*? Did that mean Lachie—?

No, surely it didn't work like that. I was human; Lachie had been human too. But dragons lived for centuries. Might he have lived longer than a normal human? The irony left a bitter taste in my mouth. Thanks to his long-lived father, he hadn't even had a decade.

I lay back against the cushions, exhausted, but too strung up to sleep.

When I opened my eyes sunlight streamed in through the balcony doors. With a clink of china Micah set a breakfast tray on the bedside table. Guess I'd been able to sleep after all.

Breakfast was only cereal and juice, but I was starving. I wolfed it down double-time, as if he might change his mind if I wasn't quick enough. He stood, arms folded, and watched every bite go down.

"What? You've never seen anyone eat before?"

He didn't reply. Strong silent type. He had a surly face, like a professional bouncer. The kind who always expects the worst of the clientele. Maybe he was terrified I'd attack him with the plastic spoon they'd so thoughtfully provided. As if I could do any damage even with a metal one. The guy was built, easily twice my weight and a good head taller.

I had him pegged as a werewolf. He gave off a faint orange glow, which reminded me of my visitor of—yesterday? Was it only yesterday I'd been fighting a werewolf in my kitchen? How time flies when you're having fun. I rotated my shoulder experimentally. Hardly a twinge.

He was taller than my werewolf, but I guessed there were no height requirements. Not that I knew much about it, other than—thank God!—that it took more than a scratch to create a new wolf. How many werewolves hid in plain sight among us ordinary folk? Now that I could see the orange glow, would I find them everywhere, like cockroaches scuttling in the dark?

When I'd finished he took the tray and left me to discover how slowly time can crawl when you have nothing to do but stare at the wall and worry. By the time someone tapped politely on the door I was going crazy and it was only ten o'clock.

"Come in." High-class establishment, indeed. I was a prisoner. Who knocked at a prisoner's door?

Jason did, apparently.

"What do you want?" I turned away from his lying face before I could give in to the urge to punch it. His stupid glowing aura did nothing to improve my mood. What was wrong with me? Why could I see these weird colours?

Because he's a dragon and you have the sight. Stop whining.

"Have you eaten?" Jason asked. "Is there anything else you need?"

I stared stupidly. For a moment I appeared to be having two different conversations at once.

Only I didn't know who the other one was with.

He was taller than I remembered, looming over me as Micah had done. I stood, forcing myself to unclench my fists, and lifted my chin. I would not be intimidated by this lying sack of shit.

"So you're a dragon. Explains a few things, I guess. So …
when you said fidelity wasn't in your nature, you weren't
kidding."

God, why did I say that? As if I cared any more about his
stupid affairs.

"No. I wasn't. I'm sorry about that." He sounded genuine,
his blue eyes guileless. "I never meant to hurt you, you know.
We were just too different."

I'd forgotten what a good actor he was.

"It doesn't matter now." An urge to slap that caring look
off his face made my palms tingle, and fury tightened my
chest. How had I ever thought he was handsome? "You
betrayed me. I thought you had my back, and you sold me
out."

He gave me a quizzical look.

No, that wasn't right. I hated him for his carelessness, for
thinking he was above the law, that he could drink and drive. I
hated him for not cherishing my baby with every fibre of his
being. For living when Lachie died.

"Kate." He sat on the bed and patted the spot beside him.
"I want to help you. You know I'm on your side."

His eyes bored into me, so sincere. A wave of dizziness had
me swaying where I stood. He held my gaze as I crossed to his
side, took my hand as I sank down next to him. His hand felt
warm and comforting.

"You know I'm here for you, don't you?"

I nodded. I remembered now how beautiful his eyes were,
such a clear sky blue. So many of our fights had ended with me
gazing into them and remembering all the reasons I loved him.

"Tell me about this." He drew something from his pocket; a stone about the size of a small marble. It was black, with pretty silver lines. I'd seen it somewhere before. I only glanced at it for a moment, then lost myself in his eyes again. So beautiful. "Where did you get it? Did you find it? Did someone give it to you?"

I opened my mouth to answer but no words came. I wanted to tell him—*don't tell him*. Pressure built inside my skull. I'd do anything for him. *Backstabbing bastard.* Anything he wanted. *Kill him.*

A wave of fury surged through me. I leapt to my feet, screaming defiance.

"Get out of my head, you sonofabitch!"

He fell back, pure astonishment on his face. I spat words at him like missiles.

"Why did I trust you again, you worm? You're pathetic. You were never fit to be my consort!"

The door crashed back against the wall. Nada stood there, Micah at her shoulder.

"What's going on? What are you doing in here with her?"

Jason rose, still with that stunned expression on his face. Too slow to hide the stone.

Nada pounced. "What's that?"

She snatched it from his hand. Abruptly he came out of his trance, shooting her a venomous look.

"Give me that."

"Why?" She held it tantalisingly out of reach. "What is it? Is it hers?"

The look she gave me was contemptuous. My fingers crooked into claws. I longed to tear her apart.

"Give it to me. Now." Jason spoke through gritted teeth. Obviously he felt as I did about the griffin upstart.

"Or what? You may not have noticed, but all your pets have gone with Valeria. No one is going to jump to do your bidding. Least of all me." She stood with her hands on her hips, like an adult telling off a small child, the stone hidden in one fist. A muscle jumped in Jason's jaw.

I folded my arms. The enemy of my enemy is my friend? No, but I was prepared to enjoy the show. Let them fight. There would be an opportunity for me in it somewhere.

"You forget yourself," said Jason, steel in his voice.

Nada stepped in, so close her face almost touched his. "I am not the one conspiring with a piece of human trash. I am not the one keeping secrets from my mistress. I think *you* forget *your*self, and your place here."

He stared at her with contempt. "My place is at Valeria's side. You're a fool if you think that place will ever be yours."

Nada's mouth twisted. "Say what you like, but stay away from this woman till Valeria gets back. We'll see who the fool is then." She still thought we were conspiring against her precious mistress somehow. "Micah, I want you outside this door twenty-four seven. No one comes in unless I say so."

Lucky Micah. The big man nodded, not complaining at being given babysitting duty.

Jason laughed. "You're going to bother Valeria with your petty jealousy *now*? Excellent plan! She'll be thrilled at the mess you've made."

She glared at him with naked hatred. "My jealousy, this stone, your woman—whatever it takes. Anything to bring you down."

Jason looked at the stone and shrugged. "It's a piece of worthless rock. Knock yourself out."

He moved to the door and spoke to Micah. "If anyone wants me, I'll be in the mountains with Valeria. Try to keep Nada on her leash while I'm gone."

He walked out. Nada glared at his back, then crossed with quick strides to the glass doors that led out on to the balcony. She stared down at the courtyard. In a few moments I heard a car start and crunch across the gravel.

"Running to Valeria won't save him." She walked out without even glancing my way. "Remember—no one in or out but me."

Micah nodded and locked the door behind them. I stalked over to the glass doors myself. How dare they lock me in here like some piece of baggage to be collected at their leisure?

Fists clenched, I looked out on the sunlit courtyard and planned a thousand painful deaths for Jason and the mad griffin bitch.

CHAPTER THIRTEEN

By mid-afternoon my inventiveness had run out and my temper had climbed back down out of the stratosphere. Oh, I was still mad—at these freaks for holding me against my will, at Ben for getting me mixed up in this in the first place, at Jason for ... well, for being Jason.

No one had come or gone since he'd stomped off in a tantrum. Typical Jason move—it brought back a lot of memories.

Knowing he was a dragon made sense of a lot of things. No wonder I'd always found it so hard to stay mad at him, whatever he did, however many other women he slept with, always promising this was the last time. My sister had accused me of being a doormat. I'd thought so myself.

Turns out I wasn't so spineless—just charmed into forgiving him. My skin crawled at the memory of him forcing his will on me. It had felt like a fog invading my mind. Such a sickening feeling of helplessness, like being a prisoner in my own body. He'd been so sure he could still get me to do or say anything he liked, just like the old days. But I'd fought back, and hadn't that shocked him!

Better get used to it, arsehole.

And this was the man I'd chosen to father my child. *Good job, Kate.*

If Lachie had been half-dragon, what did that mean? It was hard to imagine my scrawny little munchkin as something quite so imposing. Scales instead of curls, claws instead of grubby little-boy fingernails. Not that it mattered any more. Jason had seen to that.

Time to stop dancing to his tune, or that of his so-charming griffin associate. That was a strange relationship. Where did the power lie? Nada had made no secret of her hatred of him, but empty threats seemed the best she could manage without the absent Valeria's say-so.

Now there was someone I didn't want to meet. Best to be long gone before she arrived.

The balcony door was out. Shame I didn't have a bobby pin—I might have used it as a lock pick. Not that I had the faintest clue how to pick a lock, but I itched for action and mere details weren't going to stop me.

Kicking my way through the glass, while it might make me feel better, was bound to attract attention. The way I felt right now, that didn't seem such a bad thing. Restless energy fizzed inside my skin, desperate for release. My shoulder itched like the devil, but it wasn't sore any more. My headaches and sickness had melted away too, leaving me ready to take on the world, or at least a werewolf or two. Only the tiny voice of reason reminding me what had happened in my last encounter with a werewolf led me to the en suite, where the window wasn't locked.

It wasn't big, either, but big enough for someone my size, though it might take some acrobatics. I stood on the bath and fiddled with the flyscreen. Somehow I managed to get it off without dropping it outside. Then I hoisted myself up and got my head and shoulders out the window.

Immediately I saw the problem: a sheer drop onto sandstone flagging. Even if I could wriggle myself around and get out the window feet first, it was too high. I'd be lucky if I only broke my legs.

A white-hot knot of rage tightened inside me. The blue vault of the sky beckoned, tantalisingly close. I wanted to spread my wings and leap out into that vast blue emptiness, free of this prison. Free of this lump of useless flesh.

How dare they keep me here against my will? Who did they think they were?

I brought my gaze down from the clouds to the gravelled driveway below, the garage and the high sandstone wall around the property. On the street behind, a small Asian woman walked her fluffy white dog past the back gates, enjoying the sunshine. I ground my teeth. Even the stupid mutt on its leash had more freedom than I.

Something about the woman penetrated my ferocious sulk: the way she carried herself, or something in the tilt of her head. I knew her.

I leaned forward, the window sill cutting into my ribs, toes grazing the edge of the bath. She glanced up, apparently casually, and our eyes met through the wrought iron gate. Then she was gone, hidden behind the wall again.

I eased myself down from the window and picked up the flyscreen. Micah's deep voice growled something in the corridor outside my room, and I froze, but he didn't come in. My hands clenched on the screen. Just let him, and he'd be wearing this as a necklace. A terrible longing to smash his head like a watermelon filled me. I could do it so easily. Filthy dog.

Whew. Easy there. What the hell was the matter with me? I sank down on the edge of the bath. Was this schizophrenia? Where were all these violent thoughts coming from? I felt like Dr Jekyll being taken over by Mr Hyde.

A small but distinct snap sounded under my hands. I'd broken the aluminium frame.

Who was I kidding? Schizophrenia didn't make you throw up stones or see auras around people. And it certainly didn't give you the power to fight off your sleazebag ex's psychic assault.

Something had happened to me—or more likely, been done to me—and it was all tied up with those lost moments in the garden with Leandra. Just as well she was already dead—I could have killed her for the mess she'd made of my life. Admittedly it hadn't been all sunshine and roses before, but at least people hadn't been lining up to kill me before she'd stuck her nose in.

To have any chance of figuring it all out, I had to escape. I eyed the broken flyscreen, weighing my options. It didn't take long. If the window was the only way out, there was only one thing to do.

I raised the broken screen and slammed it down as hard as I could into the bath.

Then I bolted into the bedroom and scrambled under the bed, heart racing.

A voice in the corridor: "What was that?"

A dust bunny tickled my nose as I pressed my face against the carpet, trying to make myself as small as possible. Most people, presented with an open window and an empty room, would leap to the obvious conclusion, however unlikely it seemed. Hopefully werewolves were no more likely to think things through logically than anyone else.

The door opened and a pair of black boots came in, paused, then hurried to the bathroom.

"Shit. She's gone!"

Another pair of boots joined the first. "Out there?" Micah's voice. "She's crazy. Get downstairs and find her. She can't have gotten far after a fall like that."

I listened to their feet thudding down carpeted stairs, heard the shouts as others joined them. I'd kicked the nest good and proper, and now all the little ants were scurrying. It was enough to warm a girl's heart.

I slid out from under the bed. No time to lie around. When they couldn't find me, someone would use their brain and realise I could never have jumped from that window. I had to get moving.

First I had to find Ben. I hurried down the corridor in the direction they'd taken him, heart pounding. What now? Knock on every door and hope Ben answered and not some werewolf?

The room next door seemed too close. They didn't want us whispering secrets through the walls. At the one after I brought my lips to the crack between the door and the frame.

"Ben?" I didn't dare raise my voice, but it still sounded loud in the empty corridor. I glanced over my shoulder, jumpy as a teenager trying to sneak out of the house. And how *were* we going to get out of the house, even if I managed to find Ben and free him? *Later. One problem at a time.*

No one replied, so I moved on to the next door. Only three more before the corridor finished at a set of double doors.

"Ben? Are you there?"

I heard movement, then his voice, deep and low. "Kate?"

Weak with relief, I leaned against the door. "Are you okay?"

"I'm fine. Was all that commotion you? What did you do?"

"Long story. I'll tell you later. How are we going to get you out of there?"

"See if you can find the keys. Try Nada's office. It's the one at the end of the corridor."

"How do you know?"

"Been here before. Hurry, before someone comes. And be careful."

"Okay." Hearing his voice made me feel better. A faint scent of pine forests reached me through the heavy oak panels, or was that my imagination? "Don't go anywhere."

I listened at the double doors at the end of the corridor. Nothing. Probably everyone was out looking for me. And if I wasn't quick they'd find me, too.

I eased the door open and slipped inside.

The walls were lined with bookshelves, but Nada's taste ran to romances and soft porn rather than accounting texts or the usual kind of legal tome found on office shelves. I suppose it counted as an office, because it contained a desk, but it didn't look like a place where any real work happened. The leather chair sat square behind the desk, pushed in neatly, as if it rarely saw use, and the desk itself, though large enough to dance on, held nothing but a computer and a neat organiser full of pens.

I glanced around. Armchairs and coffee table, no filing cabinets—what kind of office didn't have filing cabinets? It looked like the desk drawers were the only place to store anything. Noiselessly I padded across the deep soft carpet and opened the top one. More pens. Office supplies.

No keys.

My palms started to sweat. Time was running out. I rifled through the other drawers, horribly aware of the noise I was making. Where else could they be? It had to be somewhere handy. I got down and peered under the desk. A secret compartment maybe?

"Looking for something?"

I jumped, slamming my head on the underside of the desktop. Nada stood in the doorway, flanked by Micah and another guy who could have been his twin. Same dead eyes and surly expression. Nada's face lit with glee, her smile mocking as I crawled out from under the desk.

She had something in her hand. "This, maybe?"

I stared, my vision narrowing. I didn't see the men move as I lunged across the room, only felt them as they slammed me back against a bookshelf. Half a dozen books tumbled around me, but I only had eyes for the stone.

She had the channel stone.

I twisted and struggled in Micah's grip, but I might as well have tried to wrestle a statue. There was no moving him. Nada's laughter floated behind us as he hauled me back down the corridor and locked me in my room again. Someone shouted from behind a closed door.

Long moments passed before I realised the voice had been Ben's. By then my throat was raw from screaming obscenities. I stared out the balcony doors, blind to the view; that damned black stone filled my head. The channel stone. How could I know its name but not its purpose? I longed for it, with a physical craving more desperate than a pack-a-day smoker giving up cigarettes.

Seeing it again had caused me, quite literally, to lose my mind. I'd become someone else, my consciousness completely taken over with the need to possess it. All thought of keys or escape had vanished in a roar of need. Awareness of it still thrummed through my body.

Madness. I hugged myself hard, trying to hang on to Kate, to find myself again in the midst of strangeness. Poor Ben. He must be worried sick, hearing me dragged screaming down the corridor. Deep purple bruises flowered already on my arm where Micah had manhandled me back to my room.

The source of the bruises appeared in the courtyard below, another couple of thugs in tow, and I stepped closer to the glass to watch. After a moment a regular convoy emerged from the garage—two vans and a four-wheel drive like the one we'd arrived in last night. Surly guys streamed out of the house and piled in. Wherever they were going, it didn't look like a social call.

"Give my regards to Alicia," said one who appeared to be staying. I had to strain to hear through the glass.

Micah frowned. "Let us worry about Alicia. You focus on your own job. I don't want to hear you let the girl escape again."

"No problem, boss. Don't get your fur singed, okay?"

Micah growled and the guy skittered back inside like a kicked puppy.

Finally Nada came out and got into the four-wheel drive with Micah. I felt a sudden wrench. What the—?

It hit me then—the channel stone. Somehow I knew Nada had it. I swear I felt a tug as the car moved off and the distance between us grew. Unconsciously I turned in its direction as it disappeared around the house, as if I were the needle of a compass and it my true north.

Bloody hell. I sank down on the bed. I knew then, as well as I knew my own name, that I had to get that stone back.

CHAPTER FOURTEEN

I woke from a dream of blood and terror. My body felt unfamiliar, as if I were wearing someone else's skin. Though my chest heaved with the pain of remembered agony, my groping hand found nothing but the bandage around my shoulder.

The room was dark and the house still; it must be the early hours of the morning, when even the late-night revellers have gone home to sleep and the streets are empty. Not even a ticking clock broke the silence. The mound of cushions I'd hurled off the bed made a strange lumpy silhouette by the locked door, like a collapsed hay stack. The one pillow I'd kept was warm beneath my cheek.

I could have been the only person alive in the whole mansion. I knew most of them had cleared out with Nada— I'd only seen Kicked Puppy Guy all day. He'd brought my dinner and refused to speak. Evidently when Micah kicked someone they stayed down.

In the silence I heard the faintest click and rolled over, seeking its source. Cool air caressed my face.

I'd hardly registered that the balcony door stood open before a dark shape moved in the shadows by the bed. I inhaled sharply, but before I screamed the house down it stepped into the moonlight.

"Luce!" My whole body sagged with relief. "What kept you?"

She froze. Then I saw the knife, raised to strike, blade glinting in the moonlight. I scrambled away in a tangle of sheets, heart pumping. Why was everyone trying to kill me all of a sudden?

I slid off the bed and backed away till I hit the wall. The bed between us would no more protect me than the kitchen bench had kept the werewolf at bay. She was small, but she looked like she knew how to use that knife. She was also stark naked.

Time stopped as we stared at each other. Her eyes were lost in shadow, impossible to read. Why did I say that? I didn't know this woman.

At last she lowered her hand. "Who are you? And how do you know my name?"

A damn good question. Pity I had no answers. Part of me insisted I knew her: her pretty Chinese face always wore that serious expression. The long silken fall of her black hair was always pulled back in that business-like ponytail. Her hands looked delicate, yet I knew how capable they were. How handy with a knife, for instance.

The other part of me had never seen her before in my life.

And yet ... the feeling of relief persisted, despite the knife and the disturbing lack of clothes. The cavalry had arrived! It made no sense—particularly as it was clear she had no idea who I was. The knife made it obvious her intentions weren't friendly, and I shrank back against the wall, uneasily calculating my chances of getting past her to the balcony door. The odds weren't good.

How did I know her name? *Search me, lady.* I blurted the first thing that popped into my head instead.

"How'd you get up here?"

A fair question, in my view. No ladder leaned against the balcony, no rope hung down. It seemed even more curious than her nudity.

"I flew," she said, deadpan.

She was joking, right?

She crossed to the interior door and tried the handle. "Why is this locked? Where's the key?"

"How would I know? I'm a prisoner."

She looked me over, her gaze cold. "So you're working for Alicia?"

Goddammit. Why did everyone assume I must be working for someone? "Look, I never heard of Alicia or Valeria before yesterday. I don't know anything about any crazy dragon war, and I wish all you people would stop blaming me for things I haven't even done."

"Keep your voice down." She considered me for a long moment, completely unfazed by her own nakedness. It was impossible to tell what she was thinking, but she went back to the balcony for what looked in the dark like a huge bunch of keys, the kind of thing a chatelaine might have worn in the olden days.

"What are you doing?" I asked as she knelt by the bedroom door.

"Getting us out of here," she said.

"Can't we go back the way you came?"

She ignored me, slipping an L-shaped piece of metal off her giant key ring and inserting it in the lock, followed by something else that looked like it belonged in a dental surgery. Okay, so they weren't keys but lock-picking tools. That explained how she'd managed to get in. I'd never seen anyone pick a lock before. Were they all criminals in this brave new supernatural world? And naked ones, at that? I hardly knew where to look. Such a fabulous lot of new experiences I was having lately.

It was obviously trickier than they made it look in the movies. She gave up on the dental device she had and chose another from the ring.

I watched, trying to piece things together. She could have flown out the way she'd come. She was a wyvern, after all. That would be why the lock picks were on such a big ring, so she could grip it in her claws as she flew. And why she was naked. If you only meant to turn human long enough to murder a sleeping woman you wouldn't bother bringing clothes.

This all fell into place in my mind, click, click, click, like the tumblers moving in the lock. Wyvern, check. Fly in, fly out. Check.

Leave the dead body behind.

I broke out in hot sweat all over. This had never been meant as a rescue. She'd come to kill me. And how the *hell* did

I know she was a wyvern? A few days ago I wouldn't even have been sure what a wyvern was.

She eased the door open and peeked out into the corridor.

"So you're breaking me out of here?" Glad she'd changed her mind. Though she barely reached my shoulder, I didn't fancy my chances if I had to take her on.

She glanced at me as if I were something nasty she'd found on the bottom of her shoe—if she'd been wearing any—then gathered up her tools.

"But that wasn't part of the plan, was it?"

"You talk too much," she said.

"So what's the plan now? How do I know you're not going to kill me if I come with you?"

"You don't."

She didn't add "you'll just have to trust me" or any other vague reassurance.

"Then I think I'll say 'thanks, but no thanks'."

The knife reappeared with alarming speed. "I don't remember giving you an option."

That seemed a persuasive argument, so I slipped my shoes on and went out into the hall.

She jerked the knife to the right. "Down the stairs."

"Wait! We have to break Ben out too. I can't leave without him."

"Will you keep your damn voice down!" she snarled.

Too late. A door opened further down the hall and Kicked Puppy Guy came out. I froze.

He went for his gun, but Luce was quicker. The knife whizzed past my nose, and I heard a wet thunk and the guy's grunt of pain.

Luce shoved me toward the stairs. "Move!"

I moved, with her on my heels. Our feet made no noise on the thick carpet as we pelted down the stairs.

Another door slammed overhead, followed by the shrill of an alarm. Our guy must have hit a panic button, which meant more thugs arriving soon. Not good. I skidded round corners, following Luce's terse directions: "through here! this way!" I hoped she knew what she was doing, because I was completely lost and disoriented in the dark.

I slammed my shin into a chair as we raced into the kitchen. She hurled it to the floor behind us, then toppled them all down the long table as we passed. Someone was right behind us, but dodging the crashing chairs slowed him down. We burst into the yard mere seconds ahead of the pursuit.

"Come *on*!"

Luce snatched at my hand and dragged me behind her. The first guy burst out the door and got off a wild shot.

We zigzagged across the yard. I hunched low, expecting to feel a bullet rip into me any second. Behind us someone shouted, but no one fired again. Luce damn near pulled the back gate off its hinges, and we flew out into the street.

A white sedan idled at the curb. Luce wrenched the back door open and we piled in.

"Let's go!" said Luce. "What are you waiting for?"

"What's *she* doing here?" the driver growled. "I thought you were going to kill her."

My heart nearly jumped out of my chest. It was the werewolf from my kitchen.

"Later, Garth," Luce said. "Shut up and drive."

CHAPTER FIFTEEN

The drive was short but tense. Garth did as he was told and didn't say a word, but his anger was plain in the stiffness of his thick neck and the way he slammed the gear stick through the changes.

Garth. The monster had a name. He probably even had a job and a family to come home to, just like a normal person. My heart raced as I stared at the back of his head, surrounded by the now-familiar orange glow. Well, not quite like a normal person. There was that whole turning into a werewolf and attacking people thing. I shrank back in my seat, my body instinctively recoiling from the danger he represented.

Not that I was much safer with Luce. Her aura was blue. Werewolf or wyvern—choose your poison. Either way there were claws and fangs. She watched me the whole time—not in a threatening way, but as if she were trying to work something out. The faint puzzled crease down the centre of her forehead was the most expression I'd seen on her yet. At least she'd put some clothes on.

I turned away to watch the dark streets slide by out the window, trying not to let my fear show. The road was wet. Must have rained earlier, when I was asleep. Another late-night car trip. No wonder I was so bloody tired. And with every one my situation got worse and worse. Almost punch-drunk now, I reeled like a fighter who'd taken too many blows to the head. What now? Had Luce rescued me only so Garth could finish the job he'd started in my kitchen?

We turned in at a large motel, its *No Vacancy* sign flashing a brilliant red. The car crunched its way across the gravel yard and pulled up in front of door 13. Lucky number 13.

"Move," said Luce.

I got out. I could smell moisture in the warm air. Probably more rain on the way. No lights showed at the row of windows that marched down the length of the building. Either the other rooms were empty or their occupants were asleep. Not much point yelling for help either way, given what any would-be rescuers would find themselves up against.

Garth unlocked the door and shoved me inside. I stumbled and fell to the gritty carpet. Jerk. I wished I still had my pepper grinder; I'd show him a thing or two. I glared up at him, and he returned the glare with interest, stalking past and hurling the car keys down on a rickety table.

He turned to Luce as she came in and shut the door.

"It's later," he said, "so start talking."

"Get her up off the floor."

She pushed past, ignoring his temper, and switched on the bedside lamps, revealing a typical room layout. Bed with two small chests either side. A round table with two mismatched chairs, and a cupboard cum wall unit opposite the bed that housed a TV and an electric kettle. Above the bed hung a tired print of a beach scene. A small bathroom opened off the entryway.

The lamplight did little to dispel the gloom. The place was still dark and dingy, like cheap motels everywhere. The carpet smelled of smoke and old greasy takeaway. I got up, keeping as far from the angry werewolf as possible in the small room.

He clenched his big fists and squared up to her. "How about I rip her throat out instead? What the hell is your problem? You were supposed to kill her."

His eyes actually turned yellow as he spoke. The wolf hovered very close to the surface.

Luce wasn't impressed. He was head and shoulders taller than her, but she got right up in his face and slapped him hard.

"If you try turning wolf on me, I'll shove your head so far up your furry arse you'll be able to eat what you had for breakfast all over again."

She had a big temper for such a tiny person, and the wolf backed down. He sank onto the bed, lowering himself beneath her. If he'd been in wolf form he probably would have shown her his belly.

"Garth's a little emotional," she said to me. "Don't mind him. Have a seat."

She indicated the table jammed into the corner. Apart from the bed it was the only other place to sit. I took one chair and she took the other. Garth stayed on the bed, not meeting anyone's eyes. He wore a Darth Vader T-shirt, and he looked like a sulky kid—but my experience with werewolves was pretty limited. Maybe they were always grumpy.

There was a stain on the seat of my chair that might have been food, or blood—or anything really. I tried not to sit on it and looked around. No way out except the front door. I'd be lucky if the window on the back wall even opened. My chances of climbing out with an angry werewolf in the room were slim to none.

Luce leaned forward, pinning me with a stern look, as if she understood my little survey of the room. "You may be under the impression I'm a reasonable person, because I haven't let Garth kill you yet. Don't make that mistake."

She was preaching to the choir here. I was already convinced this petite Asian doll was far more dangerous than the hulking werewolf.

"I'm going to ask you some questions, and you are going to answer completely and truthfully. If you don't, things will go badly for you. Very badly. Do you understand?"

I nodded, mouth suddenly dry. Maybe Luce was short for Lucifer. Her matter-of-fact attitude was far more menacing than Garth's angry posturing.

"Good. Let's start with something easy. Who are you and why were you locked in Valeria's keep?"

"My name's Kate O'Connor. I work for my friend Ben in his costume shop, and sometimes I do these special courier jobs for him."

She was quick. "You mean you're a herald?"

"I told you!" Garth roared, leaping to his feet. "She was there! She did it!"

"Shut up, Garth! Let her talk."

I waited till he sat down again. The guy was a powder keg waiting to blow. "Well, kind of. I mean, yeah, I did the jobs, but I didn't know about any of this shifter stuff. I thought there were just a lot of secretive people around who didn't want the world knowing their business. And then this urgent job came through …"

I gave her an edited version of the events of that afternoon—as much as I could remember of it, anyway. It didn't seem like the smartest move to mention visions of my hands dripping blood to these two, so I left that part out.

"… and then I went down to the local shops to get some Panadol—" Probably best not to mention the glowing people either. "When I got home the power was out and next thing I know a werewolf jumps me in the kitchen. But you know that part already."

Luce glanced at Garth, who now paced impatiently in the space between the TV and the bed. He seemed to have a problem with sitting still. "Yes. Garth is … impulsive. He was meant to be gathering information. I prefer to act on facts, not gut instinct."

The werewolf stopped pacing long enough to snarl at me. "She's lying! Are you going to believe this garbage about losing her memory? Bloody convenient, if you ask me."

"But nobody did, so keep your mouth shut." Her aura flared a brighter blue as she stared him down. Did that mean she was close to changing herself? Or did changes in the aura reflect the shifter's emotional state? So much I didn't know. "You were telling me how you ended up Valeria's prisoner."

"Right. Well, after Ben saved me from your friend here, we hid out while Ben tried to find out why I was attacked." I met Garth's glare with one of my own. He certainly didn't look like someone who'd been shot a couple of days ago, though he had a wild look to him, as if he'd been running on adrenalin for a while and needed a good sleep. I knew how that felt.

His pacing made me nervous. Would he attack again? I watched him out of the corner of my eye as I continued. "He told me about the shifters. Said he had lots of contacts. I guess one of them must have sold him out, or maybe you weren't the only ones looking for me, because Nada turned up on the doorstep with a couple of thugs and took us back to the house in Mosman. I'd never heard of Valeria or Alicia before Garth accused me of working for them, but Nada thought I was in league with Jason, which is even more ridiculous. I mean, sure, he's my ex-husband, so at least I *know* him, but I'd rather jump off a cliff than do anything *he* wanted."

"*You're* the one Jason married?" Surprise flashed across her face, then hardened into deep suspicion. Damn it. Garth made me so nervous I'd started babbling. Why did I even mention Jason?

"That traitor!" Garth rumbled.

I glared at the werewolf. "Trust me, whatever he's done to you, he's done worse to me."

"You were married for five years," Luce said. How did she know that? "You expect us to believe that in all that time you had no inkling Jason wasn't human?"

"I don't care if you believe it or not. It's the truth." It made me sound like an idiot. Hell, it made me *feel* like an idiot.

How do you miss something like that? "But I don't see what our marriage has to do with anything. Until tonight I hadn't seen him in more than six months."

In fact, I could have told her down to the day how long it had been: the last time had been at Lachie's funeral. Seven months and two days ago. But she didn't need to know that.

"But Nada accused you of working with him."

I shrugged. "Nada didn't seem exactly rational where Jason was concerned. I told you, I'm not working with anybody. I didn't know any of this even existed till two days ago."

"What did Nada think you two were up to?"

That was a tricky one. Why hadn't I kept my mouth shut? "I'm not sure. She said Jason had killed Leandra, but maybe she thought I had something to do with it." And maybe I did. Damn, I wish I could remember.

Garth threw his arms up in exasperation. "*Jason* killed Leandra? Do you think we're stupid? He wasn't even there!"

"She said he poisoned her." She also said I'd stabbed Leandra to death. Basically, no one knew diddly-squat. Especially me. No wonder Luce and Garth were suspicious.

"Really. Then why did we find her with her chest cut open right after *you* left? You thought you'd make sure of it in case the poison didn't work?" Garth whirled on Luce. "This is crap. There was no poison. How much more of this do we have to listen to?"

She ignored him. "The woman in the garden—what did she look like?"

Sick. Like someone dying of poisoning, come to think of it. "Elegant. Taller than me, blonde hair. She was wearing a grey business suit."

Luce nodded. "And what did she give you?"

"An envelope. The usual sort." *Please don't ask me who it was for.*

"Did she say anything to you?"

Help me, Kate. "She knew my name—but I don't remember anything else."

Garth loomed over me, his eyes glowing yellow again. "This whole story stinks worse than three-day-old fish. I say we kill her now."

I shrank back in my seat, clenching my teeth on half-truths and omissions. There had to be something I could tell them to help my situation.

"She did give me something else, though." At least, I thought she did. Where else had it come from? Hopefully it didn't prove me guilty of some heinous crime, but with Garth so set on blood I had to risk it. "A black stone."

Mentioning it awoke a strange longing in me. I felt the stone's loss like a missing tooth, a space where something should be.

"A black stone." Garth's voice was heavy with disbelief. "Why would she give you a black stone?"

Luce leaned forward, face intent. "A stone? Or more like a disk, about so big?" She made a circle the size of her palm with her fingers.

"Definitely a stone. About the size of a marble."

She flicked a glance at Garth. "Could be some kind of geas."

"Do you still have it?" Garth asked.

I shook my head. "Nada's got it."

He rolled his eyes in another *how convenient* comment. Clearly he refused to believe anything I said.

"Never mind the stone," Luce said, brushing his objections aside with a wave of her hand. "Earlier tonight, when I first entered your room, you said something to me. Do you remember?"

What kept you? I wasn't likely to forget such a peculiar experience. I'd felt so happy to see her. At last, someone I could trust! But I'd never met her before in my life.

Shame the feeling had gone. Her expression now gave me no clues as to whether she was friend or foe. At least with the werewolf I knew where I stood.

"Why did you say that?" She leaned closer, her gaze intense. This was the crux of the matter. She'd come to kill me, and those three little words had changed her mind. But if she expected rational explanations, she'd come to the wrong place.

"I've been having some ... visions ... since I, ah, met Leandra. They're more real-feeling than dreams, and they come when I'm awake, more like memories. But they're not. At least, not of anything that's ever happened to *me*.

"I had this one about you. I don't remember much now, but you were in an old warehouse. Your face was swollen and bruised, and you had ... burn marks." I swallowed. Remembering the damage to the delicate creature in front of me made me feel ill. That much of the vision was still crystal clear. I could recall the emotions, but not the details.

"I had the feeling I'd been searching for you for a long time. I was desperate, but I wouldn't give up hope. And then I found you, and there was so much blood … I thought you were dead." Like a broken doll abandoned on the concrete floor by some careless giant's child. "But you opened your eyes, and whispered 'what kept you?' and I had to laugh. And then you started laughing too, and … and that's all I remember. The feeling of relief. It seemed so real, even though it wasn't my body in the vision—like in dreams, where you can be someone else, but it's still you inside. And then tonight, when I opened my eyes and saw you, the feeling came to me again from the vision, of how thankful I'd been to see you … and I guess it just slipped out."

Wow, that sounded lame even to me. I didn't need to look at the werewolf to know how impressed he'd be.

Luce's poker face was much better. They could have invented the word "inscrutable" for her.

"That was Leandra," she said, and her voice wasn't quite steady. Maybe not so inscrutable after all. "Leandra found me, when I'd given up hope."

"So what?" Garth, of course, was still spoiling for a fight. "She could have heard it anywhere. It doesn't prove anything."

Luce didn't even spare him a glance. Her dark almond-shaped eyes never left my face. "I've never told anyone that story, and I'm pretty sure Leandra didn't either. No one else knows."

She stood and turned away, as if she'd caught Garth's restlessness. I watched her pace, horribly aware my life depended on her. There wasn't much I could do if she decided to let Garth have his way.

Suddenly she whirled and caught Garth's arm. I jumped, heart hammering, but she only tugged him into the bathroom with her.

She shut the door to keep their conversation private, but insulation isn't a huge priority in cheap motels. Though she kept her voice down I still heard her words, echoing off the tiled walls.

"I believe her."

Garth started to argue, but she cut him off. "Even if she did hear that story somewhere, why would she say 'what kept you?' now? She had no way of knowing what that moment meant to us. It was as if Leandra spoke to me!"

"Leandra could have told her about it before she was killed," Garth protested.

"For heaven's sake, Garth! You're so set on revenge you're not using your brain. 'Please, dear herald, delay stabbing me to death for a moment while I tell you this deeply personal and entirely irrelevant story from my past.' Is that how you think it went down?"

Whatever Garth thought, I didn't get to hear it as she ploughed on. "I think you're right. Leandra did tell her, but as a kind of password, because she needed a way to let me know I could trust this woman that wouldn't be obvious to others."

"Like who?"

"Like Jason, or whoever really did kill her. I think this stone she gave her is a geas, her last message to us."

"Geez, Luce, you're going too fast for me." Welcome to my world, buddy. It's confusion city here. "A geas? But they're always on scales."

"Well, maybe some kind of trigger spell. I won't know until I see it."

There was a long silence. When the big werewolf spoke again, it sounded as if every word was dragged out of him against his will. "I guess we need to find it then."

For once we agreed on something. Every time someone mentioned that damned stone I felt a hollowness like a gnawing hunger. It could be a geas—whatever that was—or a piece of bloody unobtainium for all I cared.

I just knew I wanted it back.

CHAPTER SIXTEEN

I slept fitfully for the remainder of the night, fully clothed on the queen bed, Luce stretched out next to me. I wasn't used to sharing a bed with another person any more, and I woke up every time she rolled over. Under the bandages my shoulder itched like crazy. Hopefully that was a good sign.

Garth slept on the floor by the door, curled up with his tail tucked round his nose. I contemplated a bathroom break sometime in the small hours but the instant I swung my feet off the bed he came awake, yellow eyes gleaming in the dark. He growled, an ominous sound which raised the hairs on the back of my neck, and I decided I could wait till daylight after all.

The sound of the TV woke me. I'd fallen into a deep sleep at last, and it was nearly two o'clock in the afternoon according to my watch. Two talking heads discussed the highlights of the Sydney Festival in bright happy tones while Garth, human again, crunched his way through a bowl of Coco Pops. Guess he'd slept late too. There was no sign of

Luce, which made me nervous. No one wants to be alone with a homicidal werewolf.

I sat up. His bowl brimmed with little brown balls shedding their chocolate coating into a sea of rapidly browning milk. Pure sugar masquerading as breakfast cereal. The last person I'd seen tucking into it with such gusto had been Lachie, but he'd had the excuse of being five years old at the time.

"What?" Garth grunted. "Did you expect me to eat raw meat for breakfast?"

I shrugged. I hadn't given much thought to the typical werewolf diet, but I would have expected a little more protein. He'd be high on a sugar rush in twenty minutes.

"Where's Luce?"

"Out."

Guess he didn't like breakfast conversation.

In the bathroom I finally gave in to the maddening itch and peeled the bandage back to check my shoulder. I stood there so long, staring at my arm, it was a wonder Garth didn't burst in, thinking I'd somehow escaped.

How was this possible? I ran a tentative finger over the fine white scars on my arm. No bleeding, no scabs—not even reddened, healing skin. These scars looked as if I'd been clawed years ago. Hurriedly I checked my stomach, checked everywhere, but it was the same story. Less than forty-eight hours had passed, but I could barely see the place on my stomach which had hurt so much. The scar had faded to such a thin white line it took some finding.

Wow. I stared at my reflection. The mirror was spotted with age and the light from the single globe was dim, but it sure looked like me staring back. Only I'd never had super healing powers before. *Supernatural* healing powers.

Back in the main room Garth resolutely watched TV, pretending I wasn't there. I studied the back of his head. I'd never seen exactly where Ben's bullet took him, but it had brought the werewolf down and stopped him dead in his tracks. I shuddered, remembering the hideous thing sprawled on my kitchen floor among the broken plates. He'd certainly *looked* dead, at least for a little while. Must have been a shot to the heart, or somewhere equally vital, for an effect like that. Yet he sat there eating Coco Pops as if nothing had ever happened.

Supernatural healing powers indeed. Was Ben's friend wrong? Was I turning into a werewolf after all? I tried a snarl, wondering how it would feel to have a wolf's teeth, a wolf's jaw.

Of course Garth picked that moment to look around.

"What the hell is your problem?"

I blinked. "Need caffeine. Want some coffee?"

He glared. Did all werewolves have a monobrow like that? "The only reason you're still alive is that Luce reckons we need you. You'd be dead already if it was up to me. So forget coffee and chit chat."

Something inside bristled at his tone. Stupid dog. Always the threats and the one-track mind. "You're not a morning person, are you? Do you want coffee or not?"

He turned back to the TV with a growl. They were on to the weather now. Some blonde was all breathless and amazed at how many days in a row the temperature had hit the high thirties lately. Had she forgotten it was summer? Happened every year. The media had been at their usual fear-mongering for weeks, reporting the build-up of fuel with morbid glee. There was always some expert warning this year could be the worst bushfire season for years. They said it every year.

I made coffee and chose a little box of cereal for myself—one with a lot less sugar than Garth's. I watched him as I ate. He wore a black T-shirt with Darth Vader on the front and the words *World's Greatest Dad*. His hair was military-short and greying at the temples. I was rubbish at picking people's ages but he could have been in his early forties, though his body was in such good shape it was hard to tell. No flab hiding underneath Darth Vader. Had he been a werewolf all his life? I knew nothing about him. Why, for instance, was he so intent on avenging Leandra? I knew all about the pain of losing someone important to you, but even though I hated Jason, murdering him had never occurred to me.

"So … Leandra." I said. "She was just your boss? Or a friend?"

He gave me a look of disgust and kept on shovelling Coco Pops.

"What will you do now she's gone?" I persisted. Were there werewolf accountants? Shop assistants? "Will you work for Valeria or Alicia, or do something else?"

"Work for Valeria or Alicia?" He laughed, a short, bitter sound. "They wouldn't have me even if I wanted to."

"Why not? Jason changed sides, didn't he?"

"Dragons can get away with things wolves can't." His bitter tone spoke of experience. "But Alicia's a loser and Valeria's a prize bitch—I wouldn't be caught dead round either of them."

"And Leandra was better than them?"

He smiled. "Leandra was the most vicious of the lot. She would have been the heir by now if Jason hadn't sold her out, the bastard."

A noise at the door brought him instantly alert, but it was only Luce. In the daylight I could see dark shadows under her eyes that hadn't been apparent last night. Her gaze swept the room as she closed the door behind her, as if searching for threats. They were both so jumpy.

The room didn't look any better in daylight—the stains and scuff marks on the furniture were even more obvious—but there were no bogeymen waiting to leap out at her. And I didn't even want to think about what kind of bogeyman it would take to frighten a werewolf and a wyvern.

"You two look cosy."

Garth rolled his eyes and got up, taking his bowl back to the bench. "How'd it go?"

"No sign of them. The keep's deserted."

"The house at Mosman, you mean?" I asked. "There's no one there?"

"Empty as broken eggshells."

I laid my spoon down. Suddenly I'd lost my appetite.

Where was Ben?

"What do you think they're up to?" Garth asked Luce, but I answered for her.

"I heard them talking about an attack on Alicia. They said Valeria was in the mountains getting ready. It sounded like it could be any day now."

Luce dropped into Garth's chair and considered me thoughtfully. "What kind of attack?"

"I don't know. But they all went off somewhere last night. Only a couple of guys stayed to guard Ben and me." And now they'd left too. To move Ben somewhere safer? Or something worse?

Luce looked at Garth. "Sounds like Valeria's finally making her move. Patience pays off after all." Under the table she clenched her fists. Not so inscrutable today. For the first time I realised Luce too had lost someone she cared about. "First get Leandra out of the way, then attack Alicia while she's off guard. Nicely done."

Very nicely, as long as you weren't Leandra. A dizzying rush of hatred for Valeria swamped me. Adrenalin surged, urging me to get up, move, *fight*. I fought it down. I had to think.

Would Alicia be prepared? More likely cowering in a hole somewhere, knowing her. Her strategy all along had been to hide out and hope the rest of us killed each other off, leaving her the field. She must be shaking in her designer shoes by now.

I started pacing, my mind racing, trying to block out the sound of the TV. The weather girl had moved on to the inevitable bushfires. The TV showed footage of flames roaring through gum trees at Lithgow, on the other side of the mountains. Any minute now they'd wheel out the expert. I glared at the TV, images of fire filling my mind.

What had that thrall of Valeria's said to Micah? Don't get your fur singed? Perhaps that had been more than just a cute way of saying "be careful".

"She's going to burn them out," I said.

"What?" Garth looked confused.

Luce was quicker. Her agile mind was part of the reason she made such a good head of security. That and sheer ruthlessness. "Are you certain? Did you hear them say so?"

I shrugged. "It's what I would do. Alicia's been playing it safe too long. She thinks she's impregnable in that fortress of hers, but she's forgotten what dragons *do*."

"Make everyone else's lives miserable?" Garth suggested.

"Breathe fire." I knew I was right. Couldn't they *see*?

Luce tapped her fingers on the table. "And that's what you would do, is it, if you were a dragon? You seem pretty well informed for someone who claims she only found out dragons existed two days ago."

I stopped pacing, a chill stealing over me. Deliberately set a fire and try to kill people? No, of course I wouldn't. What kind of lunatic does a thing like that?

A werewolf?

"Still, if you're right—and I can't see any other reason for Valeria to be lurking in the Blue Mountains—we need to stop her."

Garth nearly choked. "Are you nuts? Why should we get in the middle of a fight between those two? To save Alicia? I don't give a rat's arse what happens to her! Let them kill each other off."

"That's the problem, though—they won't. Alicia will die, and then Valeria becomes the heir. There's no way I'm letting *that* happen, after she killed Leandra." Luce slapped her hands on the table and held Garth's gaze till he dropped his head in submission. "We'll do whatever it takes to stop her. If it means working with Alicia, then so be it. We also need to get hold of that stone and find out what it does. If there's a message there from Leandra, it might be something we can use against Valeria. That stone's important."

I felt that too, with a bone-deep knowledge that had nothing to do with logic. I needed that stone, hungered for it almost. Once I had it I'd crush that worm Valeria.

"What are we going to do with *her*, then, while we're chasing around the Blue Mountains?"

"We'll take her with us."

He rolled his eyes. Impudent dog. "We can't trust her."

"We can't trust anyone." Luce was brutal, as always. "The only reason I trust *you* is because you were with me when Leandra died. As far as I'm concerned, everyone else is suspect."

"What about the other herald? We going to spring him too?"

Ben! I'd hardly given him a thought. A wave of guilt rose up inside me, drowning out the dark hunger that insisted on finding the stone above all else. Ben was more important than a stupid piece of rock.

"Yes!" I said.

"No," said Luce.

We glared at each other.

"You're hardly in a position to be making demands," she said.

"Fine," I said. "I need help rescuing my friend, and you don't even know what your precious stone looks like without me."

Outside doors slammed and feet crunched on gravel as people packed up, getting ready to leave. Someone shushed a whinging child. Inside silence reigned as Luce and I engaged in a battle of wills.

"Perhaps we can work together," she said at last. "For the moment."

A wealth of menace hung in that last phrase. Heaven help me once we found the stone if she decided I was no longer necessary.

One problem at a time. First we had to find Ben and somehow rescue him—the three of us against a dragon at the height of her powers, with all her resources and an army of followers.

Still, it wasn't exactly a fair fight. We had Luce on our side.

CHAPTER SEVENTEEN

Leura House was a lovely old wooden mansion with large verandas all around, built in the 1880s. Set in beautifully manicured grounds, it lay across the rail lines from the village of Leura in the Blue Mountains. Very picturesque. Probably a favourite photo spot with the local brides.

Garth drove past at a sedate pace, slow enough to check the place out but not so slow as to look suspicious. Though it was summer the eucalyptus-scented mountain air had a nip to it. Leura itself was a pretty little tourist trap full of antique shops and tea houses. Lachie and I had stopped there once for afternoon tea after hiking nearby. He'd been a bit young to appreciate the spectacular scenery, finding the hot chocolate at the Leura café—"they gave me *two* marshmallows, Mummy! A white one *and* a pink one!"—the most memorable part of the day.

We'd had a quick look around the shops, but he'd been sick of walking, and we hadn't ventured as far as Leura House. It was surrounded by other homes, some modern, some not so much. Some of the older cottages looked as though they'd been here since soon after Blaxland, Lawson and Wentworth had made their epic journey across the mountains and discovered the wealthy grazing lands on the other side.

Luce had spent the drive up hunting Valeria with nothing more magical than good old google-fu, typing a search for accommodation into her phone as Garth drove.

"Try Lilianfels," Garth said, peering at the list. It was a luxury resort at Katoomba, near the tourist mecca of the Three Sisters. Lachie and I had admired it that long-ago afternoon. Well, I had at least. Lachie had been more interested in scuffing patterns in the dirt with the toe of his shoe. "Dragons love their creature comforts."

She nodded and dialled the number. "Hello, could I speak to Nada Kusic? ... Oh, she must be delayed. Could you put me through to Jason Hepburn, then? ... Never mind, thanks for your help." She hung up and looked at him. "Not at Lilianfels."

"They could be using false names," I said.

"Not Valeria's style. She doesn't care who knows she's coming. She thinks she's untouchable now."

She dialled another number and went through the same routine, with no more luck. On the third try her dark eyes sparked. "They're putting me through!" She hung up, a smug look on her usually expressionless face. "Leura House. A 'stately old home', according to the website."

"Valeria's probably got the whole place booked out." said Garth.

If she did, it wasn't obvious from the road. There were no cars out front, but a driveway that curved around the building suggested parking out the back, so for all we knew the place could be packed.

A man leaned on the railing of the upper veranda, a lazy trail of smoke rising from the cigarette dangling from his fingers.

"Well, at least he's not glowing," I said.

That didn't mean he wasn't on Valeria's payroll, of course. There'd been humans at the Mosman house.

Luce's head whipped around as Garth pulled over further down the road. "Glowing? What do you mean?"

"You know." I gestured at them both. "The auras or whatever you want to call them. Different colours."

Garth looked mystified but Luce's eyes narrowed. "You can *see* them? What colour is mine?"

"Blue."

"And Garth's?"

Why was she asking? "Orange. Micah's was too."

"How long have you been able to see these auras?"

Oops. "Since … since I met Leandra." Was she mad because I'd forgotten to tell her about it? Or suspicious that it could have slipped my mind? It *was* pretty screwy, but it wasn't the most unusual thing that had happened to me in the last few days by a long shot. I rubbed uneasily at the white scar on my arm.

"I've heard of them." The ice in her voice could have frozen Niagara Falls. "Leandra told me when I asked her how she always knew."

"You mean you can't see them?" But wasn't that how the shifters could tell who else belonged to their little freak club?

"No one can see them," she said, "except for the dragons."

I met Garth's eyes in the rear vision mirror. They were full of suspicion, and the monobrow was drawn into a furious scowl. I glared back. Had I asked to be dragged into their crazy world?

He was first to look away.

"What now?" he asked Luce. "Sneak in after dark?"

Luce stared out the windscreen at nothing. The fingers of one hand tapped absently on the armrest as she thought.

"They won't recognise this car. No one got a good look at it last night. Let's drive around the back and have a look."

He looked doubtful, but he put the car into gear. "You're the boss."

We did a U-turn and headed back the way we'd come. The wrought-iron gates stood open and Garth turned in. My skin crawled, imagining eyes at all those windows watching us pass, but there was no one in sight. Even the smoker had disappeared.

A familiar black van sat all alone in the empty car park. Through the large windows on the ground floor we could see a restaurant where a couple of staff moved from table to table. It was nearly six; they were probably getting ready to open for dinner.

Garth pulled into a parking spot but left the motor running.

"Looks pretty empty," he said. "It's tempting."

Luce nodded.

"But it's broad daylight," I objected. They weren't going to be any help rescuing Ben if they walked in and got caught.

Garth gave me a disgusted look. "Here's an idea: let's dangle you as bait and see if anyone takes a shot."

"I'm serious. They know what you look like."

"Your concern is touching," Luce said. "But if most of them are off somewhere else, the ones who are here aren't going to be hanging around reception. They're most likely guarding your friend. It could be our best chance to take him. If we wait for dark the others might be back."

Good point. All right, I was sold.

I looked up as I shut the car door. The windows above were all empty, but I felt their presence like eyes. Was Ben in one of those rooms? I sure hoped so. Chasing all over the Blue Mountains with Luce and Garth looking for homicidal dragons would be a lot more comfortable with Ben along.

Inside it smelled of furniture polish and something wonderfully garlicky wafting from the kitchens. The walls were panelled in dark wood, and a worn Persian runner led from the entry to a large mahogany reception desk. The foyer was empty except for an overweight Labrador stretched out on the cool tiles. It thumped its tail on the floor in welcome, then heaved itself to its feet and waddled over. I patted the smooth head and it wagged absentmindedly till it caught Garth's scent. With a reproachful look at me it backed off, disappearing behind the desk as fast as its arthritic legs could carry it.

Voices sounded in the restaurant but no one came out to greet us. It wasn't a big hotel—probably only ten or twelve rooms. Most likely the receptionist also doubled as a waitress or chambermaid too.

We peeked into a large lounge where a fire was laid in the massive fireplace. It probably got cold at night, even in summer, at this elevation. No one there either.

Luce pointed up the grand staircase and Garth nodded, leading the way on silent feet. For such a solid guy he could move quietly when it suited him. I ghosted upstairs in their wake, my heart thumping nervously.

On the first floor we crept along listening at doors, our footsteps lost in the thick carpet. The lower half of the walls was panelled in the same dark wood as downstairs. Above the rail they were painted the colour of dried blood. All was still. No one home.

Guess I wasn't cut out for a life of intrigue. Knowing that any moment someone could open one of these doors, or come up the stairs behind us, set my nerves on edge.

At the end of the hall a smaller staircase continued up to another hall that sloped up and around a corner. Must have been an attic once, or servants' quarters—no point bothering with level floors for mere servants. The sound of a TV drifted faintly from around the corner.

Still in the lead, Garth strode confidently around the bend and rapped on the lone door at the end of the corridor.

"Room service!"

I froze, uncertain what to do, but Luce moved up behind Garth. Guess they'd done this kind of thing before. Footsteps approached the door. As the handle began to turn Garth hurled himself against the door.

The guy who'd been opening it fell back with a cry as the door slammed him in the face. Luce and I rushed in on

Garth's heels as a second man rose from his chair. Garth bore him to the floor, where they flailed and grunted. Luce snatched up a table lamp and watched for her chance. When the other guy rolled on top, hands clenched around Garth's throat, she smashed it over his head. He went down like a sack of potatoes and lay still.

Garth clambered to his feet and checked on the first guy. He was dazed and groaning, his nose gushing blood. Garth punched him in the head, putting him out cold, then kicked him on to his side. The casual brutality made me wince.

Suddenly I registered the other person in the room. I flew over to the big four-poster bed where Ben lay, cuffed to the bedpost with cable ties, and ripped the gag away from his mouth.

"Are you all right? Did they hurt you?"

"Better now," he said, as Garth sliced through the ties. He looked exhausted, but his smile warmed my heart.

I grabbed him.

"Thank God you're okay." His arms around me felt so good, I never wanted to let him go again.

His kiss left me in no doubt he felt the same. When I finally came up for air, he wore a serious expression. "How did you get here? Who are your friends?"

Garth snorted, probably at the idea of being mistaken for a friend of mine. I ignored him. "Luce and Garth—friends of Leandra's."

"Oh." He eyed Luce, his expression guarded. "I thought I recognised you. You're Leandra's security chief, aren't you?"

"Former security chief."

"I'm sorry. I heard she died."

"She didn't *die.*" Garth clenched his massive fists and stepped closer. "Somebody *killed* her."

"Don't look at me," I said.

Ben put a protective arm around my shoulders. "We had nothing to do with it. We're heralds, not fighters. See, there's my charm."

He crossed to a table by the window. Our charms nestled side by side on its polished surface, his on its leather thong, mine on a silver chain. I slipped mine around my neck again.

Garth wouldn't leave it alone. "I thought those things were supposed to protect you. Maybe you're only pretending to be a herald."

He stepped closer, aggression in his hunched shoulders and clenched fists. He made the generous-sized room feel smaller. I eyed the elegant couch and the delicate legs of the side tables. How long would they last if Garth decided to start another fight in here? Ben was taller but Garth had a good twenty kilos of pure muscle on him.

"'Those things' nullify any aggressive magic in the herald's vicinity, but they don't stop bullets. If someone waves a gun in my face, there's not a lot I can do."

"Garth," Luce snapped. "Protecting the herald is only a by-product. They're really meant to reassure the clients that the herald isn't bringing any magical surprises with their delivery."

She turned to Ben. "So why would Valeria break the queen's peace and snatch two heralds out of their bed? It certainly looks like you're involved."

"That wasn't Valeria, it was Nada. Who knows why she does anything? She's mad as a cut snake."

"But Valeria must have known. Have you seen her?"

"She was here last night."

"And what did she say?"

"Nothing much. I got the impression she wasn't that interested in me."

Garth swore and Luce held up a slim hand to forestall another explosion. "Then why was she holding you? She must have said *something*."

His face was bleak. "I think she wants Kate."

"Me?" All three looked at me, Garth's face suspicious as ever, Luce's impossible to read. "Don't tell me she believes that rubbish Nada's spinning about me and Jason?"

He shrugged. "Don't know. They didn't say anything in front of me. But there's something going on there."

"Bloody convenient," Garth muttered.

Luce silenced him with a look. "Very. But also entirely probable. She hasn't got this far without being paranoid. Frankly, I'm surprised she let you live, having taken it this far. Perhaps she's still a little afraid of Elizabeth. Maybe she thinks as long as she wins the proving the queen will overlook the abduction of her heralds."

Horrified, I edged closer to Ben, breathed in his familiar Ben smell. I couldn't bear to lose him now.

"So what happens now?" he asked. "Are you going to let us go?"

"I don't have what I came for yet."

"And what's that?"

"A black stone. Have you seen it?"

He shook his head.

"It's not here," I said. If I concentrated I could feel it, pulsing on the edge of my awareness, but nowhere close by.

She stared. "How do you know?"

Damn. When would I learn not to blurt out the first thing that came into my head? Luce's stare would unnerve anyone. Sharks probably looked like that just before they ripped you in half. I licked my lips.

"I just do."

And wasn't that the freakiest thing? Why did I feel this bizarre connection to that stupid stone? What was a channel stone even *for*?

Ben looked from one to the other of us, confused, but he'd have to wait till I could get him alone. I wouldn't be telling Luce I'd remembered its name, that was for sure. There were already too many things I couldn't explain. Maybe Ben had heard of channel stones, even though he hadn't recognised it when I'd shown him.

"Garth, search," she said.

He turned the room upside down, looking as though he enjoyed the excuse for a little mayhem. I winced as he toppled the delicate tables to check their undersides. He ripped everything out of the carved wardrobe and emptied the drawers on to the floor, scattering T-shirts and underwear all over one of the unconscious men who lay there. He even went through the pockets of the two downed men. It was soon clear the stone wasn't in the room. I resisted the urge to say *I told you so*.

"It seems you're right," she said. "Which means it's probably gone to Alicia's with the rest of them." Her gaze rested on Ben. "Do you know where that is?"

"I've delivered there before. She has a house on the ridge overlooking the National Park."

"Then that's where we're going. You can wave your Hermes charm and get us in to see Alicia."

Hermes—of course. Not Robin Hood, but the messenger of the gods. Which meant the dragons thought of themselves as gods, I guess. Arrogant bastards.

"They're not going to let you in just because you're with me. Heralds work alone."

"We'll work something out."

"Look, no offence—I appreciate the rescue and all—but it won't work. You'll endanger us all for nothing."

"But we have to!" I blurted. That damned stone nagged at the back of my mind, impossible to ignore. "They helped me rescue you, now we have to help them."

"No, we don't," he said gently. "This isn't some game where each side keeps score. The proving is dangerous stuff. We need to stay right out of it."

"But I *want* to help." Panic tightened my throat. I had to persuade him. I needed that stone back, though I couldn't tell him so. The first question would be "why?" and I had no answers. "If we don't get to the bottom of this business with Leandra, I'll never be safe."

Ben looked less than thrilled at the thought of being dragged in front of another dragon. He glared at Luce.

"What's the point of seeing Alicia anyway? How's that going to help get your stone back if Valeria's got it?"

"It won't," she said. "But I have to warn her that Valeria's about to unleash dragonfire, or Valeria wins and I never see the stone again."

"Unleash—? But that's taboo!"

She pinned him with a hard stare. "So's kidnapping heralds. Do you really think that will stop Valeria?"

CHAPTER EIGHTEEN

They like to call them villages up here, these suburbs sprawled either side of the Great Western Highway as it snakes its way up the mountains, as if harking back to some romantic cobblestoned English ideal. But they're as full of concrete, glass and asphalt as any other part of Greater Sydney. McDonald's hasn't gained a foothold, which is a source of great pride among the residents, but there's not much else to show you're in the mountains, till you round a bend and catch a glimpse of tree-covered slopes falling away to the side of the road.

"Can you smell smoke?" I asked.

Garth, at the wheel again, frowned at me in the rear vision mirror. "You can smell that?"

"Sure." It seemed pretty strong to me, but Luce and Ben shook their heads.

"How come your nose is as good as mine?"

It was a fair question. Suspicion was his natural state, but for once he had a point. Was I going to turn into a werewolf? Or did I have to wait till the full moon? But surely Garth of all people wouldn't be asking if that was the reason. He'd know if he'd infected me.

So why was my sense of smell as good as a werewolf's?

"There were fires at Lithgow this morning," Luce said. "Maybe they've spread."

Maybe. There was certainly enough fuel. The bulk of the Blue Mountains was national park—hectare after hectare of bushland, all dry as tinder at this time of year. Its beauty made the area a popular place to live, but every summer the residents paid the price with months of living on alert. Some years bushfires raged unchecked in the more inaccessible areas, burning out thousands of hectares. If it was a really bad year, homes were lost, but every year the threat of fire hung over the area like a pall of smoke.

I stared out the window and sighed. It wasn't only the heightened sense of smell. There was that conversation in the motel last night. Even though Luce had dragged Garth into the bathroom to whisper to him, I'd still overheard. Much as I'd have liked to blame it on shoddy insulation, taken with the acute sense of smell and my new party trick of seeing auras round shifters, it all pointed to some supernatural explanation.

And the aura thing had started *before* Garth attacked me.

I let my head fall back against the seat and tried to ignore the other three. They'd been arguing since we'd left Leura, and all through the meal we stopped for on the way.

"Even if they let *us* in, they're not going to accept you two," Ben said for the third or fourth time. "They must know who you are."

"There are precedents," Luce said, "if you go back far enough."

"From what I've heard of Alicia, she's even more paranoid than usual for a dragon. She's never going to trust someone so highly placed in a rival's camp."

"I don't see why we're bothering with Alicia anyway," Garth grumbled. Luce started to speak and he cut her off. "Yes, I know, I know, we don't want Valeria to win, but why not go straight after her? Forget Alicia! You know what it's like once an attack starts. It's all confusion and screaming. And the sun's going down. There's bound to be a chance to get to Valeria."

He was eager as a child begging for a new toy—and I'd had some experience with that. Life with Lachie seemed further away than ever. The biggest drama on an average day had been standing in checkout lines, saying no to Lego and lollies. When had things become so surreal? In the back seat I snuggled next to Ben, who'd morphed from best friend to … well, something much more than friendly. He worked for Magic Fed Ex and apparently so did I. In the front seat, a werewolf begged his wyvern boss to let him kill a dragon. Partly to avenge a dragon's death I may or may not have had a hand in—but I'd never know if I couldn't recover my memories—and partly to get back a magic piece of rock. Mustn't forget that part.

On reflection, "surreal" hardly did it justice.

Glimpses of red and pink sky peeked through the trees ahead, but it was nearly dark. We'd turned off the highway and drove along smaller roads, past houses perched among the trees and up on sandstone bluffs, their lights softly glowing in the dusk.

Gradually the houses thinned out, becoming grander as the blocks grew bigger. The road climbed higher and higher, till we were running along the ridge line, densely forested valleys falling away to either side. In daylight the view would have been spectacular.

We rounded a corner and Garth stomped on the brake, jolting us all forward against our seatbelts. A huge gum tree lay across the road.

As soon as we got out, the sap-and-sawdust smell of freshly cut timber hit my nostrils.

"Well, that was no accident," said Luce, surveying the clean cut made by what must have been a super-large chainsaw. "Looks like we walk the rest of the way."

"Do they know we're coming?" Garth glared into the darkness at the side of the road, looking for something to attack. "Is Valeria trying to stop us?"

Luce snorted. "Don't flatter yourself. Valeria's not scared of us. This isn't to keep anyone out. It's to keep someone in. I bet any other access roads to Alicia's are blocked too. Valeria doesn't mean there to be any survivors."

That wasn't the most comforting thought. People persisted in building on these ridge lines because of the glorious views, but they were the most dangerous place to be in a bushfire. Fire could race uphill faster than a person could run. Or a wolf. Luce was probably the only one of us with a fighting chance if it came to that.

Garth stopped at the fallen giant and lifted his head. He appeared to be sniffing the air.

"What?" asked Luce. "Is someone there?"

"No." He laid a hand on the trunk and scowled as if he thought he could move the tree by sheer bad temper.

"Come on, then."

The trunk came nearly to her chin, but she vaulted lightly over and looked back expectantly. There were no streetlights out here, and with her dark hair she was barely visible in the gloom on the other side. The rest of us stood outlined in the car's headlights.

I looked at Ben and he shrugged.

"I think it's another couple of kilometres from here." He boosted me over, his big hands warm on my waist, just as the headlights switched themselves off, plunging us into darkness. Garth still hadn't moved.

"Hurry *up*, Garth," Luce said.

But instead of joining us he hauled his T-shirt over his head and started unbuckling his belt.

"What are you doing? No! Stay human."

"This is bullshit," he said, kicking off his shoes. "Two kilometres? By the time you walk there and stand around arguing with the guards it'll all be over. And that's assuming they don't kill you on sight. I'm going to find Valeria."

"Garth!" Luce's tone was icy. "Stick with the plan."

"There *is* no plan," he spat, but the last word came out half-strangled as his body hunched forward. Again I heard that awful crunching as his bones shifted and reformed. I reached for Ben's hand in the dark, the sound bringing the terror of that experience in the kitchen rushing back.

But he didn't even look at us. The wolf bounded into the trees at the side of the road and disappeared.

After a moment of stunned silence Ben cleared his throat. "Is he always so ..."

"So impulsive? So pigheaded?" Luce bit each word off with precision. Then she sighed. "He used to be my most reliable man. He hasn't been himself since Leandra died."

Well, there were a few of us in that boat.

"I've never seen a shift before." Ben's voice held a note of wonder.

"Lucky you," I said.

"Look sharp," Luce said. "Let's try and get there before he gets himself killed."

We followed her down the road, dark now but still radiating the day's heat up at us. Now that my eyes had adjusted, I could see well enough to dodge the pot holes, though I could make out nothing in the darkness under the trees on either side. I looked around anxiously as we walked, wondering where the tree-loppers were now. My back crawled with that horrible feeling of being watched, but the only movement was a light wind stirring the scrubby undergrowth and rattling dry leaves. We were all on edge: it showed in Luce's tense shoulders and the way Ben moved protectively closer to my side.

The road wasn't wide, and the gums met over the top, leaning toward each other with a whisper of leaves. We walked through a black leafy tunnel, though the clean scent of eucalyptus was overwhelmed by a smoky taint to the air. The road turned to dirt under our feet, and I wondered if we'd entered the national park by mistake till a high stone wall appeared on our right. It was old, all its sharp edges softened by years of weather, but it meant business: broken glass embedded all along its top glinted in the faint light from the other side. I guess good fences make good neighbours, but it didn't say much for dragon society that their homes all featured drastic security measures. Not the friendliest bunch. I tried to remember if there'd been such a wall around Leandra's place, but came up with the usual blank where those memories should have been.

After more than a kilometre of wall, we finally found a gate. A whole gatehouse, in fact, brightly lit, with a bored-looking man sitting in it. The set-up was more like something you'd find at a big commercial site than a private home. This Alicia must be serious about security. The guard came to life when we appeared out of the darkness, stepping out with suspicion written all over him.

"Move along, please," he said. "This is private property."

"We're here to see Alicia," said Luce. "Tell her Lucinda Chan is at her gates, requesting an audience."

"What is your business with my lady?"

Luce fixed him with an arctic stare. "I'll tell her myself when I see her."

He stepped back into the gatehouse and spoke into a phone, watching us through the glass the whole time as if afraid we'd storm the fortress if he turned his back. Personally, I wasn't up for anything more strenuous than a cup of tea and a good lie-down. The excitements of the last couple of days and the lack of sleep were starting to tell, and fortress-storming was no longer an option without Garth, if it ever had been. I wondered where he'd got to—hopefully he was still in one piece.

The guard put the phone down. "Wait one moment, please."

I actually yawned while we waited ... for one moment, then another and another. The dragon Armageddon might be about to hit, but I couldn't stay on high alert any longer—my adrenal glands just weren't up to the strain. My need for the stone had pushed me this far, but if someone didn't wave it under my nose soon I'd be out on my feet. I tried to sense its position, as I had at Valeria's house, but either it was too far away or I was too tired; all I could get was a vague yearning.

Ben looked even worse than I felt, with dark shadows under his eyes and a scruff of stubble. He couldn't have gotten much sleep last night either. I leaned against him and he kissed me, soft and sweet. Something inside sat up and took notice. Maybe some things were worth staying awake for.

"I can smell the smoke now," he said.

I nodded, uneasy. It could be nothing, of course. Often Sydneysiders smell smoke when the fires are a hundred kilometres away—it depends which way the wind is blowing. On the other hand ... again I thought of Garth, out in the bush somewhere. Had he found Valeria's people? Not that I should care if he ran into trouble or got caught in a fire. Stupid dog.

A car came down the driveway from the house—another four-wheel drive. Seemed to be the car of choice among the supernatural set. This one didn't look as if it spent any time off-road, given the gleaming shine of its hubcaps in the glare of the gatehouse lights.

The guy who got out looked equally well-cared for, tall and slim in a tailored suit which flattered his slenderness without making him look like a drainpipe. If it hadn't been for the bright green hair he could have been a model for Young Businessman of the Year. His aura glowed a greenish brown, like khaki.

"Lucinda," he said, "how lovely to see you again."

He made no move to open the gate, despite his welcoming tone.

"Hello, Adam. Aren't you going to invite us in?"

"I'm not sure that would be in my lady's best interests."

"Why?" Her gesture took in the three of us. "Do we look so threatening?"

"Your reputation precedes you, my dear, even if we hadn't had … ah … previous experience. Lady Alicia is not in the habit of entertaining the intimates of her rivals."

Luce folded her arms. "Perhaps Lady Alicia isn't aware my patron is dead."

"We did hear a rumour to that effect," he admitted. "One wonders what your purpose could be, if so, for coming here."

"Perhaps if one opened the gate one might find out."

Ben stepped forward and indicated the two of us. "We're heralds. We claim right of entry."

Adam arched one green eyebrow. "Show me your heraldic insignia."

I lifted my charm out of my shirt and held it out. Ben did the same. He squinted at them for a long moment. What did he see, apart from a simple silver charm?

"They appear to be genuine." His voice betrayed a hint of surprise. I suppose we did look a suspicious bunch.

"Let us in, Adam," Luce coaxed. "We're unarmed, and we're on your side."

"One moment, please." He turned away and spoke into his phone, explaining the situation to someone on the other end. Alicia, perhaps? I couldn't hear the reply.

"The heralds may enter," he said when he hung up, "if they have a letter or geas to deliver. Unfortunately Lady Alicia is not able to offer hospitality at this time to Ms Chan."

"Lady Alicia won't be offering anything to anyone if she doesn't see me *right now*," said Luce.

"Threats will make no difference," he said.

"It's not a threat. You don't know what's coming, Adam. I'm trying to help you."

He ignored her and turned to Ben. "Do you have a letter?"

Ben threw Luce a look that said *I told you so* plainer than words. "No. The message is verbal."

Adam spread his hands in a gesture of helplessness. "Then I'm afraid I can't admit any of you. I must ask you to leave the area immediately."

The gate guard stepped forward, his hand resting on the gun holstered at his side. His meaning was plain.

Luce ignored him, her attention focused on the green-haired man. "Adam, if you value your Lady's life, you have to let us in."

He shifted uneasily, unnerved by her intensity. "Tell me what you know and I'll speak to her."

"No. I have to speak to her myself."

"My lady won't allow that. How can she be sure this isn't some trick to gain access? We only have your word Leandra is dead."

"Is Alicia so craven a lone wyvern terrifies her?"

"*Lady* Alicia sees no point in taking unnecessary risks."

Luce held his gaze with hers. "Trust me, Adam, this one's necessary."

He shrugged. "Then there's only one thing to be done. You'll have to swear to Lady Alicia."

CHAPTER NINETEEN

"What kind of creature is Adam?" I asked a short time later. Was the green hair natural? I was prepared to believe almost anything at this point.

He'd left us in a room with one wall floor-to-ceiling glass, overlooking a cleared, park-like area at the side of the house full of flowering shrubs and fruit trees. It was lit by powerful floodlights, making the scene almost as bright as day. Inside two leather lounges faced each other in front of a massive fireplace that probably saw heavy use in the colder months. At the moment it boasted an artful arrangement of pine cones and native blooms.

The short ride up the driveway had passed in tense silence. No one had spoken since Luce agreed to his terms, and the silence was making me twitchy.

"A leshy," Luce said. She gazed out at the floodlit gardens, her back to the room. "A kind of forest spirit. Alicia has several in her employ. They like it up here in the bush."

"I've never met one before." Ben joined Luce at the window. "Are they always so tall?"

She shrugged. "Unlike the rest of us, they can take any size or shape they please. In Europe they used to run with wolf packs a lot, or hang out with bears. They're sociable creatures. But yes, their natural humanoid form is long and lean."

Rather like Ben himself. Next to Luce he looked like a giant. She barely came up to his armpit and looked more like a kid standing next to her dad than a grown woman.

He looked down at her. "What's involved in this swearing business? She's not going to make you a thrall, is she?"

"No. Only humans can be enthralled."

"But?"

I'd sensed a "but" there too. The look of shock on Adam's face when she'd agreed to his terms of entry told me he'd only offered because he was sure she'd refuse. And then the shock had changed to triumph, and I knew Luce had let herself in for something bad. Her face now was expressionless, as usual, but something in the way she stood, a certain sag to the shoulders, hinted at her unease.

"But by swearing to Alicia I bind myself to her and her cause for life."

That didn't sound *so* bad. I mean, betrayal seemed to be in fashion among shifters. Loyalty for life only meant as long as you wanted it to.

"Can't you cross your fingers while you swear or something?"

She frowned at my flippancy. "Dragons aren't stupid enough to rely on your *word*. The swearing involves a binding magic that will kill me if I go against her. It's an old ceremony seldom used any more. Most people won't agree to give up such power to anyone."

"Then why would you?" Ben looked horrified. "You don't even *like* her. Why didn't you tell Adam about Valeria and leave it to them to deal with? You don't have to get involved."

She turned. Her face was its usual mask, but her spine was rigid. "I'm already involved. This is personal now. Alicia's been hiding up here since the proving started, waiting for the others to kill each other off. She's got no idea what Valeria's capable of. They're not prepared. Valeria will chew them up and spit them out, and *I can't let that happen.*"

"You'd spend the rest of your life tied to Alicia just to stop Valeria winning the proving?"

"Not to stop her winning." Her face twisted into a feral grin. "To destroy her. To get that stone back and avenge Leandra."

"But Leandra's dead. She doesn't care if you avenge her or not." I couldn't see why it mattered so much to her that she'd take such a drastic step. Unless something was forcing her? "You're not doing this because you were bound to Leandra first, are you?"

She shot me a contemptuous look. "Of course not. No one but Alicia would dream of asking such a thing. Besides, even if I *had* been bound to Leandra, bindings are severed by death."

Adam returned with a drink tray, ending the conversation. Ice clinked in tall glasses of water flavoured with lemon slices. About to take a sip, I slammed the glass down on a handy table instead, seized by a sudden unreasoning terror. I sank on to the nearest lounge, lost in a memory of terrible pain. I saw a glass, and Jason's smiling face. Last time I'd drunk something like that … last time I'd *died*. My stomach cramped in sympathy.

"Are you all right?" Ben sat next to me, a worried look in his dark eyes. "You're shaking."

Adam and Luce stared at me in surprise. Heat rose into my cheeks.

"I'm fine." A half-hearted smile didn't seem to reassure him, funnily enough. *You're not dead, you idiot. Snap out of it.*

Several other people entered, creating a welcome diversion. Three of the men looked as though they could have belonged to the same basketball team as Adam and had the same khaki-coloured aura, so I figured them for leshies too, though none sported Adam's outrageous hair colour. One carried a tray with an odd assortment of objects—a white cloth, an ugly, malformed bowl and a small knife. The others were human, as far as I could tell—no glowing auras, at least. They were built along the same muscular lines as Garth, probably bodyguards for the woman who followed them.

She was supermodel good-looking and made the most of it in a clingy black dress slit up the side to show off shapely tanned legs. Long hair foamed over her shoulders in a dark cloud. Her aura blazed red, far brighter than Jason's had been. This must be Alicia, dragon queen-in-waiting. She was the most beautiful woman I'd ever seen, and I hated her on sight.

She paused inside the door and surveyed the room, one hip tipped forward, leg jutting out the slit in her dress. *How to Make an Entrance 101: be sure to stand in a way that shows off your assets.* Check.

Were all dragons this full of themselves? She and Jason would make a pretty pair—though there might be a fight for the mirror.

When I finally dragged my gaze up as far as her face, I found something strange lurking in her expression. Nerves? A touch of fear, even?

She stared at Luce. From the intensity of her expression she probably hadn't even noticed Ben and I were in the room.

"Is everything prepared?" The question was clearly directed at someone else, but she didn't take her eyes off Luce. The man with the tray stepped forward.

"Ready when you are, my lady," Adam said, coming to his side. I wondered about Adam's job description. Butler? Bouncer? Bed toy?

Alicia glided further into the room and took the knife from the tray. The blade was only short, but it looked sharp. Strange symbols were carved into the hilt, but I only caught a glimpse as Alicia's long fingers closed around it.

"Come, Lucinda," she said.

Luce stepped forward, her body relaxed now, despite her earlier doubts. She'd made her decision.

A fierce protectiveness welled up inside me. She looked so small standing in front of the willowy Alicia. I knew she was stubborn and strong-willed, but even for her this was a drastic step. I hoped she knew what she was doing.

Alicia drew the blade across her own forearm. For a moment it seemed nothing had happened and the room held its breath. Then blood began to well from the cut, and Adam caught the drops in the ugly little bowl.

It looked like some blind potter's first attempt, and I wondered why the elegant Alicia suffered such a deformed piece in her house, until it began to glow softly. Right. It must have some magical significance.

"My blood for you," said Alicia.

No one moved as Adam set the bowl back on the tray and picked up the cloth. The sound of tearing was loud in the silence as he ripped it in two and used one piece to bind Alicia's arm.

With her blood still coating the knife Alicia took Luce's hand and sliced a deep cut across Luce's arm in the same place.

"My blood for you." Luce's voice was calm and strong as she watched her blood drip into the bowl to join Alicia's. The glow about the bowl intensified.

Adam bound her arm with the other half of the cloth then offered the bowl to Alicia, who raised it to her lips and drank.

Eww. Gross. Luce drank next, then wiped her mouth with the back of her hand, leaving a smear of blood across her face. Nobody else moved, eyes locked on the two in the centre of the circle.

Alicia watched Luce, hunger in her eyes. The glowing bowl lit their faces from below, casting weird shadows. The atmosphere was so tense you could have heard a pin drop. What were they all waiting for?

Then the light from the bowl died and Luce's blue aura shivered and flashed bright red, the exact colour of Alicia's. I drew in a shocked breath and Alicia glanced my way, as if noticing me for the first time. A millisecond later Luce's aura shone its usual soft blue hue. I would have thought I'd imagined that flash of red except for the smug smile now plastered on Alicia's face. Clearly she'd been waiting for it.

She sank into an overstuffed armchair and crossed her fabulous long legs as the leshy with the tray disappeared. The bodyguards took up positions on either side of her chair as she inspected each of us in turn, settling on Luce with a sneer that still held more than a trace of smugness.

"The famous Lucinda Chan," she said. "My sister's vaunted security chief. Perhaps I was lucky after all, that you resisted all my offers to tempt you away from Leandra's entourage. *I* could have been the one killed on my own grounds."

Luce's jaw moved, as if she was clenching her teeth, but her voice remained calm. "That could still easily happen."

The bodyguards moved as one, their hands reaching into their jackets for the guns holstered there.

"Are you threatening me?" Alicia asked, her tone amused. She waved one elegant hand and the bodyguards relaxed their ready stance. "You know you're physically incapable of harming me now."

"Not at all. Merely pointing out you're in grave danger. Valeria has this property surrounded and cut off. We believe she means to burn you out."

"She's welcome to try. We're completely bushfire-proof here."

In the air-conditioned comfort of her house I couldn't smell smoke any more. But that didn't mean we were safe. The view out the window told me nothing. Floodlights showed fruit trees separated from the house by a wide expanse of grass, clipped short. A sensible precaution in a bushfire-prone area.

There should be nothing the fire could latch on to close to the house. But beyond the lights loomed the bush: a dark, amorphous mass. No stars shone through the heavy cloud cover. Who knew what lurked out there?

"You may be bushfire-proof," I said, "but are you dragon-proof?"

Alicia laughed, a mocking sound. "And you would be one of the supposed heralds?"

"There's nothing supposed about it," Ben said.

She eyed him as if he were a bug she'd like to step on. "Whoever heard of a herald delivering a verbal message? I'll grant you the charms were real enough. Perhaps you stole them. I'm sure my mother will be thrilled to hear the whole story. She takes a rather dim view of people messing with her precious heralds."

"That didn't stop Valeria from kidnapping us," I said.

She turned the bug-squishing look on me. "That's a big hole you're digging for yourself there, accusing a dragon of interfering with the heralds. Though I suppose it's no more ridiculous than suggesting she would break the oldest taboo."

Some of her leshies tittered dutifully, though Adam didn't seem to share their amusement. His gaze kept straying to the window, a worried crease between his green eyebrows.

She directed a megawatt glare at Luce. "I don't see what you hope to achieve by coming to me with this outrageous story."

"Your ship is about to go down," said Luce, "and you can't even see the iceberg. Valeria is *winning*. Is that what you want?"

"According to your own story, my house is surrounded and cut off. What would you have me do?"

"Fight. The time for running and hiding is over. Valeria means to end it here, right now."

Alicia tossed her hair over one magnificent shoulder. "Valeria is not the only one with plans. Don't underestimate me, Lucinda."

The door banged open. A leshy rushed in, bringing a whiff of smoke with him. "My lady, there's fire sweeping up the north valley."

Obviously this wasn't the north side of the house—the view remained unchanged. But wait ... those clouds hung awfully low over the trees.

Not clouds. Smoke.

"Start the pumps and get the men out with the hoses." She stood up. "Everyone to your assigned positions."

"Where do you want me?" Luce asked as the room emptied.

"Go with Adam. He'll show you what to do." She looked at Ben and me with calm indifference. "You can wait in the library. I've lived up here a long time. We've dealt with plenty of bushfires before. It's quite the spectacle, but nothing to be afraid of."

She waved a dismissal and we followed Luce and Adam out. Alicia acted as if she were offering us a treat—a ringside seat at a bushfire! Yeehaw. That was one spectacle I could have happily done without.

***

Most days, the library's huge picture windows probably boasted a magnificent outlook across a valley carpeted in the dusty green of gum trees. Right now the view was lost in smoke and darkness. A great pall hung over the valley, lit from below by an ominous red glow.

"No sign of flames yet," said Adam, watching his fellow leshies rush around outside. Someone had turned on a roof sprinkler system, which gave the bizarre impression of rain, as water trickled down the enormous pane of glass in front of us and droplets spattered the ground outside. A team of leshies stood ready with hoses and shovels, presumably to deal with any embers which flew in ahead of the fire front. Embers were usually the cause when a house went up, often landing on the roof out of sight and starting fires inside roof cavities.

I swallowed and inched closer to Ben. Despite Alicia's confidence, Adam seemed uneasy. I was with him—this wasn't something to treat so casually.

"We should get out there and help," I said. I felt like a sitting duck behind that vast expanse of glass. "Don't you have fire shutters for these windows?"

A huge white cloud of smoke billowed about halfway up the slope at the back of the house, ghostly pale against the night sky.

"The fire brigade has been summoned," Adam said. "You're much safer in here than out there, believe me."

"The fire brigade won't be coming." Luce sounded as cool as ever. "I told you, the roads are blocked. Nothing will get through. If you're relying on them you're in big trouble."

"We're not relying on anybody. As Lady Alicia said, we've been through this before and we know what to do." He gestured at the activity outside the window. "If the fire comes this way we will close the shutters, but in the meantime Lady Alicia would like you to observe."

Outside one of the hose-wielding leshies went down in a tumble of long limbs. Probably not what Alicia had meant us to see. "What the—!"

Dark figures moved in the smoky tree line. Another leshy stumbled, hose spraying wildly as he clutched at his arm. Shouts of alarm filled the smoky air.

"We're under attack!" Adam's face paled. I had the feeling he'd believed us all along about Valeria, but loyalty to Alicia had kept him quiet. He met Luce's eyes. "Come with me."

He probably meant only Luce, but Ben and I tagged along. Hell, I wasn't staying here on my own if Valeria's forces had arrived. My heart pounded. But where was safe?

Not outside, but that was where we went, plunging down a set of steps and into a frightening world. Straight away I started to cough; the smoke was thick and the heat intense. The flames were close now, roaring up the slope with a noise like a jet engine, and stinging embers pelted us as we ran.

"Get behind the barn!" Adam shouted. "Try and stay out of trouble."

I barely heard him over the noise of the fire front. Ben caught my hand and dragged me behind him into the lee of the barn, where at least we were protected from the embers. The wind drove them almost horizontally before the front, like sand in a sandstorm. My bare arms stung with a dozen welts that were already blistering.

The barn had its own sprinkler system, and we hugged the wet walls, letting the cooling spray soothe us. Ben ducked inside and returned with an axe and a shovel, which he passed to me.

"What am I supposed to do with this?" I shouted. Dig my way to freedom? "Where did Luce go? We have to help her!"

"Stay here," he shouted back. "Remember we're heralds, even if nobody else does. Self-defence only."

He stepped protectively in front of me, axe at the ready. Self-defence only. Right. As if I would run out and attack someone with my trusty shovel.

I strained to see what was happening through the choking smoke. Visibility was down to only a few metres. I blinked tears away from my stinging eyes and searched for Luce as figures loomed out of the smoke then disappeared again.

The leshies gave as good as they got, now that Valeria's forces had lost the initial advantage of surprise. Right in front of us, one dodged a knife thrust from a hard-eyed man. The knife scored his arm and green blood dripped. The leshy snarled, baring pointed teeth, then snapped his fingers. Strands of grass surged out of the ground in response and whipped around the knife-wielder like green tentacles. They dragged him down so fast the guy didn't even have time to scream before he disappeared into the churning earth. I swallowed hard and shrank back against the barn wall, but the leshy took no notice of us. Sprouting thorns all over his body, he plunged back into the smoke in search of another opponent.

Another seemed to remember his race's ancient affinity for bears. A grizzly appeared out of the haze, towering on its hind legs over the man who faced it. The man backed away, a look of desperation on his face, as he emptied his pistol into the snarling bear. The bullets may as well have been flea bites for all the notice the bear took of them. It swatted the gun away and seized him in its massive claws. The man screamed, and I turned away as the sound abruptly cut off. I didn't want to see what happened next.

There were wolves among the attackers, and some on Alicia's side too. Three ganged up on a leshy, snarling and growling as they dragged him down like an animal and tore into him. Two others rolled across the ground not far from us, biting and snapping at each other in a frenzy. One was black like Garth. Could it be him? I couldn't tell. Luce had disappeared into the haze; I hoped she was safe.

Not that any of us were. I eyed the wall of flame headed our way, lighting up the night with an eerie orange glow. It flared the height of the gum trees, roiling and snapping in their crowns, spitting burning debris ahead of it.

I leaned closer to Ben and yelled in his ear. "They need to stop fighting each other and start fighting the damn fire!"

Could none of them see the danger?

I was soaked to the skin from the barn's sprinkler system, my hair dripping in my eyes, but I knew that was scant protection. The heat was scalding; the air so hot and smoky I could hardly breathe. Maybe the fire would go around us. All it needed was a wind change to set it on another path.

But as I stared at the looming wall of flame I knew that was wishful thinking. Unless the leshies had some magic tricks up their sleeves we were in real trouble. Not even firefighters, with trucks and proper hoses, would stand a chance.

The grizzly-leshy still fought, its deep, full-throated roars rising above the noise of the fire. I couldn't see as many of Valeria's men. A couple were down, unmoving on the grass, but most had faded back into the gloom. Some of the leshies had rushed to their hoses, trying to stop the grass from catching. Looked like Alicia's side had won. I searched for Luce again, unsettled. Was it just me, or did that seem too easy?

No time to think about it now. I glanced back at the house, with its huge picture windows now protected by steel shutters. We had to get back in there. The heat out here was blistering.

Gradually another noise became apparent over the roar and crackle of the fire, a kind of rhythmic whumping. Helicopter? Could be one of those big firefighting jobs that scooped up megalitres of water then dumped them on the fire from above. My eyes stung and watered from the smoke, but I strained to pierce the gloom, searching the dark skies above the flames.

"There!" I caught Ben's arm, heart in my mouth. "Is that—?"

A shape, glimpsed through smoke, but all wrong for a helicopter. A plane? No. It arrowed through the sky, in and out of the roiling smoke cloud. An impossibility, looming larger, huge wings labouring. She really was going to do it. My mouth dropped open.

"Dragon!" Ben screamed. "Get down!"

The nearest leshies heard him and turned, faces wreathed in horror. One was Adam; he ran for the dubious cover of the barn where we sheltered.

"Inside, quickly!" Ben grabbed me, but Adam stopped him.

"No!" he shouted. "This way!"

He ran towards the fire. Was he crazy? The dragon was nearly on us, so close every beat of its massive wings battered at the fire below, sending it gusting and writhing in unexpected directions. We stumbled after him, coughing. Into the mouth of hell, it felt like, the roaring flames billowing waves of heat against us.

The dragon passed overhead, long and sinuous, tail flicking behind it. The light of the fire reflected gold and orange off the glinting scales of its underbelly. Screams and shouts pierced the smoky air, and then came a noise like a thousand furnace doors opening at once. A concussion wave knocked me screaming to the baking ground, Ben half on top of me.

And Alicia's house erupted in a spectacular fireball.

CHAPTER TWENTY

I lay stunned, my head ringing from the blast. Fear held me immobile, a deep ancestral terror that set my pulse racing and my body trembling. I was a mouse frozen in place by the screech of a hunting owl. The dragon filled my vision as it soared on past the flaming wreckage that a second ago had been Alicia's proud mansion.

Its body glittered and winked, reflecting the fire from a thousand mirror-like scales. It was hard to tell what colour it really was. Its head looked disturbingly crocodilian and its bat-like wings brought to mind every half-remembered nightmare of things that dropped from the night skies on to the unwary. I thought I'd been frightened when Garth had turned wolf in my kitchen, but that was nothing to what I felt now.

I might have lain there frozen till the fire front rolled right over the top of me but for a hand that reached down and hauled me to my feet. A green hand.

Adam had lost his urbane humanity and now looked all leshy. His hair had turned to grass and his eyes glowed a brilliant emerald. His other hand had a firm grip on Ben's bicep. Ben looked like he needed the help standing up, as dazed as I felt.

"She's coming round for another pass," Adam shouted over the roar of the flames. "Come on!"

He dragged us toward three giant water tanks grouped together a little way back from the barn. Closer to the advancing fire front. My insides churned with terror. Dragon or flames? Either way meant death.

We crawled into the gap between two of the tanks and hunkered down. My legs shook so much I had to sit, knees pulled up to my chest. I dragged my shirt up over my nose and mouth, gasping for a breath that wasn't full of smoke. I was light-headed and panting in between coughs. Much more of this and I'd pass out from the heat. My skin prickled with it and my eyeballs burned in their sockets.

Above me Adam sprouted vicious four-inch claws on one hand and raked them across the side of the tank. The screech of metal set my teeth on edge. Water gushed from the slashes all over us.

I looked up at the small slice of sky between the tanks and caught a glimpse of the dragon banking on one wingtip. Despite the heat a shiver ran down my spine.

Down on ground level chaos reigned. The fire had started its run across the lawn with a roar like a jet engine. All the combatants had scattered, seeking shelter. One group of leshies hid in the barn, while another couple sprinted for the garage. In a moment they reappeared in one of the four-wheel drives, its headlights bouncing dizzily as it crunched across burning debris.

"They'll never make it," said Ben, even as spot fires leapt ahead of them into the trees lining the driveway. "They'll get trapped somewhere on the road."

Adam made a noise of distress. I heard the buffeting of the dragon's wings again and this time I saw as flame belched from its mouth, engulfing the barn in an instant. The sprinkler system had no chance against the white-hot heat of the dragon's breath. The poor bastards trapped inside probably didn't even have time to scream before they vaporised.

The fleeing car zigzagged in a desperate effort to avoid its fate. The dragon followed with a lazy wing beat. Beside me Adam coaxed the grass into a thick sodden blanket with desperate fingers. It poured across the ground and into our little hidey-hole, knitting itself into a thick carpet. The fire front roared at our backs. He pulled the heavy blanket over us, shutting out the noise and light.

The last thing I saw was the four-wheel drive exploding.

The next two minutes were the most terrifying of my life. The noise as the fire front leapt over us was indescribable, like a thousand freight trains roaring down on us. Every second I expected to be incinerated by the dragon. But we stayed safe under Adam's dense blanket of grass and earth, protected by the water gushing from the tank all over us. There was nothing for the fire to catch hold of, and after an eternity of heat and smoke and terror we emerged, still in one trembling piece, hardly able to believe we'd survived.

Adam stared at the blazing inferno that had been the mansion. "I can't believe she did it." His voice trembled ever so slightly. "To defy every edict and actually take trueshape in a populated area, for any mundane to see. It's an outrage. And for *this* she thinks to become queen?"

Sounded like a pretty fair bet to me. After all, she was the only candidate still standing. Clearly Valeria thought the end justified the means—and who was left to argue?

I put one hand on the leshy's slender arm. He had that dazed look I knew so well. "I'm sorry. You've lost a lot of friends today."

He turned his glowing green eyes on me. "Thank you. But there's no time yet to weep. Your friend Lucinda was right. We must fight."

The rhythmic thump of wing beats heralded the dragon's return. Oh, Lord, not again. There were only a couple of outbuildings still standing. Was she determined to burn everything?

"Don't throw your life away for nothing, mate," Ben urged. He caught hold of Adam's arm as the leshy made to crawl from our shelter. "You can't take on a dragon, and getting yourself killed won't bring Alicia back."

The dragon settled on the burnt grass near the blazing barn, sending a whirl of sparks eddying through the smoky air. God, it was huge. I felt the vibration through the ground beneath me as massive clawed feet touched down.

Adam bared pointed teeth in something halfway between a grin and a snarl. "But my lady is not dead—at least, I hope she's not. We have a fire bunker beneath the house. It is her custom to seek shelter there when danger threatens."

I could hardly tear my eyes from the dragon. Something about it called to me. I wanted to touch it, to—*be* it? To take to the skies, feel the wind in my face as I soared. Without realising I started to move towards it.

Ben caught my arm and hauled me back. "Hey! What are you doing?"

It wasn't quite so graceful on the ground with its massive wings folded away. A man approached, and the huge head swung to regard him. He looked like a toy next to the creature's bulk.

As I stared, mesmerised, the dragon's outline flickered. At first I thought it was an effect of the fire's heat, but then the dragon kind of *shimmied* and disappeared.

In its place stood a naked woman.

Whoa. How did *that* work? Werewolves were one thing—the mass of a wolf and an adult human were very similar, after all—but this boggled my mind. How did that huge creature become a woman less than a tenth its size? Where did the rest of it go?

The woman in question had large breasts and a mass of dark blonde hair braided around her head, which was all I could make out from this distance. She surveyed the damage she'd wrought with evident satisfaction, unconcerned with her nakedness. The infamous Valeria.

The man offered her a white garment, which turned out to be a long white dress when she slipped it on. Very Greek goddess-like, and pretty much the last thing I would have chosen to wear to a bushfire-cum-shootout. But hey, I wasn't a homicidal dragon. What did I know?

She said something to the man and he laughed. With a start, I realised it was Jason. I'd been so focused on Valeria I hadn't even recognised my own ex. And the bastard stood in the middle of all this death and destruction, laughing. A body lay practically at his feet.

That body suddenly leapt for his throat. Not dead after all. As if at a signal, leshies materialised from the ground. They must have been using Adam's camouflage trick with the living grass blankets. Valeria's surviving men poured from one of the outbuildings, and suddenly there were struggling figures scattered everywhere.

Adam sprinted toward the action and Ben scrambled out after him, hefting his axe.

"He's going to get himself killed! Stay here and keep your head down."

So much for self-defence only.

I clutched my shovel, heart in my mouth, terrified Valeria would turn dragon again. But she backed away from the onrush and headed for the house with half a dozen men, leaving Jason to direct the fighting. Probably going to make sure Alicia was dead.

Ben swung the axe at a man Adam had just dodged. He blocked the blow with an upraised arm against the axe haft. I winced. That would have broken most people's arms. I looked closer, squinting against the smoke. A tell-tale orange glow surrounded him. Werewolf. They must be made of stronger stuff.

Lachie and I had learned taekwondo together for a while, so I knew all about the bruises a good sparring match could inflict. I'd made it as far as brown belt, but I harboured no illusions as to my abilities. These guys were professionals, and this was no polite sparring match. The werewolf struck back and Ben leapt away, narrowly avoiding the knife blade he wielded, then spun into a series of kicks. The last one sent the knife spiralling away. Seemed Ben knew what he was doing. As long as he kept the wolf too busy to shift he should be okay.

Further on I caught a glimpse of Luce through the smoke, struggling against an ordinary human. Thank God she was still alive—I hadn't seen her since we'd left the house. Wonder where she'd ridden out the firestorm. She landed a blow that sent the guy reeling and darted back to help Ben.

I looked around for Garth, the last of our little band. Scanning the smoky distance, I nearly jumped out of my skin when the water tank behind me reverberated with a blow.

Snarling and snapping, two wolves rolled past, locked together, each trying to find the other's throat. One was black and the other more brindled, with brown streaks among the darker fur. They were clearly on different sides of this battle, but which was which?

I sidestepped, hefting my shovel, trying to stay out of their way. I should hit one, but what if I picked the wrong one? The black one might be Garth—but then so might the other. I'd only ever seen him in wolf form in the dark, and admiring the colour of his coat hadn't exactly been a top priority.

Then again, maybe neither of them was Garth. How did I know a strange werewolf would appreciate the rescue? I might have to fight them both.

I lifted the shovel, hesitating. Black or brindled? The black wolf had lost an ear, and bled heavily from deep gashes on its chest. It still fought, but couldn't seem to get back on top. It yelped as the brindled wolf raked its belly again, and twisted in a futile effort to get away. The brindled wolf snarled and sank its teeth into the black wolf's throat.

Enough. I raised the shovel and slammed it down on the brindled wolf's head.

CHAPTER TWENTY-ONE

The black wolf whimpered and tried to wriggle out from under its opponent, but the brindled wolf was out for the count. I dropped the shovel and got down on my knees and heaved at its bulk. God, these things were heavy. The black wolf watched, yellow eyes intent. It made no move to attack though my efforts must have hurt it. At last I managed to shift its unconscious opponent enough to free it. With a groan it dragged itself clear and collapsed in the mud around the water tanks, its sides heaving.

"Is that you, Garth?"

The creature didn't seem so fearsome any more. It lay panting, its eyes closed. I edged closer. Blood oozed from a deep wound in its throat, bright red. Too much blood.

"Garth? Are you all right?"

Maybe if I applied pressure to the wound … I reached out and laid a nervous hand on the fur of its shoulder. No reaction. Well, at least it was in no shape to attack me.

I needed something to make a pad.

What are you doing, fool? Forget the wolf. Where's the dragon?

I staggered to my feet, wildly looking around. I had to stop the bleeding. What did I care what Valeria was doing?

But the channel stone …

I shuddered and closed my eyes, aching with need. Where was it? I reached out, strained with all my senses, but I couldn't feel it at all. It must be far away.

My eyes popped open again at a sound at my feet. The black wolf lay still as stone, no longer panting.

"Garth!" I dropped to my knees. The fur beneath my hands began to retract, the dark body stretching and sliding.

But that wasn't the sound I'd heard. I whirled just in time to avoid a kick to the head from a very naked, very pissed-off man.

It was my old friend Micah, lips curled back in a savage snarl. The brindled wolf was gone. Damn. Looked like my taekwondo skills were going to be put to the test after all.

I lurched to my feet and aimed a kick at his knee. High kicks look flashy but if you bust someone's knee cap the fight's over. Our teacher had drilled into us that your first choice when faced with a fight is always to run. Next best thing is to disable your opponent straight away, before they get a chance to hurt you. Especially if that opponent is a werewolf with supernatural healing abilities, I suppose, though somehow that had never come up in class.

Micah sidestepped my kick and lunged in with a punch that would have knocked me out cold if I hadn't managed to dodge it. The water tank rang with the blow. I swear his fist left a dent.

I danced around, trying to keep between him and Garth, hands up ready to protect myself. At least he didn't have a weapon. Apart from supernatural speed and strength, that is. I coughed, desperate for a breath of air that wasn't full of smoke. I needed Ben, or Luce—even Adam would do—but I didn't dare take my eyes off him to look for help. And calling out would make no difference, with the barn on fire at my back. No one would hear me over the roar of the flames.

He threw a punch that I managed to block, but the contact sent a shock of agony all the way down to my toes. I got one of my own in, driving my fist into his solar plexus. That got a satisfying grunt out of him but didn't slow him down.

My arm throbbing from the block, I circled warily, weaving away from his blows. He was way too strong for me. Another block like that and I wouldn't be able to use my arm at all.

He lashed out again, catching my jaw as I danced back, not fast enough this time. Pain exploded through my face and down into my neck. I snapped out another kick, then dodged back.

Too far. My foot caught on something and I went down heavily. Micah's leering face loomed over me as I lay there, too winded to get up.

"Say goodnight, sweetheart."

My groping hand found what I'd tripped on. As he closed in I swung the shovel with all the strength I had left. It made a most satisfying *thunk* as it connected with his ribs.

I scrambled up as a line of blood appeared across his ribcage. There was murder in his eyes, but I felt no fear, only a sudden towering rage. How dare this dog lay his filthy paws on me!

Garth sat up, then struggled to his feet, barely able to stand. "Get out of the way. I can … take him."

I ignored him. Brandishing my shovel, I advanced on Micah. "Get away from me, you dog. You dare raise a hand to me? You should be down on your knees begging forgiveness."

He met my gaze and I caught him, pinned him with my glare. His fury melted away, replaced with horror at his temerity.

Slowly he sank down on his knees, head bowed in contrition. "Forgive me, mistress."

In one tiny corner of my mind, part of me watched in astonishment. *Whoa, what's happening?* Garth staggered against the water tank, glancing between us with a look of confusion.

I ignored them both, casting around to see what was happening. The water tanks blocked my view of the burning house, where Valeria had gone, but I could see Jason. That would do. He would tell me where to find my channel stone.

"Stay here," I ordered Micah. "See that this one comes to no harm."

Protectiveness was a new feeling. I shouldn't care what happened to a mere wolf, but the human's emotions had infected me, leaching across the barrier between us. My arm throbbed from the blows she'd taken to save him. I suppose it made sense to preserve a valuable asset.

I marched off, ignoring the aches of my body and the chaos around me. Jason struggled with the leshy Adam, who'd found a gun somewhere. They were locked together, fighting for control of the weapon. Inch by inch, Jason forced the leshy's straining arm around till the gun pointed back at the green face.

The gun boomed and the leshy fell. Jason looked up, chest heaving, and saw me for the first time. His jaw dropped, a look of horror in his eyes. "Kate? You're … you're glowing!"

"Where is my channel stone, you filthy lizard?"

He jumped, then glanced around almost guiltily. No one listened, but still he lowered his voice to a whisper. His face was white with shock. "Leandra?"

"Give it to me, traitor, and I'll make your death an easy one."

He stared, dumbfounded. Impatient, I slapped his face, sending him staggering. I was not accustomed to waiting for answers.

His face darkened. "How the hell did you get in there, you toxic bitch? Kate, of all people! Are you trying to destroy me?"

He slapped me back. As I stared in shock—he dared assault me so openly?—he retrieved the dead leshy's gun and levelled it at me.

"How many times do I have to kill you?"

Micah leapt between us in a blur of pale flesh. He must have circled around behind Jason. The gun went off as they struggled for possession in a replay of the previous tussle between dragon and leshy, but this time werewolf muscles came up triumphant. Jason raised his hands as Micah pointed the gun at him.

"Flee, mistress!"

"Yes, flee, Leandra, before your compulsion dissipates and he starts shooting *you*."

"Not without my channel stone. Where is it?"

He shook his head, mocking. "I don't have it. Can't you tell?"

Of course I could. Jason smirked, careless of the gun levelled at him. Behind him the smoke swirled like a storm front about to break.

"Have you seen it?" I asked the werewolf. "A black stone with silver tracery? It's mine. This traitor stole it from me."

Micah frowned, though he never took his eyes from Jason. "Nada had something, about the size of a marble. I didn't get a good enough look to see what colour it was."

Nada. My lip curled. Always meddling in the affairs of her betters. Griffin upstart. "Where is Nada now?"

"Be silent, Micah!" Jason snarled. "To me, men! Seth! Ciaran!"

Did he think me powerless? "Shoot him."

Micah obeyed, putting a bullet through Jason's shoulder. He fell to the ground, writhing and moaning, hand clutched to his shoulder as though he might bleed to death. Ridiculous.

"Put the next one through his heart." Not that it would kill him. Only destroying the heart completely would do that—but the pain would be excruciating. "Where is Nada?"

For the first time it struck me as odd that she wasn't here. The woman had been Valeria's constant shadow since the proving had begun, jealously guarding her position at my sister's right hand. If Valeria sneezed, Nada was there with a tissue. Yet she wasn't present for the moment of her mistress's greatest triumph. What could be more important than that?

"She was hunting something for Valeria. Pretty excited about it too." Micah nodded at Jason, panting on the ground, white face twisted in pain. "Something to do with him, I think. Said she was going back to school."

Jason twitched at that.

"What? What does that mean?" I kicked him, feeling a satisfying crunch of ribs. "What school? Does she have the channel stone? Tell me!"

Jason groaned and spat blood on the ground. He looked up at me, his gaze intent. "Katie, if you're in there, you've got to stop her."

Garth appeared out of the smoke, giving Micah a wary berth. He clutched at his abdomen as if holding himself together. "Come on, Kate, what are you doing?"

I looked wildly from one to the other, torn in ways I couldn't understand. Stop who? What was going on?

"This guy's got a gun," Garth persisted. "How long before whatever you did to him wears off? Valeria could be back any time—let's get the hell out of here."

Jason's blue eyes never left my face, beseeching. "Go to King's, Katie. Hurry."

God, I felt so dizzy. My head spun. Must be the heat. I wiped my sweaty face with a shaky hand. It came away smeared with ash and grime. He hadn't called me Katie in years.

Through the haze I saw two men running towards us. Garth's voice became more insistent. "Kate, come on!"

That was my name, wasn't it? The other had gone, and I was alone in my head again. Garth tugged at my hand and I let him pull me away.

"Where's Ben? And Luce?"

"Don't worry about them. Luce will look after him." He dragged me across the smoking ground, following the path of the fire front between trees whose crowns still burned. Blackened grass crunched beneath our feet. I could feel the heat of the ground through the soles of my shoes. "Let's get you out of here."

His big hand was rough with callouses but strangely comforting. Why was he being so nice to me? He just didn't seem like Garth without the death threats. He threw me a quick glance as we ran. There was awe in it, mingled with a hefty dose of confusion and more than a dash of fear. Pretty much mirrored my own feelings.

My memory had returned, rushing back in like a flood breaking through a dam wall. With it came other memories and a dark knowledge that was never mine, but belonged to the stranger riding shotgun in my head.

Jason had called me Katie. He'd called me Leandra.

And I was both.

CHAPTER TWENTY-TWO

Garth hustled me through a scene from hell, one hand clamped tight around my arm. We couldn't see more than a few metres for the smoke that lay heavy over everything, swirling with sudden wind gusts and the movement of half-glimpsed figures around us. Most of the humans were clothed, though some were as bare as Garth, obviously having just shifted. Others still wore animal form, and some of the leshies were almost vegetable, in a nightmarish Day-of-the-Triffids way. My eyes streamed from the smoke's sting as I staggered along beside my naked rescuer. My chest felt tight, squeezed by iron bands, making every breath a painful battle.

The inferno of the burning house lay ahead, a flaming beacon in the smothering grey world. The fire called to me. *No, don't look!* Panic bubbled just below the surface. *I am not a dragon. I am not a dragon.*

Garth staggered as a bullet whined past.

"Are you hit?" I yelled.

He shook his head and veered left, his face a bloody mask of determination. He looked like hell—drenched in blood, one eye swollen shut—but he moved fast. Coughing and gasping for breath, it took all I had to keep up with him. I hardly knew where I was. *Who* I was. If he hadn't been half dragging me I would have fallen.

A figure materialised out of the smoke and dark: Micah, gun in hand, also stark naked still. Part of me—a small, hysterical part—found that very funny. There were certainly drawbacks to the shifter lifestyle.

"Mistress! Let me help you."

He cracked off a shot, and a man I hadn't even seen dropped just behind us. There was no way I could tell which side he'd been on; I hoped Micah knew what he was doing.

"Stay close," Garth growled. "Watch our backs."

Micah nodded and fell back a step, gun at the ready.

"Slow down," I begged between coughing fits. "Can't … breathe."

"Not much further." He wasn't having as much trouble, though the left side of his head was covered in blood and he was still hunched over in pain. Obviously shifters had more efficient physiques. Maybe it was worth having to buy new clothes all the time. "It'll be clearer on the road."

I doubted that, but I had no breath to argue. We circled around the burning house. Fire roared and leapt like a live thing among its twisted timbers. Searing heat forced us to keep our distance. No one could get close to that raging inferno and live.

Smoke billowed and swirled around us, hiding and then revealing nightmarish glimpses of struggling figures. My eyes stung, so dry it felt as if they'd been boiled in their sockets. I peered into the smoke, straining to see where we were going.

A sudden gust revealed a handful of figures between us and the house. They saw us at the same time.

"Run!" Micah shouted. "It's Valeria!"

The smoke billowed again, hiding Valeria just as she opened her mouth to yell orders. We couldn't hear her over the roar of the fire. Micah planted his feet and fired, but Garth didn't wait around to see the outcome.

He dragged me down the driveway between the burning trees, while flames crackled and spat overhead. Micah's gun barked again and again, but we saw nothing of the struggle through the choking smoke. At least it hid us from our enemies.

We made it to the gates, past the smoking ruins of the gatehouse, and burst out on to the road. Heat seared my feet through my shoes. The rubber soles were half-melted. The fire had jumped the road and now roared through the bush on the other side, heading away from us toward a low sprawling property. I heard the shrill screams of terrified horses among the crackle of flames as we staggered down the road.

I cast a fearful glance over my shoulder. The smoke swirled, obscuring the burning house. I couldn't see Valeria or Micah. Then, over the other noises, a regular thumping sounded above us. Not again! I cast around for somewhere to hide, but the bush burned on both sides of the road; there was nowhere to run but straight ahead. My heart pounded as we charged down the road hand in hand, Garth urging me on. I craned my neck, trying to spot the dragon in the sky. Lost in panic, it didn't occur to me that the rhythmic beats were too close together to be a dragon's wing beats.

"Chopper!" shouted Garth.

Sweet relief flooded through me. We stopped for a moment and I bent over, hands on knees, sobbing for breath. I could hear myself wheezing like an asthmatic as I dragged in smoky air, each breath stabbing painfully. A massive helicopter passed overhead, flying low through the smoke. It trailed a giant sack of water beneath it, which it released on the other side of the road. Water cascaded down, sending great clouds of steam hissing up through the blackened trees.

I looked back at Alicia's burning house. Through gaps in the smoke I saw flames licking hungrily along bare framework, the skeleton of the house exposed. "They must think Alicia's place is a lost cause."

Garth's insistent hand tugged me into motion again. "They'll put everything into trying to save places that still have a chance. Just as well—nothing they've got would put out dragonfire. That's gonna keep burning till there's nothing left."

A branch crashed down onto the road as we passed, so close the scorching heat beat against my back. My blistered arms stung and my eyes burned from the smoke. I bent low, trying to find cleaner air, but the smoke hung everywhere, and my lungs felt clogged with it. So much for the air being clearer on the road.

We were staggering like a pair of drunks by the time we passed beyond the immediate fire zone. Smoke still filled the air, but the trees either side of the road remained green, untouched by flame. A little further on we came to the original roadblock, the big old gum Valeria's men had felled, and there, on the other side of it, was our car. I scrambled over the rough tree trunk and collapsed gratefully against the white sedan.

"You got the keys?"

Garth just looked at me. Right. No clothes. Where exactly would he be hiding a key?

He bent down and pulled something from under the car, behind the back wheel. "We keep a spare back here."

Good idea. "What holds it on? Magic?"

"Blu Tack."

He grinned at the look on my face, the first real smile I'd ever seen on him. If it weren't for all the blood and grime it might have been an improvement. As it was he just looked feral. His clothes still lay scattered where he'd dropped them; now he picked them up and got dressed. I sagged over the bonnet, coughing, while I waited for him to unlock the car.

"Let's go." He dropped heavily into the driver's seat.

Holding a conversation was much easier now that he had the familiar Star Wars T-shirt and jeans back on. Not that he'd seemed to care, but casual nudity wasn't my thing. Particularly blood-soaked nudity. Sadly the clothes didn't do much for his overall appearance. He still looked awful. A gash on his cheek bled sluggishly, and one of his ears …

"What is *that?*"

"What?" A shiny pink knob of flesh sat where his left ear should be. He touched it, then shrugged. "Must have lost an ear in the fighting. It'll grow back."

"Really?" That pink growth was a new ear? "You can regenerate body parts?"

Panicked laughter welled up, and I forced it back down. There was nothing to laugh about. *I had a dragon inside me.*

"Neat trick, huh? Shifting fixes pretty much anything. Except for silver, of course."

Oh, of course. I eyed his face, pale beneath the blood. "Does it hurt?"

"Like the devil." He hesitated. "Beats being dead though. You saved my arse with that shovel."

He looked away, as if expressing gratitude was difficult. Guess he didn't get much practice at it.

"After I tried to kill you, too."

This was the longest conversation we'd ever had—and probably the only one that hadn't ended with him threatening me. As an apology it needed work, but I'd take what I could get.

"Well, we all make mistakes. So you don't think I killed Leandra any more?"

"I know I took a knock to the head back there. Maybe I dreamed the whole thing." His battered gaze never wavered from my face. "But I think we both know Leandra's not dead."

I drew in a sharp breath—and nearly coughed up a lung. But I was glad of the diversion. He'd said it, and now it hung in the smoky air between us. I didn't know what to say, so I took refuge in practicalities.

He had blood matted all through his hair. I recalled the sound of his head slamming against the water tank. Could be concussion. And the way Micah had kicked him too—maybe internal injuries.

"Get out of there. You're not driving."

"I'm fine." He squinted up at me with his one working eye.

"You can hardly see where you're going." I took his head and felt all over for bumps, as gently as I could. One on the back of his head was the size of an egg.

"I can see the two of you. You both look like shit."

"Nice. You don't look so hot yourself, you know."

"When fighting werewolves you have been, look as hot you will not."

I glanced down at the Darth Vader T-shirt. "Thanks, Yoda. You're a big Star Wars fan, huh?"

"Absolutely. Han shot first, you know."

I shook my head. How much weirder could this day get?

"Out." I got hold of one muscled arm and hauled. Reluctantly he allowed me to help him out. "Are you really seeing double or are you just being a smart-arse?"

"Bit of both."

I got him settled in the passenger seat and started the engine. Then I sat, staring out at the smoke and the eerie yellow light. I heard the wail of a siren in the distance. The fire brigade was on its way. The massive tree blocking the road behind us was going to be a problem for them.

"What are you waiting for?" said Garth. "Let's go."

"We have to go back. We can't just leave them."

Ben would never abandon me—and I'd run out without even knowing if he was still alive.

"We can't go back." He leaned closer, the expression in his one good eye fierce. "Luce would be the first to tell you—your safety's more important."

"I don't care." I grabbed the door handle. "I can't leave Ben."

He reached across and stopped me with one big hand over mine. "He's got Luce. She's worth any five others in a fight. She'll keep him safe if anyone can. You're more important." A look almost of wonder came over his battered face. "When Valeria finds out about you …"

Adrenalin rushed through me at the thought, and something more—a confused welter of fear, hatred and exultation. Yes, when Valeria found out, I'd better be miles away. I had only a battered wolf for protection until I found the stone.

He was right. The human would be safe enough. It was more important to go after the stone. What was that bitch Nada doing with it? I clenched the steering wheel, knuckles white. Jason's fear had infected me. What was he afraid of?

"Stop her"—had he meant Nada? Stop her destroying the stone? Or had he been addressing his human female, telling her to stop *me*? Either way, why would he care?

I frowned at Garth, mind racing. In the end, it came back to the channel stone. I felt its lack as a pain beneath my breastbone. I had no choice, compelled like a common thrall to seek it out.

"Mistress?" Garth whispered, eyes wide. "We have to get you to safety."

I started the car. The wolf laid his head back and closed his eyes. He was injured—I should get him to hospital. Concussion could be nasty.

No. Ridiculous. The wolf would heal, or not. It didn't matter. The channel stone was more important.

I huffed out a breath, shaking my head to clear it. *Get out!*

"Garth! Don't go to sleep." His face was pale, almost grey under the dirt and ash and blood.

"Not sleeping," he grunted. "Thinking."

"Must be a new experience for you."

Best to keep him talking. If he lapsed into unconsciousness I wanted to know about it. My body trembled as if I'd just run a marathon, but at least it felt like mine again. I kept sneaking looks at Garth as I drove, torn between my inner struggles and a growing concern for him. I'd seen him heal unnaturally quickly before, but so far he didn't seem to be improving.

"I heard Jason call you Leandra." He rolled his head toward me and opened his eyes. Well, the one eye that would still open. "And I … I felt her … I don't know how to explain it. The way she stands. Even her voice—it's deeper than yours, you know. And the way you compelled Micah—only a dragon can do that.

"But I know she's dead. I saw the body. And I thought you killed her—but Jason said he did … and now … Shit, my head hurts. I don't know what to think."

Well, that made two of us. I couldn't even be sure it was *me* doing the thinking. A stranger kept looking out of my eyes, a ruthless stranger whose coldness was alien to me. My whole body tensed, as if I could keep her out by sheer willpower.

I drove a little way in silence. It was the most god-awful mess, and I was pretty sure if Garth was picking sides between me and Leandra I wouldn't be coming out on top. But he was all I had right now.

And if all else failed I could probably take down a concussed werewolf.

"Ben got a call for a courier job. It was urgent, and they asked for me by name." Ben had been pleased—said it showed I was building up a reputation for a quality job. Ha! How wrong could you be? That Leandra was a stone-hearted bitch. "The pick-up point was right across the other side of Sydney, and it took me nearly an hour to get there. The place was a mansion, but I'd been told not to go to the house but to let myself in through the side gate. There was a beautiful garden around the back."

Garth nodded, eyes shut again. No need to tell me he knew the place well. The scent of roses came to me again, their glorious reds and pinks glowing in the sun as I walked past on the sandstone path. I'd followed the path as it meandered under the trees and past the pond with the red Japanese bridge. And there she was.

"Leandra was waiting for me in the garden. As soon as I saw her I knew something was wrong." She'd been so pale, her beautiful face grey and sweating, her body shaking as she fought the urge to hunch over in agony. God, I could feel that pain now, like an animal tearing at my intestines. I shuddered, hatred for Jason welling up inside. I would rip him apart, feed on his organs while he screamed for mercy.

"That filthy traitor poisoned me. He contacted me and begged for a meeting. He swore he wanted to come back to me." The steering wheel creaked ominously as my hands tightened on it. "Why didn't I kill him then? I didn't trust him for a moment, but I made myself vulnerable to him, like a fool."

There was a distinct crunch under my hands, and a crack appeared in the steering wheel. The wail of the siren was closer now. As we rounded the next bend a fire engine roared past in the other direction, lights flashing.

"I met him in a public place. I took the thralls. Every precaution! And still he managed to poison me."

Garth cast an uneasy glance at the speedo. "Slow down, mistress. Why didn't you tell us you'd been poisoned?"

I waved an impatient hand, still fuming at my remembered stupidity. "You could have been in on it. Luce called while I was with him, and he used the distraction to slip the poison into my drink. I didn't know who I could trust. So I told the thralls to get me a herald and make sure it was Jason's woman."

"Why her?"

"There was a chance Jason still cared for her. The only thing better than killing him would be doing it in her stolen body."

CHAPTER TWENTY-THREE

I sat on the bench beneath the graceful boughs of the jacaranda, arms wrapped round my stomach. Its green-dappled shade couldn't cool the fire in my veins as the bane leaf burned its way through my system. Swaying leaves faded in and out of focus as I shook, each breath harder to draw in than the last.

Where had he found it? Such a rare plant. So feared by dragons it had been all but exterminated from the world. It had been long years since one of our kind had succumbed to its deadly toxin, but the memories were still fresh, handed down through the generations. Tasteless. Colourless. Odourless.

But not painless, as I could now attest.

Sweat broke out all over me and ran in undignified trickles down my face. I hunched over as another agonising cramp racked me. They were coming closer together now. Time from ingestion to death was rarely more than three hours, and there was no known antidote.

At best, I had another hour.

Where was the damn herald?

Alone in the garden, I sat my own death watch. I'd forbidden the thralls to leave the house, cutting off their panicked pleas with orders to make sure no one disturbed us once the herald arrived. Orders gave them a way to serve, which always made them feel better, though the panic was barely contained. They wanted Luce, or even Garth, to relieve them of the burden of responsibility. I couldn't trust anyone, so I had forbidden the thralls to call them.

I heard the click as the side gate opened. At last! I forced myself to stand, though my legs trembled. I would not be found languishing on a seat.

Pretending to gaze at the roses, I watched her approach out of the corner of my eye. She was dark-haired and apparently heavily pregnant, pretty in an unremarkable sort of way. There were a hundred such as her on the street every day; I couldn't see what Jason had found so alluring. I felt a sudden misgiving—perhaps there was nothing here to work with.

But I had no other options, so she would have to do. She stopped a few paces away, and I turned to meet her gaze fully. There was a hardness there I liked, a tilt to the chin that said she didn't care what the world thought, lines that spoke of suffering and lessons learned. She was more than she'd first appeared.

Another spasm seized me and I shifted unsteadily.

"Are you all right?" she asked, a little warmth creeping into her businesslike mask. Human females couldn't seem to resist the urge to nurture and defend. So unlike dragons. She stepped closer, one hand outstretched as that urge warred with the need to remain aloof and professional. Silver glinted at her throat as she shifted— a chain that no doubt held the symbol of her office.

"Help me, Kate," I whispered, allowing fear to show in my eyes, pouring every ounce of the terror that swelled in me into that look. Less than an hour left. I couldn't compel her while she wore

that charm but normal human decency would serve for the moment. They did so love to play Good Samaritan.

"What's wrong?" She started forward and helped me to the bench. Her grip on my arm was strong and capable. "Are you ill?"

As she bent over me, her Hermes charm swung free from the sack-like maternity dress she wore. I doubted she was truly pregnant; her movements were too swift and sure. Besides, she'd run another job for me only a couple of months ago and I didn't remember any pregnancy. Doubtless it was part of the game the heralds played with the watchers who'd come out of the woodwork for the proving, trying to shake off pursuit.

You could spend all your time chasing off one set, only to have another take their place. And it wasn't only my sisters' people; our mother also liked to keep up with events, as did other factions like the wolves or even the goblins. Some of the overseas queens had spies on the ground for the proving too, nor were they above trying to influence the outcome. I had long decided either to ignore them or to use them to feed misinformation to my sisters. Today's effort should be doubly amusing, since there would be no delivery.

At least not one they could see.

"A momentary faintness. Please, sit down. I just need a minute to catch my breath."

She sat, with an anxious glance back at the house. "Should I call someone for you?"

The thralls had obeyed orders to stay out of sight. "There's no one home. I have a very important delivery for you, and I didn't want anyone to see it. I can trust you to take care of it, can't I?"

"Of course." She nodded, but her eyes had a wary look.

"That's a lovely necklace you have there," I said, as if noticing it for the first time. "May I see it?"

She leaned closer, holding the charm out for inspection.

"I'm sorry, I don't have my glasses. Would you mind …?"

I made a little helpless gesture and she obligingly lifted the charm over her head and offered it to me.

Another spasm racked me and my hand shook as I took it. So easy. The first part of the great gamble had paid off. I knew she was new and I'd heard there was something unorthodox about her appointment. There'd even been rumours she knew nothing of shifters—and now they were at least partially borne out. No one had told her of the protection the necklace afforded her.

Of course, I could have produced the gun from my pocket and forced her to hand it over, but then she might have run, and I couldn't actually shoot her if it came to that. She was the perfect instrument for my revenge. I couldn't wait to see the look on Jason's face as his ex-lover murdered him. It had seemed to me he still bore a candle for her, that the hatred weighed much more on her side than his. How delightful to see him betrayed in his turn.

I smiled as I closed my hand around the charm.

"Thank you, Kate. You don't mind if I call you Kate, do you? We're going to get to know each other so much better, after all."

She frowned, not yet alarmed, but the wariness was back. I had to smile, despite the pain, as her clear green gaze met mine. I had her.

"You're going to do something for me."

I leaned in and forced my will on her. The green eyes lost their sharp focus and her face went slack.

"Of course. What would you like?"

First I gave her the letter. I didn't want her seeking help before I was strong enough to take control, so I planned removing her memory of this interview. The letter would direct her somewhere safe and isolated until I could assert control of her body.

I waited till she had stowed it safely in her bag, then handed her the hunting knife that nestled next to the gun in my pocket. I was a regular little arsenal today, both weapons taken from one of the thralls. Normally a dragon had no need of any such.

Today was not a normal day. I grimaced with pain, but Kate continued to stare with that dreamy smile, not noticing as sweat ran down my face. I stank of fear and sickness and the garden was beginning to blur. Not much time left.

"I want you to take that and make a cut here," I said, unbuttoning my silk blouse to show her the place. "A deep one, mind. You need to get right down to the bone."

"But that will hurt you."

Confusion chased the smile from her face and I felt my grip on her mind weaken.

"Look at me, Kate."

I forced my way back in, soothing and shaping, moulding her will to mine. It would have been easier to simply enthral her, but she'd be significantly less useful to me afterwards. I needed an unbroken mind for my new home.

"Right here." I guided her hand so the tip of the knife pricked my skin. Both our hands were shaking. Sunlight reflecting off the ornamental pool behind her dazzled my eyes. I blinked, but it made little improvement, my vision fading as the poison did its deadly work.

She drew the knife back. A tiny drop of red clung to its point. I closed my eyes, heard the rush of breath as she exhaled, then pain exploded in my chest.

She struck so hard the blade lodged in my sternum. I felt the tug as she freed it, then dragged it down in a long slicing cut. Whimpering with pain, I fought to hold on to consciousness.

"Yes. That's it," I gasped. "That's it. Now … reach in."

My body spasmed in agony. I tried to hold on to her shoulders but felt myself slipping, and she laid me down on the grass. When I opened my eyes the world wheeled above me: green leaves, blue sky, and her face looming over me. Fear fought its way to the surface as my control faded. Blood pulsed from the deep slash down my chest, covering her hands and splashing her face and the ugly smock she wore.

No! Not now, when I was so close. "You can do this," I insisted.

I shut my eyes again and refocused. All would be lost unless I held myself together a moment more.

Renewed agony flamed as her fingers pushed inside the wound. My breath came in short sobbing gasps.

"There's a … stone. See it? Not … there … higher. Yes!" I felt the jolt as her questing fingers found it. "Take it."

A roaring filled my ears. My voice sounded faint, as if coming from a long way away. I tried to move my hand, but its weight was suddenly beyond me.

"Go on," I urged.

I tried to meet her gaze, to compel, but darkness had crept up on me. Her face hovered in the centre of my vision, no more than a pale blur. Everything else had disappeared. My soul fled towards the channel stone, seeking union.

A tugging sensation, then a terrible crack that reverberated through my body as she tore the stone free. Oh, God, the pain. I could no longer see, had no way to know if she had obeyed me. Reduced to begging as my consciousness slipped away.

"Please ... swallow it."

***

Garth's brow furrowed. Thinking wasn't his strong suit at the best of times. "What's a channel stone? Why did you want her to swallow it?"

I'd forgotten he was only a wolf.

"Dragons don't normally speak of them." We passed through quiet suburbs as we wended our way back down the mountain on the Great Western Highway. I took my eyes from the road and pinned his gaze with my own, forcing my will on him. He was loyal, but I knew better than anyone how fast loyalties could change. "And neither will you."

He nodded. "Of course."

"They are a means of channelling mass between this plane and another."

His gaze was attentive, but no spark of understanding lit his grey eyes. I may as well have been speaking Greek.

"The mass of a *dragon*, Garth. Where do you think it all goes when we take human form? Dragons are enormous. Other shifters' trueshapes are roughly human-sized, so there is no displacement of mass. But our human forms would be gigantic if we couldn't relocate the extra mass. So we send it otherwhere when we shift and call it back when we wish to assume trueshape."

"*Otherwhere?*" He didn't sound convinced. "Where the hell is that?"

I had neither time nor inclination for a dissertation on dragon lore. "It's not important. The point is, each dragon is born with a channel stone nestled next to their heart. It's the core of our ability to shift from trueshape to human form. Think of it like the tide running through a channel. It comes in, it goes out, but the sea is always the same size."

He shook his head, struggling with the concept. We came down off the mountains while he thought and joined the stream of Sydney-bound traffic. There was always traffic. Humans were like ants, scurrying to and fro on errands that only made sense to themselves. At each red light I tapped impatiently on the steering wheel. When we got onto the M4, we would make better time.

A nagging whine intruded, growing louder. Frowning, I glanced into the rear vision mirror and saw blue lights flashing behind me.

Garth twisted round in his seat, suddenly conscious of the wailing siren too. "Police. You'd better pull over."

"What do they want?"

"You were driving rather fast, mistress."

Annoyed, I pulled on to the shoulder. Three lanes of traffic whizzed past as I wound down my window.

The patrol car pulled in behind me and a uniformed officer got out, putting his cap on as he approached.

"In a hurry to get somewhere, madam?" His bored expression disappeared when he got a good look at us. "What happened to you?"

"We've been fighting fires in the mountains. My friend's hurt. I'm taking him to the hospital."

"I'm sorry to hear that. But I'm afraid I still have to see your licence."

The bottom fell out of my stomach. I didn't have my licence—I didn't have anything to prove my identity. My wallet had been left behind somewhere in Valeria's mansion.

"Oh! My licence ..." I glanced at Garth, panicked, and mouthed: "What do I do?"

He cocked his head, puzzled till he realised Leandra was gone. Then he fanned the fingers of one hand and wiggled them. "What did Obi-Wan do when the troopers were looking for the droids?" he muttered.

I glared. Him and his stupid Star Wars obsession. Was this really the time, with a police officer at my window?

Oh, right. The "force". I looked back at the cop and gave him a nervous smile. He was young, and probably not all that intimidating out of uniform.

Could I do it now that Leandra had slipped away again? Only one way to find out.

I met his eyes and stared hard, focusing my will. It felt ... right. "I don't have my licence with me, but it doesn't matter. I'm sure you don't mind."

His expression hardened. I'd faced plenty worse lately, but there was still something unnerving about the glare of a highly unimpressed policeman.

"You're driving without a licence? I'll need to see some identification, madam."

"I don't have any. The bushfire …"

I trailed off. Damn. Jason had completely thrown me with his pleas—so out of character. I had to get to King's and stop Nada. Whatever she was doing, it was something bad. I could feel it.

And she has the stone.

I clamped down hard on that thought. That was Leandra, not me. I had no need for her precious channel stone. Unless, of course, Nada meant to use it against Leandra. I stared at the policeman, willing him to let me go. Much as I wanted to be rid of my toxic hitchhiker, I wasn't leaving the job of evicting Leandra to Nada's tender mercies. Any scheme of hers would probably involve killing me too.

The cop's face looked even flintier than before. "I'll have to run a registration check. Are you the owner of the vehicle?"

"No."

"Who is?"

I hesitated, a shade too long, and he stepped back.

"Please get out of the car." There was no "madam" any more.

Panic bloomed in my chest. Could I take him down? He was a highway patrolman. Unlikely to be a crack shot.

I got out, shaking all over. The rush of passing traffic buffeted me. God—why was I even thinking like this? I couldn't attack a *policeman.*

The air still reeked of smoke—or maybe that was me. I was hot and dirty and spattered with blood. Mostly other people's.

His eyes widened as he took in my dishevelled appearance, and his hand crept closer to his gun.

"You say you were fighting a bushfire?" Clearly he wasn't buying that story.

My heart hammered so loudly I was sure he could hear it, but I moved closer, watching his gun hand out of the corner of my eye.

"Stand still!"

I froze. A door slammed behind me as Garth levered himself out of the car.

"You stay right there!" the cop snarled, and now the gun was in his hand.

Garth was a big solid guy, and looked even more disreputable than I, but I could tell from the way he leaned on the car's roof he wasn't going to be any use in a fight.

The cop retreated to his car, never taking his eyes off us, and reached in for the radio. Calling for backup. I closed my eyes.

I didn't have *time* for this.

"Officer!" I caught his gaze with mine. Easy does it. He still had the gun. "I'm sure there's been a misunderstanding."

I stepped forward, forcing my will on him, moulding him to the proper subservience. Slowly the gun hand drifted to his side.

"A misunderstanding."

"That's right. You're sorry you stopped us. My friend needs a doctor."

He blinked like a man waking from sleep and offered a slow smile. "Of course, madam. You'd better get your friend to hospital. He looks a mess. Would you like a police escort?"

"No thanks, officer. We'll be fine."

"You take care, then." He watched us get back into the car, still smiling. In a few minutes he'd be wondering why he was standing on the side of the road in the middle of the night holding his gun.

Humans. So easy to manipulate.

Sudden fury surged through me—

—and I was back. That *bitch*. She'd taken me over again. I pulled out into the traffic. My hands were shaking. The crack she'd made in the steering wheel snagged at my palms.

Garth gave me a lazy grin. "Obi-Wan would be proud."

"Easy for you to laugh, you stupid lunk. You're not the one driving without a licence."

Or the one being shoved out of your own head by some dragon parasite. How the hell did she keep doing that? There was no sign of her presence now, but that was no guarantee she'd stay buried. At least she'd done some good this time, using her fancy mind control tricks on the poor cop.

I followed the tail lights of the car in front, careful not to speed. We needed to be far away before he came back to his senses, but I didn't want to attract any more attention. I changed lanes a few times, weaving my way through the other cars, trying to lose us in the crowd. At least we were driving a white sedan and not something that stood out more.

"Kate?" Garth's expression had turned serious.

"Yes?"

"You're back?"

I gritted my teeth. "Yes, I'm back."

And he'd better not be disappointed his mistress was gone, because I was going to fight to keep her out. This was *my* body, dammit, and she had no right to it.

"Why did she want you to swallow the channel stone? Do you know?"

Yes, I knew. I knew a hell of a lot more about dragons than I ever wanted to. They were vile. A bunch of egotistical murderous users, the lot of them.

"She thought if it was part of my body, she could use it to transfer her consciousness to me. She hoped to throw me out of my own body and take over." I couldn't keep the bitterness out of my voice. She seemed to be getting better at it all the time, and it scared me. "It was a gamble, but she had nothing to lose—she was dying anyway. Too bad about *my* life. I guess dragons aren't big on considering other people."

We stopped at a set of traffic lights and I glared across at him, daring him to defend his precious mistress. "She's picked the wrong woman to mess with. I am *not* letting her win."

CHAPTER TWENTY-FOUR

"Have you ever heard of King's?"

Garth gave me a funny look. "It's a boys' school for rich brats. Near Parramatta. Isn't that where we're going?"

I glanced across at him. Though he still leaned back against the headrest, he looked better, not quite so beat up. I could stop worrying his brain was about to leak out his ears—and the little pink nub that an hour ago had only been a proto-ear now almost matched the undamaged one. Of course, he was still smeared with blood and dirt, and sporting some serious gashes. He wouldn't be getting into any swish hotels without a good wash and a clean set of clothes—but then, there weren't likely to be too many fancy hotels in our immediate future.

"Well, *that* King's, of course." I'd even had Lachie's name down there for high school. "I thought there might be some secret dragon place of the same name. Like Hogwarts for shapeshifters or something. Micah said Nada was going to King's, but what would she be doing at an Anglican private school?"

"Probably stirring up trouble." His face had a healthier colour now. He caught me looking at him and shifted uncomfortably in his seat. "What are you staring at?"

"Just fascinated by werewolf physiology. Not so long ago you were half dead—but spend an hour relaxing in a car and look at you—a new man."

"Being driven by *you* isn't relaxing."

The lights changed and I turned off the highway into the heart of Parramatta.

"And anyway, what's the big deal? Have you looked in the mirror lately?"

"What do you mean?" I checked the rear vision mirror, thinking he was still complaining about my driving. No flashing lights.

"You think werewolves are such fast healers? What about dragons?"

He gestured at me, and I looked down, confused. "But I'm not ..." I trailed off. When I'd got into the car my arms were throbbing lumps of tenderised meat, riddled with burns and blisters from flying embers. Somewhere along the way the pain had eased, and then I'd stopped noticing it altogether. Now I could see why. There wasn't a single mark on my bare arms.

I sat at the lights outside the old wrought iron gates of Parramatta Park and turned my arms this way and that, staring at the smooth unblemished skin while a cold fear seeped into my bones. The car behind me honked. Oops—lights had changed.

"I'm not a dragon," I said, uneasy now. Whatever I was, it clearly wasn't human.

"Well, you heal like one."

Did that mean Leandra was taking over? I felt a flutter of panic and swallowed hard, fighting it down. I had to stay in control.

"It's not such a bad thing, you know. Being a shifter."

The look on his face was almost sympathetic. Garth? Being nice to me? He must have been injured worse than I thought.

"Easy for you to say. You don't have someone trying to force you out of your own body."

"Sometimes it feels like that."

"How do you mean?"

He shrugged. "The wolf is hard to control, you know? It makes me do things—well, things I wouldn't have done before."

"Before what?"

"Before I was bitten."

Oh. Somehow I'd assumed he'd always been a werewolf. I sneaked a glance as we stopped at the lights outside the swimming pool, its car park dark and deserted now. On a day like today it would have been bursting with people earlier, all with nothing more to worry about than avoiding sunburn in the heat. Lucky bastards. Garth's head was turned away, looking out at the night. A million questions hovered on my lips but that averted face suggested a lot of them mightn't be welcome.

"But now you like being a wolf?" I ventured.

Another shrug. "Doesn't matter, does it, whether I like it or not. That's the way it is. You just have to deal with whatever life throws at you."

A werewolf philosopher. Every girl should have one.

"So you're suggesting I *just deal with* having a dragon parasite inside me? Let her take over? *Oh, sure Leandra, you can have the body. What do I need it for?* You'd like that, wouldn't you? You'd get your precious mistress back."

He gave me a flat stare. "Not so precious. I doubt she would have hit that guy with a shovel to save me."

Well, that was plain speaking. But how far would his gratitude go?

"Do you know of a way to get her out?"

"You must be joking. I'm just a wolf. I keep my head down and try to stay out of dragon business. Have you tried asking her?"

"No!" That came out a bit too forceful. I tried to speak normally. "I'm not going to invite her out. She takes over enough as it is without me asking for it."

"In that case we'd better find this stone and hope Luce is right about it having some kind of message for us."

That damn channel stone. I was pretty sure now there was no message. It had just been the means for Leandra to colonise my body. As to why she wanted it back so badly—it was safe to assume it wouldn't be good news for Kate O'Connor.

What if I let it go, let Nada destroy it, or whatever she meant to do with it? Maybe Leandra would die off for real, and I wouldn't be forced to share my body with her any more. I felt her surge inside me and fought her down again. Didn't like that idea, did she?

But she's part of you now, a little voice said. That same little voice which lived inside every mother and worried about every possible calamity. I knew from bitter experience that sometimes the voice was right to worry. *What if killing her kills you too?*

Garth still watched me. This time I saw sympathy in his eyes for sure. "I'm not your enemy, you know."

"Says the guy who tried to eat me in my kitchen."

That surprised a laugh out of him. "Told you—sometimes the wolf gets the better of me."

We turned on to Pennant Hills Road. King's was only a couple of kilometres further along. It was a huge place, set on over a hundred hectares of sprawling parklands, with every imaginable facility—theatres, sportsgrounds, even a fifty metre pool. A network of roads connected the various parts of the property. I'd come here for a tour when Lachie was still small, and the place was so big they'd loaded us into minibuses to ferry us around.

I'd been thinking what a wonderful opportunity it would be for Lachie. I hadn't wanted him to board, naturally, though it was surprising how many people who lived in Sydney did board their boys, even if only on weekdays. But the school had a reputation for excellence, and I'd hoped we might have been able to afford to send Lachie there for high school. That was before the divorce, of course. Living as a single mum put such expensive dreams out of reach.

We turned in through the big sandstone gates and drove down to the main car park—there were several dotted around the campus. Not surprisingly, since it was nearly eleven o'clock at night, it was empty, so I kept going. Silent buildings loomed out of the dark as we made a circuit of the grounds.

After ten minutes I'd been down every side road and dead end, with no sign of Nada. A few lights burned in lonely windows, but apart from that we might have been the only people here. At any minute I expected a security vehicle to glide up behind us and demand to know what we were doing.

Back in the main car park I pulled in behind a row of bushes and cut the engine.

"Maybe she's been and gone."

"Or maybe she hasn't arrived yet." Garth got out and slammed his door.

I got out too and frowned around at the tree-lined roads and vast dark swathes of lawn.

"Why would Nada bring the channel stone here? Do you think there are other dragons here?"

"Could be. You find money, you find dragons—and there's plenty of money here."

"Micah said she was hunting something. I got the impression it wasn't good news for Jason. She's got a huge chip on her shoulder about Jason. Thinks he and I are in some big conspiracy against her."

"Makes sense. She's probably had her nose out of joint since the day he showed up. I mean, she's been Valeria's second since before the proving began. And then a dragon muscles in and tries to take over her role." He popped the boot and pulled out a tyre iron. "She's only a griffin—hard to compete with a dragon. Bet she's been looking for a way to take him down from day one."

I indicated the tyre iron. "What's that for?"

"Something to persuade Nada to hand over the stone when we find her."

"How *are* we going to find her?" If she was even here. I glanced around, hoping by some miracle to spot a brunette with a bad attitude coming my way. "This place is so big. We could wander round for hours and never see her. Can you … I don't know … smell her or something?"

He gave me an impatient look and tapped the length of steel against his other palm. "Track her in a place like this, with a thousand people coming and going? Even wolves aren't that good. Besides, I'm not even sure I remember her scent. We're not exactly best buddies."

Damn. Short of any better ideas, I started up the path to the nearest building that showed a light. My stomach coiled into uneasy knots. I was all too aware that time was ticking away. Maybe we'd be better off staking out the house at Mosman, hoping to catch her when she came back. *And then what? Politely ask her to stop her car so we can belt her over the head with a tyre iron and take back the channel stone?*

Considering it was late at night in the middle of the Christmas holidays, I wasn't too surprised to find the building locked up tight. None of the doors we tried would open. Where was Luce when we needed her? Her lock-picking skills would have been handy.

I looked at Garth and he shrugged, then pulled out his phone.

"Who are you ringing?"

He ignored me and spoke into the phone. "Hey mate, it's Garth—how you doing? … Yeah, sorry to ring so late. Listen,

I was wondering, do you still have Nada Kusic's number? Fantastic. Thanks, mate, I owe you one."

He hung up and gave me a smug look.

"You're going to ring Nada?" Maybe I was dense, but I couldn't see how that would help. I rubbed distractedly at an ache that had started in my chest.

"I'm gonna flush her out. Let's get back to the car."

He dialled as we walked, our footsteps loud on the empty road. "Nada? It's Micah." He'd pitched his voice lower, and he did sound uncannily like the surly werewolf. "Valeria wants you back at Mosman right now."

He winked at me as Nada's tinny voice crackled in his ear. "I don't know, I'm only the messenger boy—but she ain't happy."

He hung up.

"Do you think she believed you?"

"Guess we'll find out if we see her leaving. Let's get up to the main gate."

He got in the driver's seat this time and I didn't object. If car chases were on the menu I was happy not to be driving. But there were several car parks, and more than one exit from King's. She could slip past without us any the wiser.

As he started the engine I glanced across the rolling lawn to the historic old mansion where the younger boys boarded. A dark four-wheel drive idled out the front. Pain lanced through my chest and I gasped as a wave of longing filled me. The channel stone!

I clutched Garth's arm. "Wait! Is that—?"

A dark-haired woman came down the steps with a small boy in tow. In the light that spilled from the open door, I saw a thin frame and tousled brown curls, and my heart did a familiar sick somersault. It wasn't Lachie. It could never be Lachie. My mind knew that, but my heart refused to listen to reason, and it kept playing this agonising trick on me.

"Yep, that's her," said Garth, but I'd forgotten Nada. Yearning for the channel stone surged within me, but I fought it down, still staring at the boy. About nine or ten, tall and delicately framed, just as Lachie would look if he'd lived. He even bobbed his curly head like Lachie as he walked, as if it were too heavy for his slender neck. But Nada blocked my view of his face.

She opened the back door and shoved him in, sliding in after him. Something about that shove told me he wasn't happy about going with her. Garth rolled us quietly through the car park, headlights off, ready to cut the other car off as it approached, and I craned past his big frame, trying to get another glimpse of the boy.

Garth stopped behind two sheltering bushes and yanked on the handbrake. He scrabbled at my feet for his tyre iron, then hopped out.

"Wait till they're level," he instructed, leaning his bulk back into the car to speak, eyes gleaming with a feral light, "then ram them. I'll come up on them from the other side and take out the driver while they're focused on you. Then it'll be the two of us against Nada."

He eased the door closed and ducked away, bent low. I scrambled awkwardly over the gear stick into the driver's seat, heart pounding. First driving without a licence, now ramming other cars. What a day.

The big black car turned into the road which would take it past me. I put the car into gear and waited, every muscle tensed, the urge to rush out and reclaim the channel stone almost overpowering reason. Garth was hidden somewhere among the dark trees opposite. *Don't think about the boy. Or the damn stone. Concentrate.*

Steady ... not too soon ... I stepped on the accelerator and the car rocketed forward, just as the boy's thin face appeared at the window of the other car. A pale oval in the darkness, it looked straight at me. My heart lurched and I stomped on the brake.

The black car swept past mere inches in front of my bumper bar, that heart-shaped little face staring back at me. I put my head down on the steering wheel and sobbed.

Garth wrenched open my door. "What are you doing? You let them get away!" Then, in a slightly gentler tone: "Are you hurt? What the hell are you crying for?"

He hoisted me out of the car and I fell against his chest, howling like a madwoman. For a moment he froze, then his arms came round me in an awkward embrace.

"That kid could have been Lachie's *twin*," I sobbed. "It was him! It was Lachie, it was, it was ..."

God, I really was mad. Lachie had died in May, a few weeks short of his tenth birthday. I *knew* that. But that boy! That beloved little face. Had my obsession with the channel stone played tricks on my mind, made me see something that wasn't really there? But how could a mother mistake her own child's face? My heart was breaking all over again.

Gradually I calmed enough to explain to Garth, sniffling and wiping away tears with the back of my hand—enough for him to get the gist anyway. For once he didn't snark, but he did sigh and look down the now-empty drive.

"Well, they'll be halfway to Mosman by now. Let's go get ourselves something to eat. I can't think on an empty stomach."

CHAPTER TWENTY-FIVE

I hadn't stayed at taekwondo that night because I had a headache. It was one of Jason's nights to have Lachie, so I left him there with the other mini martial artists, his yellow belt carefully knotted over his baggy white uniform, glad to forgo the yelling and kicking for once.

"Maybe you should stay, Mum," he said, his brown eyes serious. "What if you're not ready for grading in time?"

Grading was in three weeks. I was going for a high brown belt; Lachie was trying for some green tips to his yellow.

"I think I'll be okay," I said. "Besides, I haven't got my uniform on. Have fun, and I'll see you tomorrow night. Be good for Dad."

"I always am," he said, a trifle indignant. "Love you, Mum."

"Love you too, Monster."

I drove home, hoping for a quiet night, but there was no guarantee I wouldn't be getting a call in an hour from one of the other mums saying Jason hadn't showed. He'd said he'd be finished work in time to pick Lachie up, but it wouldn't be the first time he'd let me down. Since the divorce we'd arrived at an uneasy truce, but battle could break out again any time. They'd invented the word "infuriating" for Jason. Also "unreliable", "dishonest" and many others along the same lines.

We spoke when we had to, and only about Lachie. I'd forgiven one affair during our tumultuous marriage, but I drew the line at two. Even before we officially split, we'd basically been living separate lives. He travelled a lot with work, or so he said, and quite frankly, life without him was so much more peaceful I couldn't care less what he got up to. It was no way to live, for Lachie or me, so I'd pulled the plug. Though single motherhood could be hard, I'd never regretted it.

An hour passed, and then another, without a call, so Jason must have kept his word for once. I was curled up on the lounge reading—I could even tell you which book it was, the events of that night are so burnt into my brain. I never did finish that book. I had to throw it away. Even seeing it in a bookshop afterwards would bring back a wave of such grief and pain I'd have to walk out.

The phone rang, and I remember looking at the clock, thinking *well, at least it won't be Jason.*

"Kate?" It was a man's voice, but all weird and high-pitched, as if someone were squeezing his throat. He sounded so strange it took me a long moment to realise it *was* Jason. "There's been an accident."

Terror lanced through me, swift and sudden, and the book slipped from my fingers. "Is Lachie all right?"

"We're at Westmead. The Children's Hospital." My heart lurched. "You'd better get down here."

"What's wrong?" I could barely breathe. "Is he hurt?"

"It's not good." And then he hung up.

"Jason? Jason!" I punched in his number with shaking hands, but it went straight through to message bank.

My imagination went into overdrive, picturing all the terrible ways my baby could be hurt, his little body broken. I dropped the phone on the floor and didn't even notice.

I flew to the car, the driveway rough under my bare feet. It never occurred to me to stop for shoes. My hands shook so badly it took me three tries to get the key into the ignition.

All the way to the hospital I prayed, a terrified litany of *please God please God please God.* The dark roads flicked by in a blur, until I found myself in the car park of The Children's Hospital, unaware of how I'd got there.

I must have looked a sight, running into Emergency barefoot and wild-eyed, without even a handbag to put my car keys in. I clenched them in my fist, so tight they left deep grooves in my fingers.

"My son's here," I gasped to one of the nurses on duty behind the glass partition. "Lachlan Hepburn. My ex said there'd been an accident."

My voice broke on the last word.

"Come round to the door and I'll buzz you in."

After a short delay she met me at the door, an older man at her side. They both looked so serious.

"Is he badly hurt?" *Please God please God.* "Is he in surgery? What's happened?"

The man stepped forward, his face drawn into tired lines. Behind his glasses his eyes were full of sympathy. "Mrs Hepburn, I'm Dr Rawson. Let me take you to your husband."

"It's O'Connor," I said, my lips forming words on their own. I marvelled that I could sound so normal. It was like listening to someone else speak. "We're divorced."

"This way, Ms O'Connor." With a gentle hand on my back he guided me through the corridors of Emergency. They smelled of antiseptic, and blood and pain. The way seemed long and empty, lit by the harsh glare of fluorescent lights. My panicked heart stuttered with fear.

"We have a private room for you." He opened the door to a tiny box of a room, but I wasn't listening. Jason sat on the couch, head in his hands. He looked up as the door opened, his face haggard, eyes red from weeping, and I knew.

"I'm sorry," he whispered, coming towards me. "I'm so, so sorry."

I caught my breath, hands covering my mouth. I think I staggered. It felt as if I'd been punched in the gut. I knew, but still I refused to believe. I cast a wild look back at Dr Rawson in the doorway. Nothing but sorrow in his lined face.

"If there's anything I can get you …" he said.

"Where is he?" My throat was so dry I had to force each word out, voice trembling with the effort. I had to see for myself. "I want to see my son."

Jason took my hand and Dr Rawson led us back out into the bright corridors of Emergency. They were full of noise—children crying, voices raised in argument, the beeping of machines and the constant tap of footsteps as busy nurses hurried by. It seemed another world, and I moved through it as if any minute I'd wake up and find this was all a nightmare.

Dr Rawson opened the door of another little box room and stood back for us to enter. It was dark and very cold—someone had the air conditioning on full blast. Monitors, their screens blank, huddled around a hospital bed that dominated the small space. At first I thought it was empty.

Then I realised a slight form lay under the cool white sheet.

"Why is his face covered?" I choked out. "He wouldn't like that."

I reached out, but Dr Rawson's hand on my arm stopped me. "I must warn you, Ms O'Connor, he was badly hurt in the accident. You may prefer to remember him as he was."

I caught my bottom lip in my teeth to keep it from trembling and waited, eyes welling with slow tears, until he removed his hand. Then I stepped forward and pulled the sheet away, tucking it carefully around his thin shoulders.

The doctor had been right to warn me, but I had to see for myself. The left side of his head was pulped beyond recognition, his beautiful face destroyed. I gasped in a couple of quick breaths and squeezed my eyes shut against the horror of that mutilated flesh. After a moment I leaned forward to kiss his smooth right cheek. A tear fell on his eyelid, sparkling in his long dark lashes, and I wiped it carefully away.

Lachie. My vision narrowed, till all I could see was that one closed eye, the lashes nestled on the soft curve of his cheek. Someone had obviously made an attempt to clean him up. A single drop of blood they'd missed lay among the freckles there. *Wake up, Monster.*

"Did he … did he suffer?" My whole body shook as I fought for control. I needed to know.

"I'm sure he didn't," said Dr Rawson. "Death would have been instantaneous."

That was something. I swallowed hard, my throat constricted with pain. *Death was instantaneous.*

To be grateful for such a thing was unbearable. How could I live in a world where *death was instantaneous* was a good thing? How was it right that I still lived but my baby was dead?

He wasn't even ten. I had a box of Lego stashed away at home ready for his birthday in a few weeks. We'd already sent out the party invitations.

I stroked his hair, trying to sweep it off his forehead the way he liked, but it was stiff with dried blood and wouldn't move. In the corridor outside a baby wailed and a woman's voice murmured soothing noises. Outside the world continued.

In this cold room, surrounded by silent machines, my world lay shattered.

Goodbye, Monster.

I lay my face next to his cold cheek and howled my agony into the pillow.

***

"Shit," said Garth, when I'd finished. "That's pretty rough."

I nodded, throat still choked with tears. We were at McDonald's, at an outside table near the brightly coloured playground. Even now, at eleven-thirty at night, two children played among the tubes and slides, their high-pitched squeals shearing through the noise of cars coming and going from the car park.

Sweat prickled down my spine. The night air lay heavy with humidity on my bare skin. I'd washed up in the tiny bathroom, but I still reeked of smoke. Garth smelled as bad, but his visit to the men's had removed most of the blood, so he looked a lot less frightening. His appearance had freaked out the teenagers serving behind the counter when we walked in. For a moment it looked as though they'd refuse to serve us, but they must have decided it was safer to give us what we wanted than try throwing us out. Even out here people gave our table a wide berth.

Garth was on his third Big Mac, and eyed my half-eaten burger with interest. Guess it took a lot to fuel those werewolf muscles, though it would've helped if he'd had more than a bowl full of sugar and air for breakfast. Still, breakfast was a long time ago. A long, long time ago. I was so tired I could have slept for a week. God, what a day.

I took another sip of coffee. Strong and black, but you couldn't say much else for it. It bore about as much resemblance to real coffee as McDonald's hamburgers did to real burgers. But it gave me something to do with my hands and gradually calmed my jangling nerves.

"I heard Jason's kid had died," said Garth, cheeks bulging with the last of his burger, "but it was just before he left us for Valeria, and I never found out how it happened. He was drunk, you reckon?"

I blew my nose on a paper napkin. "By the time the police tested him he was under the limit, but what else could it be? There was nothing wrong with the car, and there were no other vehicles involved. You don't slam into a tree for no reason at all."

And I would never ever forgive him.

"I'm sorry." Then he nodded at the remains of my dinner. "You going to eat that?"

Wordlessly I pushed it across the plastic table. He tore into it with as much enthusiasm as if it were his first burger instead of his fourth, bits of lettuce flying everywhere. Did he eat so messily as a wolf? Probably best not to know.

"I feel … as if I've seen a ghost." Completely gutted— again. When would I stop doing this to myself? Suddenly suspicious, I asked, "Ghosts aren't real too, are they?"

He shook his head, mouth too full to speak.

"Who was that boy? What was Nada doing with him?" Nothing good, that's for sure. But he must be important, for her to miss the action at Alicia's place in search of him. And why had Jason wanted me to stop her taking him? For I felt sure now that was what he'd meant. There'd been real fear in his eyes.

And it all added up to something that made me sick with hope and terror. Something so outlandish I couldn't bring myself to speak it out loud, for fear it might not be true. Just my heart playing its latest and most hurtful trick.

It *couldn't* be true. I was a grieving mother clutching at fantasies. But I'd seen some crazy stuff in the last few days. Was this any crazier?

Garth wiped his mouth then leaned back, arms folded. His eyes were a clear grey, the yellow of the wolf safely hidden, and the expression in them was kinder than I was used to seeing there. "You think it was him, don't you? You think that really was Lachie."

"I know it sounds ridiculous …"

He shook his head. "Never said that. But that means there's only one thing to do."

"What?"

"Dig up the grave and see."

"Dig up—!" I gaped at him. "Are you nuts? No one's going to let me dig up the grave." Even talking about it made me feel ill. It had been seven months. I did *not* want to see inside that coffin. "And what do we do then? DNA tests?"

"I'm not talking about going through official channels. You'd need a court order, and you wouldn't get one. They'd send you to the funny farm instead. No. I'm talking you, me and a shovel. Tomorrow night, as soon as it gets dark."

Just when I thought life couldn't get any crazier. Behind him a life-sized Ronald McDonald sat on a bench seat, plastic grin plastered on his plastic face, waiting for some kid to come and have a photo taken with him. If he'd joined the conversation I couldn't have been more shaken.

What do you reckon, Ronald?

Why, Kate, I think that's a fine idea. Why don't I get the Hamburglar to come and help break into the cemetery?

"Why not tonight?"

"Because I'm half dead on my feet. Even a werewolf's body needs food and sleep to heal itself. I've had the food." He yawned hugely. "And now I need the sleep."

"But what can we … I mean, will we be able to tell if—?" If it was him. My beautiful boy. Gruesome images filled my head. I had no idea how fast bodies decomposed. How could I look at what was in that coffin? God, I couldn't even bear to think about it.

What if it wasn't Lachie's body in there? What if it *was*?

"We'll know," he said firmly. "Trust me."

Funnily enough, I did. A few days ago he'd been trying to kill me, and now I felt almost affectionate towards the hulking werewolf. Life was just full of surprises.

"Why would you help me with this? Don't you want to chase Nada and get the stone back? Leandra sure does."

"You got a plan for getting in to the Mosman house and getting it?"

"No."

"Me neither. But this, I can do."

Which didn't explain why he would want to, so I stared at him, waiting for something more.

"You're a prickly bugger, aren't you? Isn't it possible I want to help because it's the right thing to do?"

I snorted. "A werewolf with a conscience?"

"Why not? We're not complete animals, you know." He threw his hands up. "All right, all right. If I'm going to help Leandra—and you—I need you focused. You're not going to be any use to me till you know. So let's go find a place to sleep and get on with it."

He stalked off to the car and I plunged after him. He was right; the need to know consumed me. I couldn't think of anything else. Even Leandra's yearning for the channel stone had died away in the face of this.

In fact, I hadn't felt her presence since she'd dealt with the cop on the freeway. She'd come out then because he was in her way, and I hadn't been able to get rid of him. Maybe if I stayed in control of the situation now I could keep her suppressed. It was too much to hope she'd given up her assault on my body—but that was a problem for later.

First I had a body to exhume.

CHAPTER TWENTY-SIX

Garth hadn't been kidding about his need for sleep. We found a cheap motel on the highway that was still open, one of those awful prefabricated jobs that look like the cleaners hose it out after you leave, and took a room for the remainder of the night. He'd dropped onto one of the beds and started snoring before I'd even shut the door behind us.

I considered pulling off his shoes but decided to leave him be. Relaxed in sleep, his face looked younger. A hell of a lot less grumpy, too. He still stank of smoke, though. We both did. I left him to whatever werewolves dream of and squeezed into the tiny bathroom to have a shower.

The spray of hot water washed away the grime, but it did nothing to relax me. My mind buzzed with impossibilities. How could Lachie be alive? I'd *seen* him, crushed and broken on the hospital bed. I'd stood at his graveside and watched his coffin sinking into the ground.

But what other little boy would Jason care so much about? I shut my eyes and turned my face up to the sharp sting of the hot water. He'd had plenty of affairs. Maybe he had other children. I had to be rational. Steam billowed about me as I considered this, my heart sinking. But other children who looked so much like Lachie? No. It was too much of a coincidence.

The shower curtain rattled aside as I stepped out on to the thin bath mat. Physically I was in good shape for someone who'd just been through a bushfire. My lungs felt clear and my skin showed no signs of burns or blisters. I swiped the steam from the mirror with my hand and checked my back. Nothing.

My reflection stared back at me. No clues there to the stranger riding behind my green eyes. Same old face.

But so much had changed in the last few days, I wasn't the same person any more. My mind shied away from thinking too deeply about that. I could make myself puke from fear and horror if I went too far down that path. Better to focus on Lachie.

I slipped my smoky clothes back on for lack of anything better and went back out into the main room. What I wouldn't give for a pair of clean pyjamas now—or even a toothbrush. But Garth had been adamant we couldn't go anywhere our enemies might be able to track us. Between the two of us, there was quite a list of them. So my place was out, and here we were in another dingy motel room, much like last night's, except this one had two beds instead of one.

And where were Ben and Luce spending the night? What had happened to them after we'd left? I still felt sick with guilt about that, however much Garth tried to assure me it had been necessary.

I sat on my bed and swiped his phone off the small chest of drawers between the beds. Garth lay on his back, one arm flung across his face. He didn't stir as I dialled Luce's number again.

"The number you are dialling is unavailable," the recorded message began, and I stabbed a finger at the End button. We'd been trying to contact Luce all night, and every time we'd gotten the same frustrating message.

I switched off the lamp and lay down, sure the snores from the other bed would keep me awake, even if my worries didn't. But they blended into the rattle and hum of the old air-conditioning unit on the wall, and before long I was out like a light.

***

It was nearly midday when I woke, and Garth still showed no sign of stirring. At three o'clock I shook him awake, unable to stand the waiting any longer.

"Congratulations, you've just won the Nobel Sleep Prize."

He grunted and rolled out of bed, staggering past me to the bathroom. The shower started up and I groaned, impatience like a lump of iron in my chest.

Still, there was nothing to be done till it got dark. Except buy shovels, of course, which we did, and more McDonald's. If I never saw another Big Mac it would be too soon, though Garth never seemed to tire of them.

After a day that felt at least a week long, he finally decided it was dark enough to get moving. We headed out along

Epping Road towards the cemetery, all the windows down to try to get some air. Outside our air-conditioned room the heat was stifling. I doubted it would get below thirty all night.

"I'm going to try Luce again," I said as we passed Macquarie Uni.

I was desperate to know if Ben was okay. He wasn't aggressive by nature. He was the kind of guy who'd rather defuse a situation with a well-timed joke than even raise his voice to someone. A few days ago I would have said he didn't have a violent bone in his body, but that was before I'd seen him shoot Garth. Obviously I didn't know him as well as I'd thought. Last I'd seen, he'd been swinging an axe and Luce had been rushing to his aid.

Now Luce was my only way to contact him, since Nada's thugs had taken both my phone and Ben's.

Trying not to assume the worst, I listened to Luce's phone ring. Maybe she was out of signal range. Quite likely, if they were still up in the mountains. Or maybe her battery was flat.

"The number you are dialling is unavailable," the same old robot voice announced.

"No luck."

Garth grunted and turned off Epping Road. The cemetery lay only a couple of blocks further on. The prospect of going there again—the first time since the funeral—gave me a sick feeling in the pit of my stomach.

"She's probably already ditched the phone."

"Why would she ditch the phone?" I watched the dark buildings slide by, bringing me closer to the moment I both longed for and dreaded. It was hard to focus on anything else.

"Alicia. Luce is bound to her now. She won't want anyone outside her circles contacting Luce, so she'll issue her with a new phone." The cemetery loomed on our left and he turned down a dark side street and ran along beside its wall till he came to the entry. Heavy iron gates barred the way. He did a U-turn and parked the car on the opposite side of the street, facing back the way we'd come. "We all change our phones pretty often anyway, to cut down on tapping."

That didn't make much sense. I stared at the massive gates. They'd stood open for the hearse and all the mourners last time I'd been here. "But if Luce wants to talk to someone she can call them herself. She doesn't have to wait till they call her."

"Not if Alicia tells her not to. You don't understand the power of a binding. Luce can't do anything now that goes against Alicia's interests. Literally, physically cannot."

That was a lot of power to put into someone else's hands. Could revenge on Valeria be worth such a sacrifice? How did Leandra inspire such ridiculous devotion?

There were no buildings on our side of the road, only bush. Garth turned off the engine and we sat in the dark, looking across at the high fences of the cemetery and the gates that barred our way. The weight of remembered grief pinned me in place. After waiting all afternoon to get here, suddenly I couldn't bear to get out of the car.

The chapels and other buildings sat in a cluster up the hill from the entrance, and lights blazed at one end. With the windows wound down we could hear music and voices, as if there was a party going on.

"I think that's the café," I said at last, trying to fight clear of paralysing memories. The look on my mother's face as the coffin slowly sank into the grave. Pink rose petals fluttering in on top of it. "Strange place for a party."

"Maybe it's a Goth twenty-first." Garth frowned at the lit windows as if he could tell from here what was going on. Maybe he could. I had no idea how good werewolves' sight was. My own had improved significantly since Leandra had hitched a ride, but I couldn't make out more than shapes moving against the light.

"Should we wait till they go?" If it was a twenty-first there could be all sorts of fun and games going on among the gravestones, and I didn't want to be caught wielding my shovel by a bunch of drunks. Plus I could put off getting out of the car and facing what was to come.

"Where's the grave?"

"Over the back section there." I pointed in the general direction, away from the buildings. Trees and hedges blocked the view.

"Shouldn't be a problem. I bet the gate's not locked. All those cars in the car park had to get in somehow."

He went over to check and came back grinning. "No padlock. It's just pulled closed. Let's go."

I took a deep breath, filling my lungs with the warm, humid air. Garth got the shovels and other gear while I hesitated with my hand on the door handle. *Come on, Kate. You can do this.*

Garth looked back, probably wondering what the hell I was doing. Good question. I could hardly cower here all night while he loitered in the road with an armful of shovels. That didn't look suspicious *at all*.

I propelled myself out of the car by sheer force of will and slammed the door behind me. The gate screeched as we pushed it open and I winced, but no one heard over the bass thump of music from the café. We cut across the grass, keeping well away from the party. No point tempting fate by waltzing up the drive with shovels over our shoulders.

The night was hot and sticky, the air heavy with moisture. At the back of the cemetery, away from the streetlights, I stumbled a couple of times before my eyes adjusted to the low light. I had a feeling that this time last week I wouldn't have been able to see this well in the dark.

Finding Lachie's grave proved challenging. I knew the general area, but I hadn't been back since the day of the funeral, and things had changed. More headstones had been erected, and the layout of the gardens seemed to have altered slightly. Or maybe my memory was faulty. The day had passed in a blur of anguish. I crawled around peering at a lot of headstones before I found the right one.

"This is it." I knelt on the grass, feeling flat and ready to burst into tears. Seeing it again, so solid and final, made my hopes seem ridiculous. *Lachlan Christopher Hepburn, beloved son of Jason and Kathryn.* Why was I here with my shovel and my crazy ideas? Could I still be in denial after all this time?

Garth seemed to sense my mood. "I'll start. You keep watch."

I nodded and moved away across the neat lawn, glad for the excuse. Memories of that day rushed back at me, none of them happy. At the funeral of an old person, there was often an element of celebration mixed into the sadness: of a life well lived, of achievements and legacies. But the loss of a child meant more than a precious life cut short; people mourned the lost opportunities, the graduations and marriages that would never occur, the children who would never be born. No one could ever know the life they might have lived, the adult they might have grown into. All lost, destroyed in an instant. The enormity of it had left me numb, buried so deep under grief I'd thought I could never climb out again. The only emotion that had burned as bright that day had been hatred, every time I looked at Jason standing on the other side of the grave.

A distant clink of glassware and a roar of laughter floated across the dark cemetery. It felt wrong to be celebrating in such a place, almost disrespectful.

Huh. I was a fine one to talk. At least the partygoers weren't digging up any gravesites.

Behind me Garth settled into a steady rhythm: the regular thunk of the shovel biting into the ground, followed by the scatter of dirt. It sounded loud in the still, oppressive air; I looked around nervously, but no one leapt out of the bushes demanding to know what we were doing.

After a time I mastered my dread enough to join him. Better to get this over with as quickly as possible. My nerves were shattered. I'd seen no signs of security, but that could change at any moment. With two of us working, we were soon down three feet or so, and Garth jumped into the hole to continue.

There wasn't room for both of us in there. The big werewolf took up a lot of space. I watched for a while, then wandered over and sat on a low garden wall, flexing my sore fingers.

Where was Ben? The fact I'd run out on him ate at me, even though it had really been Leandra doing the running. The more time passed without hearing from him, the more anxious I felt. I needed to know he was safe, needed to feel his arms around me again.

He'd adored Lachie, treating him like a favourite nephew. He'd understand how hard it was for me just to be here. And the night at Avoca had only deepened our bond. Garth was a handy guy to have around, but Ben had a place in my heart no one else could fill.

Only Garth's head and shoulders were visible now, and the mound of dirt beside the grave grew rapidly. I hugged myself tightly, sick with nerves. No mother should have to do this. What was in that coffin?

I'd stopped noticing the noise from the party. But now new noises appeared: low voices murmuring, and a nervous giggle, quickly hushed.

My head whipped around. Still some distance away, but coming closer, a couple meandered along the path, arms around each other, heads close together. They weren't quite steady on their feet. The man said something and the nervous giggle sounded again. They stopped for a kiss, then decided they still weren't far enough away from their friends and kept moving.

"Garth! Someone's coming."

The shovel clunked against something solid. Garth straightened as the two lovebirds came to an uncertain halt.

"What was that?" asked the girl.

"Probably a possum or something." Her companion tried to distract her with another kiss.

I threw a panicked look at Garth. What should we do? They'd be on us in another few steps, and there was no hiding what we'd been up to. Garth's eyes gleamed yellow, and he growled, a low warning rumble in his chest.

"That wasn't a possum!" the girl squeaked.

"It's only a dog. Nothing to be scared of. Come over here; the grass is nice and soft."

The would-be Romeo led her off the path. Still much too close. Some people just wouldn't take a hint. It was too dark to be sure, but I thought Garth rolled his eyes.

He dropped out of sight into the pit and I heard the tell-tale crunch of bones moving and realigning.

"I'm scared." The girl sat up and looked around, searching for the source of that unnerving noise. I couldn't blame her. I'd heard it several times myself and every time it gave me the horrors. "Let's go back."

Whatever the man might have said was lost as the werewolf leapt from the grave with a snarl and stalked across the grass toward them. It scared even me; I felt almost sorry for them as the girl screamed in pure terror and fled down the path. Her boyfriend obviously decided dogs might be something to be frightened of after all. He took off after her without stopping for a closer look.

The wolf loped after them, probably to make sure they didn't come back. That didn't seem likely, unless they brought a bunch of braver friends with them.

"I hope you know what you're doing, Garth."

If a mob descended on us we'd be worse off than before. I jumped down into the hole and hurled Garth's clothes up on to the grass. With a bit of luck everyone would think it nothing more than a drunken story. And who'd want to leave the party to go searching for some scary dog? Surely it was time we had some luck?

I cleared the top of the coffin with another moment's work. It gleamed pale grey through the dirt. It had been white, and so small. I swallowed a lump in my throat and pushed on, digging a spot to plant my feet either side. It was a struggle to clamber back out, and I got a face full of dirt as I flailed on the edge, legs kicking wildly.

When I looked up I found myself face to face with the wolf. I squeaked and nearly fell back into the hole.

"Dammit, Garth! You scared the crap out of me."

His tongue lolled out the side of his mouth in a wolfish grin. I didn't like having him standing over me, those big teeth so close. There's nothing friendly and doggish about a full-grown wolf in your face, especially in the middle of the night in a graveyard. My heart thumped as I scrambled to my feet. *He's on your side, remember? Calm down.* But I didn't relax till he backed off.

I got the crowbar and jumped back into the hole. It was dark as the pits of hell and smelled strongly of damp earth. I struggled with the crowbar while above me the horrible crunch of the werewolf change sounded again, followed by rustling and the unmistakeable slide of a zip.

He slid down beside me, human again and fully dressed. "Here, give me that. You'll never get it open."

I handed over the crowbar and tried to stay out of the way, which wasn't easy in such a small space. Eventually he growled in disgust and flung the shovels back out.

"Can't get any leverage," he complained. "Hop out and give me some room."

I scrambled out again, slipping and sliding as the sides of the hole crumbled. More earth rained down on the coffin with a soft pattering. I could feel it under my clothes too, and through my hair. I was dirt from head to foot.

Down in the hole Garth grunted and swore; then, with a rush and a thud, the coffin appeared over the edge like a wooden whale breeching and slammed down on the soft earth. I stared, unable to tear my gaze from it. So small.

Garth climbed out after it and shook himself like a dog, spraying more dirt over me.

"*That's* more like it," he said and got to work with the crowbar.

I waited, heart hammering, filled with a sickening anticipation. The whole party could have turned up then with pitchforks and torches, and I couldn't have taken my eyes from the dirty white coffin.

A sudden splintering made me jump, and Garth laid the crowbar down.

"Ready?"

I wasn't. I didn't want to know, and I had to know, all at the same time. But it was too late to turn back now. I nodded, trembling all over, and together we slid off the broken lid.

What did I expect to see? A skeleton, its bare skull grinning at me? My beautiful broken boy, as he'd been when I last saw him lying on that hospital bed? Some horrible mouldering in-between phase? Whatever I'd expected, it wasn't what lay in the bottom of that coffin.

"What the *hell*?"

I reached in, as if touching it could make the contents into something different, something that made sense. But the sticks remained sticks, and the shrivelled round things which looked like desiccated vegetables forgotten in the bottom of the crisper for months—well, they still looked like shrivelled round things.

Certainly nothing in there had ever been human.

I met Garth's eyes. My face must have been a picture of confusion. He, however, didn't seem surprised.

"Thought so," he said. "Didn't want to get your hopes up by saying anything till I was sure."

"Sure of *what*? What the hell *is* all this?"

"Changeling," he said. "Jason must have faked the whole thing. He switched the real Lachie for a changeling. It's earth magic. Goblins make them out of plants—sticks, vegetables, leaves, whatever. They don't hold their form for more than a week or two."

"So that means ..." I sucked in a deep breath and sat down hard among the dirt. My legs simply refused to hold me up any longer. My head swam, dizzy with possibility.

He nodded. "Yes. Lachie's still alive."

***

Back in our tiny motel room, Garth disappeared into the shower and I flopped onto my bed, dirt and all, still torn between tears and laughter. Beyond all reason and hope, Lachie was alive—but Nada had him. The bottom dropped out of my stomach every time I wondered why. I had to rely on Jason to keep him safe, and relying on Jason had never worked out well for me in the past.

My baby was alive, and I was so excited I thought I'd never sleep. But I didn't even last till Garth came out of the bathroom. I only shut my eyes for a moment, wrung out with emotion, and the next thing I knew Garth was offering me a choice of Coco Pops or Weet-Bix for breakfast.

Still on a high and feeling generous, I let him have the Coco Pops.

Our knees bumped under the tiny table. I couldn't wait to get out of this cramped and dingy place. Not even a hint of natural light crept into the room, but I felt sure that outside the sun would be shining and the sky a blaze of bright blue.

"We have to find Ben," I said. "I can't wait to tell him the news."

Today I couldn't entertain the prospect that Ben might be hurt or in trouble himself. Today was a day for miracles. If Lachie could come back from the dead, anything was possible. We'd find Ben, and the three of us would come up with a plan to get my boy back safely from Nada.

Then all I had to do was get rid of Leandra, and we could all live Happily Ever After. I tucked into the Weetbix. A good breakfast was so important when you had a schedule like that for the day.

"I rang a couple of the boys while you were asleep," Garth said. "Sent someone out to watch The Dress-up Box. He'll let us know if he shows up there."

"Great. We can head over to his place and see if he's home."

He shook his head. "Not a good idea. My guy swung past there first, and one of Valeria's stooges was watching it. It's you they want, you know, and they figure the best way to find you is through him. If he's got any sense he'll stay well away himself."

"Right." I grinned, feeling a flood of relief. "But that means he's alive, and they don't have him."

"Not necessarily. They could have him and still be watching the place, hoping you'll come looking for him."

"Geez. Are you always this positive?"

"I'm just a glass half-full kind of guy."

Jokes from Garth: what had the world come to? Seemed like everything was different this morning, and I was determined to hold on to my optimism.

Assuming he was free, where would Ben go? He had a sister in Camden, but presumably Valeria could find that out easily enough, if she didn't already know. He could be holed up in a random motel somewhere, like us, or hiding out with a friend. What kind of resources would a herald have, anyway? I had no idea.

If only he had his phone, or I had mine. How did we ever cope in the days before mobiles? Ben didn't even have a landline at home; he used his mobile for everything. Very convenient, as long as you didn't lose the damn thing.

"Give me your phone. I'll try Tanya."

If I couldn't go to Ben's house myself, maybe I could sweet-talk Tanya into taking a drive over there. It was a bit of a long shot—Ben was probably smart enough to realise Valeria would be watching for him. But I didn't know what else to do. Sydney was a big city. Finding one person among millions was too big a task for two people. And that assumed he was even *in* Sydney.

Tanya's number rang and rang, then clicked over to the answering machine. Damn.

"Hi Tanya, it's Kate. I was hoping you could do me a favour … call me back, please, on … *what's your number?*" I mouthed at Garth. He rattled it off and I repeated it.

Now what? "Maybe we should head back up the mountains."

"No point. Ben won't hang around up there, and Luce is no help to us any more."

"So what do we do?" I had no ideas, but I couldn't sit still. Lachie was out there, just beyond reach.

Garth shrugged. He was used to having Luce guide him. Being the ideas man was a new experience. "Let's go see Trevor."

CHAPTER TWENTY-SEVEN

"Are you sure you want to do this?"

Garth turned off the engine and got out. Guess that was a yes.

Together we stood on the footpath and looked up at the house above us. Perched on a sandstone outcrop, it backed onto the bush, and its green metal roof blended into the gum trees. Four motor bikes and a beat-up Holden parked on the street suggested someone must be home, though there was no sign of life. Blinds were drawn at all the windows. Narrow wooden stairs led from the street up to a large wooden deck on the front of the house.

I followed Garth up the steps, still uneasy at meeting my former—ally? associate? I couldn't remember Trevor, but anyone who made it to pack leader was a force to be reckoned with. Even Leandra had had a healthy respect for this man. Now I needed his help, but convincing him to give it would be tricky.

In front of me Garth's shoulders sat somewhere up around his ears, tight with nervous tension, and his eyes flicked constantly from side to side, scanning for threats. I knew he shouldn't be here, though on that point, too, my memory let me down, and he would only mutter something surly about pack business in explanation.

I was glad of his company, though. Braving the wolves' den on my own wasn't my idea of a good time. They would have heard the rumours by now of my involvement in Leandra's death, and I didn't want to be held to account by a pack of werewolves in the mood for retribution.

Seemed like this was the last place either of us should be looking for help.

Empty beer cans littered the massive deck. A spindly plant struggled for life in a pot by the door. Garth leaned on the doorbell, and a buzzer sounded somewhere inside.

"Don't look so nervous," he said as footsteps approached. "Remember who you are."

Was that supposed to make me feel better? I glared. I was Kate, mother of Lachie, and holding on to that truth as hard as I could was the only thing keeping Leandra at bay. Did he think I'd let her loose just to impress some werewolf?

A guy with more hair than Hugh Jackman in a bad X-Men wig opened the door and scowled when he saw who waited on his doorstep.

"What are you doing here?"

He had the familiar orange glow that said werewolf, but my nose could have told me so even with my eyes shut. He smelled of wet dog, though it was mid-afternoon and he must have been human for hours.

"Nice to see you, too, Jed. Aren't you going to invite us in?"

"You do know what exile means, don't you? Get your arse back in your car and get out of here."

Jed started to close the door, but Garth was too quick. One hard shove and Jed was flattened against the wall inside with Garth's muscled forearm crushing his windpipe.

"Do you think I'd come back here if it wasn't important? Stupid kid. Tell Trevor we need to speak to him."

He shoved the other wolf again, and Jed lurched away down the hall, still scowling. He headed for the back of the house, muttering and rubbing his throat. I caught Garth's arm.

"Maybe slightly less violence? We *are* trying to ask a favour here."

Garth bared his teeth. Perhaps he meant it as a grin, but it looked more like a snarl. Werewolves did surly much better than cheerful—at least in my limited experience.

He shut the door behind us. The hallway was dim and relatively cool given the heat of the day outside. "Wolves understand dominance."

"Okaay."

I followed him down the hallway, past closed doors on either side, to a big sunlit room at the back of the house. Three men leapt up as we entered, their scowls matching that of the injured Jed.

"Where's Trevor?"

"No business of yours, Oathbreaker."

All three were bigger than Garth, and I had to fight the urge to step back as they stalked forward. Jed smirked in the background, obviously relishing the thought of seeing us get thrown out. Or worse.

I heard the click of a door shutting in the hallway behind us, and whirled to face the new threat. A slight man with receding hair entered the room behind us.

"Stand down, boys."

Garth's shoulders went rigid at the sound of his voice, but the man ignored him.

"I'm Trevor." He offered his hand and I shook it. His grip was warm and stronger than I'd expected. "And you are—?"

"Kate. Kate O'Connor. I'm a friend of Garth's."

And that was a sentence I couldn't have imagined saying a few days ago. Strange as it seemed, it felt true.

"I gathered that." He looked at Garth for the first time, and his eyes were cold. "I assume you have some compelling reason for showing your face here again. You'd better come into my office."

We followed him into the room he'd just left. From the corner of my eye I caught Jed's crestfallen expression. Guess he'd been hoping for the throwing out to start straight away.

Judging by the look on Trevor's face, it was still an option.

I took the visitor's chair he offered in front of a big workmanlike desk. He went round to the other side of the desk but lounged against the bookshelves there instead of sitting. Since Garth had refused a seat that would have put him in the inferior position, looking up at his visitor. Stupid wolf games.

I checked his bookshelves while they sized each other up. Mainly ring binders, each labelled in neat handwriting, with a few reference books, including a complete set of Australian Accounting Standards. That's right. Trevor was an accountant. I guess even werewolves had to earn a living somehow.

At some signal known only to them, the staring contest came to an end. Garth ducked his head in submission and Trevor folded his arms, his body language more relaxed.

"What are you doing here, Garth?" The pack leader sounded tired. "You never take the easy option, do you? You've always got to stir things up some more. The pack's already on edge, and now you show up like the Ghost of frigging Christmas Past, clanking your goddamn chains in their faces."

Garth's face was stony. I could have told Trevor he was wasting his time with Dickens allusions. If he wanted to catch Garth's attention he'd need a quote from Star Wars.

Garth folded his arms, mirroring the pack leader's body language.

"Let me guess what's got their tails in a twist. The rumours of Leandra's death, right?"

"Rumours? It's a little more than rumours, mate. Looks like you're out of a job again."

"Not quite."

"Not *quite*? I heard she had her heart ripped out."

"You shouldn't believe everything you hear."

"Oh, for God's sake." Trevor flopped into the leather chair behind the desk. "Sit down, you stubborn shit, and tell me what's going on."

Garth flicked a glance at me. I nodded, and he took the chair next to mine. Trevor said nothing, but he looked at me with a new interest.

"You never explained who your friend is."

"She's a herald. I met her two nights ago at Alicia's place."

If he'd been in wolf form I swear his ears would have pricked up at that. "You were there when Valeria attacked?"

Garth launched into the mostly true version of events we'd agreed on before we came: how Leandra had given me a geas to deliver to Luce and Garth, which Valeria had stolen; how we'd gone to beg Alicia's help in getting it back and been caught up in the attack; and how Valeria had kidnapped my son to try to force me to stop seeking the stone.

"Stone? I thought you said it was a geas?"

He looked sceptical, and no wonder: a geas, a kind of magically binding task, was normally inscribed on a dragon scale.

"It is," I said. "It's an unusual kind."

"We have reason to believe Leandra's still alive," said Garth. "We think this is all part of some bigger plan of hers to win the proving."

"You think? She didn't tell you anything about this plan?"

Scepticism was rapidly morphing into outright disbelief.

"We've received messages that can only be from her."

The creak of leather as he shifted in his chair was the only sound. The venetian blinds at the window behind him were angled to block the sun, casting the room into shadow. In the dimness his aura flared a bright orange as he regarded Garth thoughtfully. The silence lengthened as he tapped his fingers on the metal arm of his chair.

"Where's Luce? I would have expected her to be all over this."

"She's still at Alicia's."

Briefly Garth explained how Luce had come to be bonded to Alicia, while Trevor's eyebrows climbed higher and higher. The pack leader rose and started pacing back and forth in the space between the window and the bookshelves. Scuff marks on the carpet suggested it was a regular habit. Must be a wolf thing. They couldn't bear to sit still.

"And what do you expect me to do? God, what a mess."

"We want you to help us get the stone back from Valeria."

"And free my son."

Trevor laughed; a short, unhappy sound. "That's all, is it? You wouldn't like me to get you the winning lottery ticket at the same time?"

"Trev—"

"Don't start, Garth. You're out of your mind if you think I'm getting mixed up in this. What do you take me for? Is *any* of what you just told me true?"

Garth leapt to his feet. Looked like it was time for the staring to recommence. Between the two of them they packed a lot of testosterone.

"All of it."

A small, reluctant smile tugged at one corner of the pack leader's mouth. "You're just not telling me the other half, right?"

An answering smile flickered on Garth's face. "I wouldn't call it half."

Seeing them like that, shoulders squared in identical postures, the same lazy half-smile on their faces, I suddenly realised.

"You're brothers, aren't you?"

His own brother had exiled him from the pack? Pity I couldn't remember what he'd done. Must have been something impressive.

Trevor frowned at me, distracted, then turned back to Garth with a sigh.

"Well, I guess I'm flattered you think I could take on Valeria. Or maybe that's the family insanity talking. But even if you told me all the juicy bits you're so obviously hiding, I couldn't help you."

"But you helped Leandra before," I said.

"Yes, I did. And some of those boys back there"—he jerked his head toward the room where Jed and his friends waited— "think that was a mistake. They reckon I've made the pack a target by supporting Leandra. That Valeria will come howling for our blood now that she's on top. They're thinking maybe a leader who makes bad decisions like that shouldn't be the leader any more."

Garth growled. "I'd like to see any of those arselickers try to oust you."

Trevor's grin showed a hint of steel. "I doubt I'm in any immediate danger. But the point is, this is not a good time to be drawing attention to ourselves. If Leandra was standing right here, my answer might be different, but I'm not risking the pack for half-truths and maybes."

I could feel Garth's eyes burning into me but I refused to look at him. We'd already agreed it was too dangerous to tell Trevor the truth about Leandra. Brother or no brother, that would be handing the man a bargaining chip that could prove too tempting.

Besides, what difference did it make? I wasn't planning on keeping her around long. Once I had Lachie back I was done with all this supernatural crap.

"I'm sorry about your son," said Trevor, "but I have to think of my family."

I glanced at Garth.

"Not him. The pack. Officially, Garth's not family any more." He strode to the door and held it open for us. Clearly the interview was over.

I stopped in the doorway and looked up at him. "And unofficially?"

"Unofficially, keeping his sorry arse alive was the best I could do. Try and keep it that way, would you?"

***

We sat in the car, weighed down by a heavy silence. I balled my hands into fists until the nails dug into my palms. There had to be something we could do.

"We could go to the police—report the kidnapping."

He shook his head. "First thing they'd do would be check with King's."

Who'd say Lachie was spending time with his father, no doubt. Nada would have thought of that.

The urge to scream coiled like a tightness in my chest. I had to get Lachie back. *Had* to. But how?

Garth started the engine and pulled away from the kerb. I didn't ask where we were going. If I couldn't come up with a plan one direction was as good as another.

A dark mood descended on me. Lachie might be alive, but I was no closer to recovering him. And meanwhile I was depending on Jason to keep him safe. "Depending" and "Jason" were two words that didn't belong in the same sentence.

Plus I had no idea how to find Ben.

Garth's phone rang, making me jump. He fished it out of his back pocket and tossed it to me. Such a law-abiding werewolf. No talking on mobiles while driving.

I checked the caller ID and my heart leapt.

"Tanya!"

"Hi, darl!" Her familiar voice lifted my spirits immediately. "How are you? How's your poor Mum?"

Mum? It took me a minute. So much had happened in the last few days, I'd forgotten I was supposed to be visiting my sick mother in Brisbane.

"Yeah, she's much better now." My God, wait till I told Mum Lachie was alive! "She'll probably be going home in a couple of days."

"That's great! Does that mean you'll be back soon? I cleaned up your kitchen for you. You lost quite a few dishes but the place is looking much better."

"Thanks. You didn't need to do that." I shot a look at Garth out of the corner of my eye. Probably should have made *him* clean it up, seeing he caused the mess in the first place.

"Oh, it was no trouble, hon. You don't want to be coming home to something like that. It didn't take long anyway. Ben gave me a hand."

"Ben?" Thank God! I let out a shaky breath.

"Yeah, you know. Six foot two, dark and gorgeous? He came round looking for you. Said he couldn't get you on the phone and thought you might be home. Did something happen to your mobile? Whose number is this?"

"Oh. It's, ah, Mum's. Left home in such a rush I forgot to pack my charger, and now the battery's dead. Did he leave a message for me?"

"No, not really."

"Not *really*? What did he say?"

"Something about Elizabethan England. You guys got some kinky sex game going on?"

"What? No!"

She laughed. "A girl can hope, can't she?"

"Tanya."

"Okay, okay. All he said was he wanted to take you for a moonlit stroll through Elizabethan England when you came home. God knows what he's on, but he seemed kind of eager. I'd say you're in with a chance there, sweetie. Don't stay away too long!"

"Thanks." I could feel the heat in my cheeks. Knowing Garth could hear every word didn't help. "Well, I'd better go, Mum wants me."

"Wait! Your message said you needed me to do something."

"It doesn't matter now. I'll be home soon."

"Okay, if you're sure. See you then."

"See you, Tanya."

"Well?" Garth said when I'd hung up.

"Ben's safe. We're meeting him tonight at The Dress-up Box."

"Too dangerous. Valeria will have it watched."

"Do you think she cares so much about one lowly herald?"

We stopped for a red light. He turned and gave me an incredulous look.

"No. I think she cares about finding Leandra. Micah will have told her by now what you did, even if Jason didn't, and she'll put two and two together. She's not the type to leave loose ends."

Great. Now I was a loose end to be snipped. I folded my arms and glared at the car in front of us.

"We have to hook up with Ben. Do you have any better ideas?"

He said nothing, his mouth a mulish line while he waited for the lights to change.

"No? Then we'll have to take our chances. If we find any watchers maybe you can eat their hearts."

His lips twitched. "You're never going to forgive me for that, are you?"

"Never."

CHAPTER TWENTY-EIGHT

We waited till full dark. Garth wanted to leave it longer, but impatience had its claws in me and I couldn't sit still. Dark was dark. Garth could turn wolf if we needed him to—it wasn't as if waiting longer made him any meaner.

We left the main road and turned into the industrial area where The Dress-up Box was located. During the day the smash repair joints, auto-electricians and kitchen showrooms bustled with cars and utes, trucks and work vans, but at night the place was a ghost town. Hectares of empty concrete and silent machinery sat behind locked gates.

We drove down streets containing nothing bigger than a discarded Coke can and cruised past the shop. The emptiness was reassuring. No one was parked out here waiting for us. Of course it also meant our lone white car, cruising down a dead-end street at nine o'clock at night, stood out like dogs' balls.

Garth turned at the top of the cul de sac and headed back to the shop. A streetlight lit the forecourt and driveway. No lights showed inside.

"Park round the back," I said.

"Just because we don't see anyone doesn't mean there's no one here," he grumbled, but he swung into the driveway and parked in the lot behind the shop. When he cut the engine the silence was unnerving. I shut the car door as quietly as I could, feeling conspicuous, and headed for the back door.

Garth followed, gaze darting this way and that, trying to see everything at once.

"Relax, would you? You're like a kid on speed."

"Last time I relaxed Leandra got herself killed."

Guess he had a point. But I suspected the real source of his nerves was something more basic. Wolves were pack animals. Though he'd been exiled from his natural pack, he'd formed a new one in Leandra's service. Now he was the only one left, without even Luce to guard his back. No wonder the poor bastard felt twitchy.

I unlocked the door and let us in. The click as it latched behind us sounded loud as a gunshot to my nervous ears. Garth's jumpiness was catching.

Only a faint glimmer from the streetlight out front penetrated the darkness. The racks of clothes formed strange hulking outlines. A hat rack by the counter loomed like some many-headed alien out of the gloom. The familiar smell of mothballs and old fabrics greeted me as I threaded my way through the racks toward the back corner where the Elizabethan selection hung. Garth ghosted along in my wake, his sneakers making no noise on the concrete floor.

I sensed his presence before I saw him but even so I squeaked as a shadow detached itself from the racks and stepped forward.

"Ben!"

I threw myself into his arms. He kissed me hungrily, and I lost myself in the fresh outdoor scent of him, the feel of his lips on mine. He was hard and warm and alive, and I never wanted to let him go.

Garth cleared his throat, and I loosened my grip, coming up for air at last. The faint light coming in the high back windows was enough for my dragon-enhanced vision to make out his beloved face.

"I missed you."

A smile warmed the dark pools of his eyes. "I missed you, too. Thank God you're okay—I've been so worried."

"Me too." I reared back and punched his chest. "What the hell were you thinking, jumping into the fight like that? What happened to 'self-defence only'?"

He caught my fist and kissed each finger in turn. "Seemed like a good idea at the time."

"I'm sorry we left you."

"I'm glad you did. Making a run for it was the smart option."

Only then did it occur to me that he knew nothing about the Leandra situation. He hadn't seen me compel Micah or been there for the confrontation with Jason. He was glad I'd escaped for my own sake.

"What happened after we left?"

The fond look on his face turned grim. "Valeria had a bunch of guys with guns stationed around the house to blast anyone who survived the fire."

I nodded. Micah had shot one of them during our escape.

"Once she was sure no one was coming out, they took off and left Jason to mop up. The leshies made that more of a challenge than he'd expected. It didn't take him long to decide it wasn't worth the effort, for a handful of leshies and a couple of strays. Probably figured there was no point taking a bullet and missing all the fun. The leshies were all for going after them—they're pretty fierce when their blood's up—but Luce managed to talk them out of it."

From the corner of my eye I saw Garth grin, and felt my own lips twitch in response. I knew her persuasion skills. Knock a few heads together first, talk later—that was Luce's style.

"I left then, and got as far as the roadblock. When I saw the car was gone I felt better—I knew you'd gotten away."

"Why didn't Luce go too?" Garth asked. "If Alicia's dead there's no reason for her to stay."

"Turns out Alicia's not dead. Adam was right—she made it to the bunker in time. She waited in there till Valeria had gone. I should have realised when the leshies didn't go to pieces. By the time I got back she'd appeared and started directing the clean-up operation."

Poor Adam. He would have been so happy to know she'd survived. I wondered if she even cared he was dead. Ungrateful cow.

"So where did you two get to?"

"We chased Nada to King's."

He stiffened in my arms. I peered through the dark, but his expression was unreadable. "King's?"

I couldn't hold it in any longer. I could feel a goofy smile nearly splitting my face in half. "You'll never *guess* what we discovered!"

His body was tense as a coiled spring. "What?"

"Lachie." My eyes stung with happy tears. "He's alive, Ben! Can you believe that? All this time, he's been alive!"

He looked down at me. No answering smile, no oh-my-God-I-can't-believe-it.

I searched his face, the moment stretching into eternity.

"You *knew*?"

I stepped back. Wire hangers squeaked on their racks as I brushed against the clothes. They shifted and rustled like a crowd of ghosts looking over my shoulder. Only Garth at my side felt solid in the dark.

"I'm so sorry, Kate."

"You're sorry?" My voice climbed an octave. "You're *sorry*? All this time—!" My mind couldn't encompass it. "You bastard."

I hauled off and slapped him as hard as I could.

No reaction.

I clenched my fists, trembling with rage. My eyes were dry; this fury ran too deep for tears. Leandra stirred inside. Another betrayal. She knew how that felt.

"I *am* sorry." He took a step toward me, anguish on his face. "Jason came to me that day and said he needed a favour. He said Lachie's life was in danger. Something terrible had happened and Leandra thought Jason had done it. She was going to kill Lachie to punish him."

"That's a lie." Leandra had never had any such intention.

"I know that now, but I didn't realise it till too late. He was my friend, or so I thought, and I knew how deadly dragon feuds could be. He told me he was going to fake Lachie's death so Leandra would have no reason to hunt for him, and he asked me to hide Lachie temporarily till he could take him to board at King's.

"When I found out he wasn't going to tell you the truth, I refused. You have to believe me, Kate. You don't know what this has been like for me."

What it had been like for *him*? As if I cared.

"That was when I discovered our friendship was only a pretence. He said if I didn't cooperate he would kill my sister's little girls. I had no choice."

"You could have told me." Garth's hands closed on my arms, holding me back. "How could you do that to me? And what about Lachie, shoved into a boarding school all alone?" He'd never spent a night away from home. My heart broke all over again to think what he must have suffered. "What did he think was going on?"

He looked away, unable to meet my eyes. "Jason told him you'd died."

I lunged at him, but Garth had me in an iron grip. My body flushed with a rage so great my skin could barely hold it in. My veins ran with pure fire.

"You *bastard*. All that time you pretended to be my friend, always there for me like some frigging guardian angel." And hadn't I fallen for it! Ben, my rock, my saviour. To think only moments ago I'd been all over him like a rash. He'd *slept* with me, knowing our whole relationship was a lie. I spat words as if each one were a drop of poison. I wished they were. "You hypocrite. You couldn't even give me one little hint?"

He spread his hands in a helpless gesture. "We're talking about Gemma and Ashlyn's lives here. He sent a wolf around to rip Gemma's pet rabbit apart. Left pieces scattered across their backyard. He said Gemma was next if you got suspicious. I couldn't risk it.

"All I could do was help you in any way I could. I know it's not enough, but I tried. I sent Lachie presents, and visited him every month, till Jason found out and ordered me to stay away."

He stepped closer, eyes pleading. "This has been a nightmare. Trust me, you can't hate me any more than I've hated myself. I'm glad you know. I'm so sorry, Kate."

I stared into his beautiful dark eyes, so sad and guilty, and I felt … nothing.

"It's not enough." I shook Garth's hands off. "I will never forgive you. I don't care if I never see you again."

I headed for the door, shoving clothes out of my way. My elbow knocked a wig from its stand and I kicked it under a clothes rack without breaking stride. Garth followed, his face carefully expressionless.

The shrill of his phone made us both jump. He dug it out and answered, then stopped me with a hand on my arm.

"It's for you." He held it out, face grim. "It's Nada."

Nada! I took the phone as if it might bite me, Ben forgotten.

"What do you want?"

I could hear her smirk down the telephone. "It's not what *I* want, sweetheart, it's what *you* want. I have something that belongs to you. What would you do to get it back?"

Leandra surged inside me, but I knew she didn't mean the channel stone.

"Is he there? Let me speak to him!"

"Uh-uh, not so fast. You can chat all you want in person, after you turn yourself in."

"Turn myself in to you?" I forced a contemptuous tone, though my heart began to pound and the shadows crowded in on me. "Why would I do that?"

"Because if you don't, your little boy is dead."

CHAPTER TWENTY-NINE

"I still think I should come with you."

Garth didn't have to add that he thought I was mad; I knew him well enough by now. A muscle jumped in his jaw; his big hands clenched the cracked steering wheel so tight his knuckles were white.

He was probably right too, but I was out of options. I watched the crowds thronging the streets, some dressed to the nines, others sporting crazy hats or face paint. A light drizzle did nothing to dampen their enthusiasm. It was New Year's Eve, and they'd come to party.

The car inched along George Street. It was eleven-thirty, and the drunks were already out, staggering and swearing their way along the footpaths and sometimes weaving erratically among the traffic. Many of them had probably been drinking all day. Alcohol was banned in the areas around the Opera House and the Domain but everywhere else was a free-for-all, and even in the patrolled areas there were ways to get around the ban if you were determined enough.

My destination was the Toaster, a steel-and-glass blot on the landscape that hulked behind the beautiful sails of the Opera House. A very expensive blot. Still, position is everything in real estate. It was the place to be for a ringside seat to the fireworks on the harbour. Valeria, of course, had a penthouse suite. And tonight, it was the place *I* had to be to stop Nada carrying out her threat.

"Don't these people have somewhere else to go?"

Werewolves generally didn't do well with crowds. I didn't care much for them myself when they made our progress so slow. I checked my watch again. 11:35.

"It'd be faster to walk." I got out at the next set of lights. Garth gave me a hopeful look, twitchy as a dog told to stay.

"Are you sure—?"

"She said to come alone. I'm not doing anything to upset her." At least not yet.

I strode off into the crowd with a confidence I didn't feel. Garth thought the plan was dodgy. Hell, *I* thought the plan was dodgy, but it was the best I could come up with. Letting Leandra out to play was a risk. More than a risk: I felt ill just thinking about it. But Lachie was in danger, and Leandra was my only weapon.

Garth called that madness; I called it being a mother.

The crowds packed in tight around the Quay: anywhere with a harbour view pulsed with wall-to-wall people. I saw party hats and feathers, and everything from evening wear to T-shirts and bare feet. I gathered invitations and suggestions from all sides, some ruder than others. Everyone was out for a good time, but there were just so many people. I threaded my way through, past the ferry terminals, the ice cream vendors and the inevitable buskers. Pushing against the human tide, I could see my destination, its steel and glass hulking above the crowds, but couldn't seem to get any closer, like one of those dreams where you keep running but never move from the spot.

Overhead a train rattled into Circular Quay station, hardly noticeable above the roar of the crowds and three or four competing sources of music. Barges were moored in the harbour, floating platforms for the fireworks. When the light show started, the massive speakers around the foreshore would pump out a matching soundtrack. I hadn't been for years; the crowds and the heat always gave me a headache, and Lachie and I liked to curl up on the couch together and watch it all on TV instead. Much more comfortable, and a better view.

Plus you didn't get jostled by drunken idiots all the time. I pushed on, fighting my way through the crowd.

It was nearly 11:45 by the time I made it to the Toaster, and then I had to wait while the building security checked their lists for my name. The concierge looked nervous, as well he might, with hordes of drunken revellers outside his door. I swallowed hard and tried to hide my own nerves.

The lift pinged and three shifters stepped out, all tall unsmiling men dressed in suits. One was a werewolf and the other two looked like goblins from their auras. Maybe I should have been flattered Nada was being so cautious, but I'd been hoping for a smaller escort. One of the goblins patted me down for hidden weapons, then gestured me into the lift. God knows what the concierge thought of that. None of them spoke.

The lift was spacious, and they gave me plenty of room. The young werewolf pressed the button for their level and the doors slid shut, reflecting our strained faces back at us in the polished steel surface. The floor beneath my feet began to vibrate as the lift lurched into motion. The werewolf seemed particularly jumpy, so I chose him.

I felt that weird internal pressure I'd come to associate with Leandra's attempts to take charge, and for once I didn't fight it. She couldn't care less what happened to Lachie; the only person who mattered to Leandra was Leandra. But for now that meant our goals were aligned. She wanted the stone—and I wanted the power to turn this werewolf to my will as she'd done with Micah.

"What's your name?" I asked him.

"Quiet," said one of the goblins, but the damage was done. The young wolf automatically looked at me when I spoke, and I caught his gaze.

He had no chance. The battle for his will was over before he even knew it had begun.

"Mistress," he breathed.

The goblins' heads twitched round. Too slow.

"Kill them."

He leapt for the throat of the nearest, face lengthening into a snout that sprouted fearsome canines. I turned on the other as he whipped a gun from under his jacket. His first shot went wide as I cannoned into him, grabbing at his arm. It sounded like the end of the world in the confined space. One mirrored wall shattered, and pieces of glass rained down on us.

The wolf snarled and the other goblin screamed in pure terror as he struggled to hold those jaws away from his throat. They thrashed wildly in the confined space. Ninety kilos of wolf slammed into my legs and I went down, losing my grip on the gunman's arm.

The gun blasted again and the wolf yelped and fell still. The first goblin lay under it, struggling for air and trying to hold the pieces of his throat together. Every breath made a nasty burbling sound. The goblin with the gun clambered to his feet and trained it on me with a shaking hand.

"Get up." His eyes were wild, his aura roiling like a storm cloud. "And I swear to all the gods if you open your mouth I'll put a bullet through your brain, whatever Valeria says."

I climbed to my feet and picked a sliver of glass out of my forearm. Blood welled slowly in the gash. I clenched my other hand around it, my head throbbing with a fury I dared not give voice to, not with a gun trained on me. Too smart to be caught like his colleague, the gunman watched my face but made sure not to meet my eyes.

Damn Valeria and her paranoia. Two I could have handled, but three was too much. Why hadn't I brought my own werewolf to the party to even things up? Just because the stupid human female was worried about her brat. Her love and fear swelled like a tidal wave inside, threatening to overwhelm me. I couldn't allow myself to be tainted by her human sensibilities. More than likely the child was dead already, and *my* hopes and *my* safety had been put at risk for nothing.

The lift chimed as we reached the highest floor. The goblin stumbled out backwards as the doors opened behind him, never taking his eyes—or his gun—off me. I stepped over the bodies and followed him. The werewolf began morphing back to human form, with the usual disgusting sound effects. With a bit of luck the compulsion might survive the change.

We entered a marble vestibule which laboured under an abundance of gilt. Gilt on the massive mirror facing the lift, gilt on all the picture frames, even on the edges of a marble hall table that supported an enormous vase of flowers. The mirror caught my expression of distaste as I surveyed it. All it needed was some red velvet and we could have been in a bordello.

"What the—?"

Three other shifters came to horrified attention as they took in the scene in the lift, and the vestibule abruptly filled with people.

Two enormous men who surely had troll blood took my arms and a solid wall of bodies formed up around me. They marched me toward double doors with yet more gilt decorating the panelling. No second prize for guessing who waited on the other side. I lifted my chin.

Valeria may have won this round, but I wasn't done yet. My channel stone was so close I could almost smell it.

CHAPTER THIRTY

We entered an enormous room, decorated in a way that screamed *I have more money than taste,* if the gilt-infested foyer hadn't already delivered that message loud and clear. Overstuffed white lounges hulked like herds of albino elephants by the floor-to-ceiling windows, and pale marble columns rose from the snow-white carpet. In fact, pretty much everything was white, and preferably with added marble. By day the effect must be blinding, with the sun streaming in those enormous windows. At the moment the view of the sparkling night city outside was spectacular.

The Harbour Bridge glowed softly, its steel arch flung across the water like some giant Meccano set. A myriad boats bobbed on the water around it, all showing their own lights, while the great white sails of the Opera House bulked in the foreground. Below, people swarmed the horseshoe of Circular Quay, jostling for the best position to see the coming fireworks. From here they looked like a pulsing carpet of ants.

Valeria lounged on one of the white leather monstrosities. She wore a long strapless evening gown, also white, with her blonde hair cascading over one bare shoulder. It reminded me of the ridiculous Grecian thing she'd worn at the bushfire. That had been white, too. Someone must have once told her it brought out her tan.

Nada sat opposite Valeria, all in black, her dark hair pulled back in a severe bun. If they had a few more people they could have gotten a job as a chess set.

"Have a seat," said Valeria, gesturing me to the place beside Nada. "We're just waiting for the rest of our happy band to arrive."

Lachie? My heart leapt and I shoved Leandra out of the driver's seat with a wave of maternal longing mixed with terror.

"Drink?" Valeria offered.

"No thanks." I wasn't falling for that one again. The leather squeaked as I shifted as far from Nada as possible.

"Suit yourself." She sipped champagne, probably something French and expensive, and watched me with a self-satisfied smile.

"Something amusing you?" I sat back, feigning relaxation, though I felt wound so tight I might fly apart any second.

"Several somethings, in fact. Ah, here he is." She set her glass down with a tiny clink as the door opened. "Jason, so good of you to join us. And look, I've invited an old friend."

Jason stopped in the doorway, eyes darting between the three of us as if trying to assess the threat. Valeria's smug smile widened at his obvious discomfort, and Nada looked like a little kid on Christmas morning. Vultures, the pair of them.

"She's no friend of mine." Jason strolled over and perched on the arm of the chair next to Valeria's. "She'd happily kill me if she thought she'd get away with it."

Typical Jason dramatics, though it was no overstatement as far as Leandra was concerned. Her anger and hatred at being so close to her murderer nearly unseated me, and a brief battle raged between us for control.

"So sad how many modern marriages end that way," Valeria mused, "with love turning to hate. Why does she feel like that, would you say?"

Jason must know where this was heading, but he played along, choosing his words with care. "She holds me responsible for the death of our child."

"But he's not dead at all, is he?" said Nada, unable to contain her glee a moment longer.

Valeria shot her a look of pure venom. She'd obviously been enjoying watching Jason squirm on the end of her hook.

"No, he's not." He squared his shoulders and challenged Valeria directly. "What of it?"

"What of it?" She took another sip of champagne. "It's a matter of trust, you see. You've been with us half a year, and in all that time you never once mentioned the child was not, in fact, dead. You can imagine my distress at having to find out from someone else that my most trusted lieutenant was keeping secrets from me."

She didn't look distressed. She gave every appearance of a woman enjoying herself immensely. But then, she always did enjoy watching other people suffer, even as a child, if the reports were to be believed.

"I went through your bank records," Nada said, "and found these regular payments to your herald friend. I knew you weren't giving him *that* much work. So I got into his account, too, and lo and behold! the exact same sums were being transferred to a private boys' school. A very expensive boarding school—and yet the herald has no sons. Who could they possibly be for?"

She gave him a look of mock confusion. Smug bitch. I'd like to punch her in the face. Judging by Jason's expression, he felt the same way.

"I wasn't hiding him from *you*," he said to Valeria. "I was trying to keep him safe from Leandra. I knew leaving her for you would make Lachie a target. She wouldn't stop trying to kill him unless she thought he was already dead."

Valeria pouted. "I'm hurt that you didn't think you could trust me to keep your little secret."

"I didn't want rumours getting back to Leandra. It was better if no one knew."

But someone else must have known—the goblin who'd created the changeling. It suddenly occurred to me to wonder what had become of him or her. Nothing good, I bet. Ben was lucky he'd still been useful to Jason, or he might have been in danger himself. Not that I cared what happened to that jerk, of course.

"And yet Leandra has been dead for days. Did it somehow slip your mind?"

"I meant to tell you, of course. There just hasn't been an opportunity. We've had more important things going on."

"You told *her*." Nada indicated me with a contemptuous tilt of her chin. "You sent her running to King's to try and stop me."

"In fact she's been in on it the whole time, hasn't she?" Valeria abandoned her languid pose. She set her glass down with a force that threatened to shatter it against the marble tabletop. "First she turns up at Leandra's place and cuts out her channel stone—funny that, I thought you said you'd poisoned her. She's there again at Alicia's, leading Alicia's troops against me." That seemed a rather generous interpretation of my role. "And then she scuttles off to King's to do your bidding."

She fixed him with an icy stare. "None of these seem like the acts of a woman who'd like to kill you."

Outside thousands of voices roared and a blast of music split the air. Midnight. The night sky lit up with colour as the first of the fireworks exploded. All around the foreshores a thousand tiny white lights flashed as people tried to take photos of the show.

"She's a herald," Jason protested. "It's sheer coincidence she was at Leandra's. And then Nada nearly screwed everything up by kidnapping her and dragging her and that spitfire Luce into it."

Valeria laughed. Red and orange fireworks exploded behind her head like a fiery crown. "A coincidence? Really, Jason, you'll have to do better than that. She cut Leandra's channel stone out. And as a result, unless I'm much mistaken, my dear sister has taken up residence inside her."

She turned the glare on me. Damn. I'd been hoping she wouldn't notice the aura. That was the risk of letting Leandra take charge. That tell-tale glow appeared every time she did. Outside the crowd roared their appreciation as the music switched to a thumping rock beat.

"You always did like to experiment, didn't you, Leandra?"

"My name's Kate."

"I don't quite understand how you did it, but I gather it's something to do with this." She opened one hand and showed me the channel stone. My pulse started to race. "Ah. You'd like that, wouldn't you? I wonder what happens if I destroy it? Shall we find out?"

A timid knock interrupted her. The young werewolf from the lift entered, hunched over submissively. He'd obviously changed clothes. Apart from a certain wildness to the eyes, nothing suggested how badly he'd been hurt just a short time before. The same probably couldn't be said for the unfortunate goblin he'd attacked.

"I thought I said we were not to be interrupted," Valeria snapped. "What do you want?"

He bowed deeply, bent almost double in his efforts to placate her. "A herald, mistress, with an urgent message."

She waved impatiently. "Give it to me, then."

"From royalty, my lady."

Which meant it had to be delivered by the herald's own hand. Must be from Elizabeth. I'd long suspected her of actively aiding Valeria in the proving. Probably not good news for me.

The herald entered, an older man with an unflattering grey moustache. Why did men insist on growing facial hair as soon as it started thinning on top? To prove they still could? He was rather stooped now but he must have been about Ben's height in his youth.

Hang on … I looked closer. It *was* Ben. He bowed to Valeria and showed his Hermes charm, as protocol required. Then he gave her an envelope sealed with red wax. As soon as she took it he bowed again and withdrew. He didn't look at me, and I made sure not to look at him again either. I might be mad at him but that didn't mean I wanted to see him cut down in front of me. What the hell was he doing? It couldn't possibly be a genuine message, could it? Coming here was a terrible risk. Valeria would be within her rights to destroy any herald found to be tampering with—or, God forbid, making up—messages.

But apparently the message was genuine. Valeria slit the envelope and pulled out a single dragon scale, gleaming silver. No mistaking one of those. And it was snapped clean in half.

Well, well, well. Alicia must have found her courage after all.

Valeria leapt to her feet, face livid. A broken scale was a death threat. Guess she didn't like being on the receiving end for a change. Lord knows she'd dished plenty of them out. Even I'd received one, though it had taken Jason six months to catch me off-guard enough to make good on it.

"Alicia is *alive?*" she roared, and flung the pieces of scale to the floor, where they winked with reflected light from the fireworks.

Outside the music thundered to a crescendo and the night exploded with light in all the colours of the rainbow. Rivers of white light began to pour from the deck of the Harbour Bridge, a foaming waterfall of fire.

Things were heating up in here, too. Valeria hurled her champagne at a marble pillar. The shattering of glass brought the timid werewolf bobbing back into the room, but when he saw his mistress's face he decided the clean-up could wait till later.

She whirled on Jason. "This is all your fault! They'd both be dead by now, and I'd be heir, if it weren't for your meddling."

Jason wiped a drop of her spit from his face. She might be a queen's daughter, but he was old and not easily cowed. "You've been listening to Nada's poison too long. I've been nothing but loyal to you since I left Leandra."

She laughed, a brittle sound nearly lost in the noise of cheering from outside as the last of the fireworks exploded like gunfire across the sky.

"You're such a bad liar. You could at least come up with something convincing instead of bleating about loyalty. You don't even know the meaning of the word."

That was rich. Pot, meet kettle. I glanced around, trying to be discreet about it. How fast could I make it to the door? They were all distracted. Even Nada seemed to have forgotten me. Her face was alight with the excitement of seeing her arch-enemy taken down.

Maybe I could lock them in and compel the young werewolf to help me. I only needed a few moments to find

Lachie and make a break for it. We could easily lose ourselves in the crowds outside.

Valeria was right up in his face, spitting her words at him. "What was the plan, Jason? Did you think you could set yourself up as a *king* with this abomination? You're mad. No one would accept this half-human thing as their queen, especially not with you behind the throne pulling the puppet strings."

All eyes turned to me. Just as I was about to make a run for it, too.

"Interesting theory," I said. I guess it made sense, given the facts available to her. Too bad for Jason she didn't have them all.

"Preposterous theory, more like," he objected. "Valeria, you are my queen. I serve you alone. Why do you listen to this griffin?" If looks could kill, Nada would have dropped dead right then. "She has her own agenda. She's been trying to turn you against me since the moment I arrived."

Nada leapt up too, and they faced each other in a tense triangle. "Don't blame me for your troubles. You've brought them all on yourself."

Jason lunged, hands stretching and reforming as he reached for her, and they went down across the coffee table in a fighting, spitting heap.

"Stop!" Valeria shouted.

They both ignored her, and she leapt out of the way. Jason had massive claws where his fingers had been, like some nightmarish Wolverine. Changing only part of the body to trueshape was a skill that normally took decades to master.

Valeria wasn't old enough. All she could do was holler impotently for back-up as the combatants crunched through broken glass and shattered ornaments.

Now was my chance. I could grab Lachie while they were all distracted.

I was only halfway to the door when it burst open and Luce and Garth and a crowd of other half-remembered faces poured into the room.

Valeria shrieked in fury and knocked Garth flying into the nearest pillar. If she couldn't perform Jason's fancy tricks, at least she had her dragon strength. Something else went flying too as she swung, and I hesitated, senses screaming. The channel stone!

Valeria slipped out the door and I fought to follow her, but Leandra was too strong. She dragged us toward the damn stone. Relief sang through me as I scooped it off the floor, even as another part of me clamoured for Lachie.

When I looked up Valeria was gone, and three of her goblins were holding the door against Luce, guarding their mistress's escape. What was going on? How could Luce be here? She took one out with a flying kick to the head as I watched. I cast a wild look around; Garth swayed on hands and knees, shaking his head. Looked like his thick skull hadn't suffered too much damage. Jason was rising from Nada's body, and that was one griffin who'd never fly again. They might never get the bloodstains out of the white carpet.

His claws were still out. Definitely time to leave. I clenched the stone in my fist, ignoring the urge to swallow the damn thing again. That was just Leandra talking, and I wasn't giving her any ammunition to use against me.

Where had Valeria gone? I was terrified I knew the answer. I bulled my way past the last goblin, leaving Luce to finish him off, and hesitated in the vestibule. Left or right?

Left. "Lachie! Where are you?"

I hurled doors open all down the corridor. I found a wine cellar, a billiard room, and a kitchen that could have featured in a magazine except for the dead werewolf sprawled on the floor. It was the nervous young one. Guess he'd been right to be scared. Yet more rooms—two bathrooms and a study—but no Lachie.

I turned back and heard the ping of the lift arriving. I rounded the corner in time to see Valeria disappear into it carrying a familiar curly-haired figure, Jason right behind her.

"Lachie!" I pounded down the corridor, but I wasn't fast enough.

He looked up and saw me.

"Mummy!" he yelled, and then the doors closed on his frightened little face.

CHAPTER THIRTY-ONE

We searched outside in vain: even the noses of the full Sydney werewolf pack couldn't have found Valeria in the heaving crowds. Garth alone had no chance. Luce shoved people out of the way with a force that betrayed her fury that Valeria and Jason had both escaped. One look at her face and no one objected to being shoved.

"It's taken me all this time to persuade Alicia to move. She might be a dragon but she has the soul of a mouse. If I tell her Valeria's still on the loose now she'll lose her nerve completely."

"Surely not. She must realise she only has to kill Valeria now to win." I only half listened as my eyes scanned the crowds for a mad blonde and a beloved curly head.

"But you—" Garth began.

I cut him off with a curt shake of the head. Luce didn't know about the Leandra situation, and with her bound to Alicia now, that was probably for the best. I had my hands full enough with Leandra. I'd thought getting the damned channel stone would have quieted her, but she raged inside me for release. I could barely think.

"Best if we finish the job quickly," Luce said, "and present her with a fait accompli. Where's Ben?"

I gritted my teeth. This would be so much easier if Leandra would shut the hell up. "Why did you have to involve him?"

"How else were we going to get inside? Valeria would be chewing on your sorry ass by now if I hadn't. Besides, he offered."

"This is hopeless." On that at least Leandra and I could agree. The crowds surged in full party mode and a sick panicky feeling bubbled in my stomach. The noise was phenomenal. The longer it took to find Lachie, the more time my brute of a sister had to hurt him. *Her* brute of a sister. God, I hardly knew who I was any more. "We'll never find them like this."

"What do you suggest?" Luce had to shout to be heard over the thumping music and the cries of raucous drunks.

"Let's head for the place at Mosman."

Valeria could have any number of safe houses elsewhere, but Mosman lay just across the harbour. In her shoes I'd be heading for the closest bolt-hole to regroup.

Luce signalled the nearest leshy, and the rest of the group struggled through the crowd to join us. I stayed close to Garth and did my best to ignore Ben, who watched me but didn't try to say anything. Just as well or I would have snapped his head off. I had no time for him now.

"The bridge is shut," Luce shouted. "We'll have to take the tunnel."

That was the drawback to living in one of the world's most beautiful harbour cities—there were only a couple of options for getting across all that water, and the main one, the famous "coat hanger" bridge, was closed to traffic on New Year's Eve. The pyrotechnics people used it to launch the fireworks, and they didn't want members of the public messing with their big display. Water taxis and ferries were out too. A nautical no-go zone extended all around the fireworks barges.

The harbour tunnel burrowed under all those megalitres of water and popped up again in North Sydney. A triumph of modern engineering that might save Lachie's life.

"Sure. Let's go."

It took a while to get back to the cars, but much, much longer to get across town, past all the road closures and diversions, dodging drunken partygoers all the way. Time was tick-tick-ticking away, and my anxiety levels were through the roof before we struggled onto the tunnel approach, only to find a solid line of traffic also trying to make its way out of the clogged city. It was nearly two o'clock in the morning before we parked in a quiet back street in Mosman and made the final approach on foot.

Completely unselfconscious, Luce stepped neatly out of her black T-shirt and pants and handed them to Garth. She shimmered and blurred, and her beautiful trueshape emerged. Her change was like a dragon transformation, clean and quick, not the wince-inducing trauma of a werewolf metamorphosis.

Of course she was much smaller than a dragon, being only the same mass as in her human form, and Luce was no giant. But you could see the relationship in the delicate tracery of her wings and her two taloned feet. Wyverns, unlike dragons, had no front legs and walked upright. Her tail was smaller in proportion to the rest of her body than a dragon's, so there was something almost kangaroo-like in her shape, though no kangaroo I'd ever seen had such wicked teeth, or a barbed tail.

Of course she risked death for taking trueshape where any passing human could see, but even if I'd been inclined to argue she wouldn't have listened. She was Alicia's now, and her every action was in service to Alicia's cause. She leapt into the air and the leshies gathered around, some going through transformations of their own. In for a penny, in for a pound, I guess. If it worked and Alicia became heir as a result she might consider the death of a few supporters an acceptable price. As far as I was concerned, no price was too high to save Lachie. *Hang on, baby, I'm coming.*

A cry, quickly choked off, was the only evidence of Luce's activities on the other side of the wall until the gates swung open and a small naked woman beckoned us through.

"I miss having hands," she muttered as she reclaimed her clothes from Garth.

The leshies streamed into the courtyard and we followed them in past two guards stretched out on the gravel, their faces swollen and contorted. Wyverns could breathe a poisonous mist toxic enough to take out a dozen humans at close quarters.

Halfway across, a bank of floodlights came on, exposing us all.

"Thought it was too easy," Garth muttered.

We hit the deck as three goblins opened fire from the corner of the house. Luce returned fire and they ducked back behind the building. A couple of leshies sprinted after them. Goblin magic was a long and complicated process, not much use in a fight. Leshies, on the other hand, could cause some real damage. If goblins were the best she could do, things were looking up.

A sudden stinging blow to my shoulder spun me around. Jason stood framed in the gateway behind us, pistol levelled at me. Okay, she had more than goblins. Damn. I clutched my shoulder and felt blood welling between my fingers. The bastard had shot me. He was obviously no marksman, though, to manage only a flesh wound at that range. I could be thankful for small mercies.

An overwhelming urge to swallow the channel stone again washed over me as I stared at Jason—Leandra, struggling for control.

"Forget it," I muttered, fighting back hard. "Not happening."

Physically the stone rode in my back pocket, but it burned like a flaming sun in my consciousness. She'd been pushing me to swallow the damn thing ever since we'd got it back. Maybe I'd heal faster if I did, but I wasn't stupid. Once that stone was part of me again, she'd win the battle for my body, and that would be the end of Kate O'Connor. And now was *really* not the time. Couldn't she see I was busy? Dammit, was he going to shoot again or not?

A familiar black shape flashed past and lunged at his gun arm, deciding the issue. Jason got off another shot but it went wide, cracking against the stone fountain in the centre of the courtyard. Then he backhanded Garth, who yelped and tumbled aside, snarling. I leapt into motion, though my arm throbbed and I felt sick with shock. My teacher would have been proud of my snap kick. A satisfying crack sounded as my foot connected with his hand, and the gun went spinning into the shadows by the wall.

I fell back, narrowly avoiding the monstrous talons suddenly sprouting from his uninjured hand. That Wolverine thing was some party trick. I danced around, trying to get in another kick without being skewered. From the corner of my eye I saw Garth climb to his feet and shake his body from nose to tail the way dogs do. He was clearly hurt but still spoiling for a fight. All the hatred he'd had for me, when he thought I'd killed Leandra, was now added to Jason's account with interest. His yellow eyes gleamed with deadly intent as he prowled closer.

I circled around so Jason's back was to the werewolf, giving me a brief glimpse of the house and the bodies struggling in the courtyard. Looked like we were winning. Garth gathered himself to spring.

Valeria's voice rang out above the fighting, loaded with command. "Stop!"

Even I felt the urge to obey. She stood on the huge balcony atop the portico, Lachie still and passive beside her. My heart leapt into my throat, and I forgot the pain in my arm, forgot everything at the sight of him.

Valeria spoke directly to me. "Call off your friends or I'll kill the boy."

Luce raised an eyebrow at me, as if there were any doubt about my response. I just hoped she'd follow my lead. My heart pounded with fear as I gazed up at him. He stood so calmly she must have enthralled him. Fury boiled through me. How dare she enthral my son like a common slave?

"Go ahead," said a new voice. "He means nothing to me."

I whirled around. Alicia! She strode in, flanked by half a dozen willowy leshies, and all hell broke loose.

"No!" I screamed, but no one heard as chaos erupted.

In an instant the leshies banded together and had the courtyard shaking as if the end of the world had come. The portico bucked wildly and Valeria staggered. She dragged Lachie back from the edge, screaming orders at her remaining goblins, who opened fire on the leshies. But with the ground heaving beneath their feet, their shots went wide.

I staggered too, dizzy with pain and loss of blood. My arm ran red, and blood dripped from my fingers to the ground. Jason seized the chance to come at me again, and I barely dodged a swipe from those massive claws.

"Don't you care that that bitch is threatening to kill your son?" I screamed at him.

"That bitch is my queen," he said, panting, "and Leandra's head on a stick is the only way I can prove myself to her. If you'd just shut up and die I'd be up there with him."

He lunged, and this time I felt his claws rip through my breast. I fell back. God, the pain. I'd never felt anything like it. My chest burned with the fire of a thousand suns. I lay on my back trying to find the strength to get to my feet while the stars swam above me.

"Kate!" yelled Ben.

His voice sounded far away. I blinked, trying to clear my fogging vision. *The stone. Take the stone.* I suppose it was too much to hope the police might join the party, with all this gunfire. But the neighbours probably thought it was fireworks.

My hand inched toward my back pocket. It was the only thing that still worked—my legs refused to obey instructions. All I could do was watch as those claws slashed at me again.

Ben slammed into Jason at the last minute, knocking the killing blow aside, and they fell out of my vision. I heard snarling, which probably meant Garth had joined the fight. It seemed unimportant now. I lay there, gravel digging into my back, vision shrunk to a dark blur, and focused on my hand, forcing it to close around the channel stone. No other options. Leandra was Lachie's only chance.

Whatever it took. Lachie was all that mattered. My trembling arm inched its way up my body.

I'd tried, but even with enhanced strength and senses, I was still human. And human wasn't good enough to save Lachie. I'd give anything for him—everything I had left. The *only* thing I had left.

If Kate couldn't save him, then Kate was of no use. I needed Leandra now.

Working on instinct—mine or hers, I don't know—I pressed the stone into the gaping wound at my breast. Indescribable pain assaulted every nerve end, and my vision darkened ominously. Dammit, I couldn't afford to black out. I lay panting, the noise of the battle roaring around me, and felt the black stone burrow deeper into my flesh, like some hideous monster tick. There are some things no one should ever have to go through. My heart stuttered with agony and horror, and the world reeled away into darkness.

Barely moments had passed when I regained my senses. I could still hear Garth snarling, and the sounds of others fighting around me. Everything still hurt, but I could move again.

I clambered shakily to my feet. The biggest slash across my breast, the one the human had pushed the channel stone into, had stopped bleeding. Already it had begun to close up. I rolled my shoulder experimentally and found the pain much lessened. Excellent.

I turned and found Garth standing over the body of an unconscious human, growling at Jason. The traitor had his back to me. I landed such a kick on him it shattered his kneecap and slammed him into the brick wall ten feet away. Most satisfying. But it wouldn't stop him for long, so I looked around for a more serious weapon.

"Ben's hurt!" yelled Luce, coming to crouch beside the body Garth defended. I left her to deal with it. I'd spotted a long knife lying on the gravel, its blade bloody. Must have been Garth's. Werewolves loved knives. They were like extra-long claws. Left to choose for themselves, werewolves rarely carried guns; knives were the weapon of preference, at least until they decided trueshape was an even better option.

Feeling more myself with every passing moment, I snagged the knife then staggered as another tremor shook the courtyard. Two leshies had taken tree shape. They tore at the house with twiggy fingers, pulling great chunks of brickwork apart. The portico teetered on the edge of collapse.

Valeria screamed her defiance and shimmered into trueshape. The portico creaked alarmingly under the dragon's weight. The tree leshies flinched back and the ones on the ground scattered like a kicked ants' nest. They'd already experienced dragonfire, and they knew what was coming. Alicia's face was a study in horror and outrage. Valeria was pushing it now. Bad enough to take trueshape out in the bush, but in the heart of Sydney? The queen would not be impressed by this flagrant breach of the rules. Even if, as I suspected, Valeria was her favourite daughter.

The ground heaved as if another dragon stirred beneath it, the leshies uniting to throw up an earth wall as protection. Their activities were too much for the tottering portico. With a dragon above and juddering foundations below, it gave up the struggle and subsided in a thunder of falling masonry. I caught a glimpse of a little boy tumbling amid the dust and debris, and then Valeria launched herself with a thunderous clap of her wings and snatched him out of the air.

Something inside me clicked at the sight of that small body dangling helpless from her massive claws. The pandemonium in the courtyard faded to nothing and my world narrowed to that one child. That one beautiful, beloved child. I had never known such love was possible. Had any dragon? I forgot the leshies and their earthworks, Jason and Alicia, Garth and Luce. Friends and enemies alike, none of it mattered compared to the rage that streaked through me like wildfire. That was *my child.* She'd taken my baby and I'd move heaven and earth to get him back.

I felt a tugging sensation inside, familiar but unexpected. Was it still possible? I reached for union and felt a rush of welcome, of homecoming. Cries of delight and terror filled the air as the courtyard shrank around me.

My head level with the roof, I realised the courtyard hadn't changed. I had grown. I could see little Luce and Garth, now a naked man, jumping up and down and hugging each other as they shouted to me. I ignored them. Jason lay on the ruptured earth, dead or unconscious, and I lifted one great foot, momentarily distracted by the temptation to make sure of it.

Then I remembered my purpose and spread my wings instead, delighting in the strength I'd thought lost forever. I leapt skyward, feeling the familiar rush of freedom as I caught the wind.

CHAPTER THIRTY-TWO

Trueshape!

I trumpeted my joy to the sky. The stars wheeled above me as I beat upward, filled with renewed vigour. I had never thought to experience the joy of trueshape again.

Valeria climbed just ahead. She craned her long neck round, saw me on her tail and hissed her displeasure. She soared out over the harbour and I followed, gaining rapidly, delighting in the feel of the air rushing under my wings. Perhaps she wasn't really trying to outpace me.

She landed on the very apex of the Harbour Bridge, above the symbol the humans had lit for their celebration. It was a stylised dove, with a sprig of olive in its mouth, emblem of peace. Now a bird of a very different kind perched above it, her armoured tail lashing across the dove's face.

I circled in and landed some distance along from her, feeling a vibration in the steel beneath my claws as it took my weight.

"So you fly, too, abomination?" she snarled, her voice a deep rumble in her chest. "You are tainted with humanity, fit for nothing but death."

Lachie stirred, still clutched in her claws, and opened his eyes. He saw me and those eyes widened in terror, and he began to scream and struggle.

"Silence!" she hissed, and he burst into noisy tears.

She laid one wicked claw against his throat. "Such a tough decision. Should I cut his throat or just … discard him?"

Quick as thought, she flung him, and he cartwheeled screaming through the sky. I leapt after him and she lunged, trying to snag my wingtip with her teeth and bring me crashing into the bridge. But her jaws snapped on air as I hurtled after the falling child.

I caught him before he hit the water, cradling him in my claws as I pulled out of the dive and beat away. Above, Valeria stooped from the bridge and plummeted toward me. She had the advantage of height and speed, whereas I was desperate to protect the sobbing form in my claws. I couldn't fight; I could only hope to dodge her. Not a winning strategy.

I changed course abruptly and ducked under the bridge just as she would have seized me. I shot out the other side and pivoted in mid-air, dropping my precious bundle on the deck of the bridge, then darted away again. It was a risk, but I thought I knew Valeria well enough, and my hunch paid off. With her blood up, she wanted to sink her claws into me, feel my flesh rip and tear, and toying with Lachie couldn't provide the same satisfaction.

She surged after me, while I ducked and weaved, the nightlights of the city wheeling dizzily around us. I led her up and around the bridge, using its great steel network of girders as a shield, and she bellowed her frustration.

"Stay still and fight!" she roared, but I was no fool. She was bigger and older than me, and I had more to lose. I needed to find an advantage, and fast.

She banked over the arch of the bridge again, almost catching me. Her tail swiped the top of the dove as she passed and knocked it loose. It dangled drunkenly, its peace offering pointing straight down at the water far below.

Many pleasure craft still floated on the harbour. White flashes of light winked from them as their passengers tried to photograph the aerial display. Did they think we were part of the fireworks? The fools should be fleeing for their lives.

I skimmed low over the water, hoping the usual draconian dislike of cold water would keep her at a distance, but she dived on me. Her wings beat in my face as her hind feet clawed for my belly. She didn't bother turning her fire on me: in dragon form we were immune to it, and so the battle must be fought in more primitive style, with tooth and claw. I twisted away, barely avoiding them. I needed a miracle.

Something to give me an edge. Something like Jason in his human form with those wicked dragon claws like scythes. But he was old and skilled.

I doubled back and beat upward, trying to get above my rival. Wasn't I skilled too? I'd experimented with form more than any other dragon I knew. I'd shrunk myself down to save Luce and destroyed a full company of goblins. And of course

I'd saved myself with the ultimate throw of the dice when I'd transferred to a human body. No one had ever attempted that before.

I dropped down toward the waves again, tasting their salt in the air. Time for one last gamble. I let my tail dangle in the water to hide what I was doing, leaving a plume of spray behind me. Then I focused my will on what I wanted, reforming and shaping.

Valeria dropped like a stone, ready to pound me into the sea. As her claws reached for me I flicked my tail up again. It was shorter now, but the spike on its end was the length of a man and wickedly curved.

I whipped it up and plunged it into Valeria's exposed breast, skewering her through the heart. Obliterating that vital organ completely.

Smacking into the water felt like hitting concrete, and our entwined bodies plunged deep. Cold water filled my nostrils. I could see nothing in the black depths. Panicked, I struggled to free myself from Valeria's entangling weight. Which way was up? I followed the stream of bubbles and limped for the surface, breaking through with a great gasping relief. Dragons were not meant for swimming.

The water around me roiled with the waves of our impact. The air rang with shouts and screams from the distant boats, but none dared approach. I waited, bobbing on the water like a vast ugly duckling, until a still blonde figure broke the surface. Valeria. Definitely dead.

Taking off from the water proved impossible, though I flailed around in a brave attempt. Eventually I gave in and paddled to shore at the base of the bridge's northern end, coming up into a park at Milson's Point littered with drunks. Some were asleep; the ones that weren't scattered, screaming, as I flexed my wings.

I flew up to where I'd left Lachie. He was gone, and my heart did a little flip of dismay before I spotted him hiding behind a lane barrier. Poor kid. Time for something a little less terrifying.

I relinquished my trueshape. *Her* trueshape? *Our* trueshape? I shook my head, too tired and worn to think about it. I still felt like Kate, but I felt like Leandra too, as if our personalities had given up fighting and fused together.

I stood on the Harbour Bridge, a woman who could turn into a dragon, buck naked, alone among the wide empty lanes and towering scaffolding except for my son, a boy who'd died months ago. It didn't come much crazier than that. I laughed, a little burble of sheer happiness, and Lachie peeped out, his eyes like saucers.

"*Mum?*"

I held out my arms. "It's okay, Monster. You can come out now."

He ran to me and I crushed him tight, face buried in his hair, breathing in his precious Lachie smell. My eyes prickled with tears.

"I thought you were dead!" he sobbed.

"I know. I thought you were too. It was all a big mistake." One that would involve some tricky explanations eventually, but for now it was enough to hold him and feel the truth of his existence.

When the sobs had wound down into hiccups he wriggled uncomfortably. "Mum, you're squishing me."

"Sorry."

I loosened my hold and he looked up, eyes wide in his little pointed face. "Are you a dragon now?"

I could hardly deny it when he'd just seen me change. "'Fraid so."

"Cool," he breathed.

Typical. I grinned and stood up, still keeping a tight grip on his hand.

"Come on, we'd better get out of here."

"Maybe we should find you some clothes first."

Good point. We strolled along the bridge hand in hand, my feet leaving damp footprints on the road surface. At the northern end we found a terrified group huddled behind a truck. Must be the fireworks crew.

"Who *are* you?" one of them asked as I approached. He was as tall as Ben, but about twice as wide.

"I'm Kate," I said cheerfully, turning my will on him, "and you'd love to give me your T-shirt."

He agreed he would, and I was soon covered to the knees in a Black Sabbath T-shirt the size of a small tent. We left them gawking after us and slipped past the police barriers and down the steps to Milson's Point. There were a lot of very excited people there, shouting about dragons and fireworks and waving at the bridge, but none of them paid us much attention. I guess we didn't look too threatening—a barefoot mum and her tired little boy—and I was more than happy to be overlooked. I'd had enough excitement already to last a year, and the year was barely three hours old.

I sank down on the lawn and put an arm around Lachie, too tired to do anything more challenging than sit and wiggle my toes in the cool grass. Sooner or later Garth would turn up. Until then I could sit here enjoying the view of the twinkling city lights, with my boy tucked safe and warm against me. Heaven.

He rested his curly brown head on my shoulder in a long contented silence. I thought he'd gone to sleep, but then a question of burning importance obviously occurred to him.

He sat up. "Mum, have you still got all my Lego?"

***

More than an hour passed before Garth showed, hulking across the grass with his usual surly frown. His face brightened when he saw us among the drunks and the all-night party crowd, Lachie curled up asleep with his head pillowed in my lap.

"You did it." He squatted on his heels beside me. The most genuine smile I'd ever seen on his face appeared as one big hand reached out to rest lightly on Lachie's hair.

"Where's Luce?"

The smile faded. "Stuck with Alicia."

I sighed. "I hoped someone would take Alicia out."

Too much to ask, I guess. It would have been the icing on the cake to have Luce free.

"Me too. Luce managed to look the other way when I left, but that was the most she could do. I figured you'd need some help."

"Thanks."

"At least Valeria went down." Garth's eyes lit with pleasure at the memory. If he'd had a tail right then it would have been waving jauntily in the air. "How'd you manage it? I thought you were a goner for sure."

"Thanks for the vote of confidence."

He had the grace to look a little abashed. I described the fight as we sat side by side, looking out across the dark water. A police launch still circled out there in the proscribed zone under the bridge. I'd watched them fish Valeria's naked body out some time ago, small and rather sad-looking in its broken human form, and seen the flashing lights of the ambulance when they'd brought it back to shore. Another New Year's Eve emergency, though a touch more exotic than the usual drunken antics. How the Emergency Services must hate New Year's Eve.

"I've brought the car round," said Garth. "We should probably go before Alicia works up the courage to come looking."

I nodded, though I hated to disturb my boy. He looked so peaceful.

"Let me," said Garth. He scooped him up in unexpectedly gentle arms. Lachie murmured something then settled again, his head nestled comfortably against the werewolf's massive pecs. Jason used to carry him in from the car like that, after a night out. Which reminded me …

"What happened to Jason?"

"Got away," Garth grunted in disgust.

Shame. I should have stomped him when I had the chance, but I'd had other things on my mind. Another time, perhaps. Nothing could dent my good mood tonight, not even Jason's survival. We picked our way past sleeping bodies, couples cuddled up on picnic rugs, and the odd still-raucous group.

"There was a bit of confusion after you took off. Still, it was worth it to see Alicia's face when she realised you were still in the game."

I wouldn't have minded seeing that myself. "A little upset, was she?"

"You could say that."

He led the way out of the park and up the street. I floated along at his elbow in an almost Zen-like state of happiness, snippets of memories and emotions from both my lives bubbling below the tranquil surface.

The inside of my head was a very weird place right now. Leandra's memories were as clear as my own, though I could no longer sense her lurking as a separate presence. Even some of my own memories looked different seen through the prism of Leandra's knowledge. I could find no division any more. I was us, and we were me—not quite Kate, and not exactly Leandra either. A new whole, bigger somehow than the sum of its parts.

Better? Who knew? Right now I didn't care. I reached out for at least the hundredth time to stroke my sleeping son's head. Happier? Absolutely.

We finally reached the car, and I sank into the back seat with a sigh of relief. It had been a long night.

"Where to?" Garth asked.

I shrugged. What did it matter? My world was right here.

"The ambos took Ben to Royal North Shore," he added, a little too casually.

Ben! He'd taken that slash Jason meant for me. How could I have forgotten? I sat up straighter, some of my euphoria slipping away.

"How bad is he?"

"He'll live." He laid Lachie gently in the back seat next to me and buckled him in. "Might have some impressive scars though."

I stroked Lachie's curls back from his forehead. He shifted in his sleep but didn't wake.

I had trouble remembering why I'd been so angry with Ben. I could hardly blame him for wanting to protect his nieces. Would I have done any differently if someone had threatened Lachie's life?

"His arm was pretty bad. Some gashes on the chest and shoulder too, but the arm was the worst."

"What are we waiting for, then?"

In the rear vision mirror I caught a glimpse of his smile.

The trip to Royal North Shore didn't take long, and we were soon striding into the emergency department. Garth carried Lachie, still sleeping, since I refused to be parted from him.

The place was jumping with people. Falls and brawls, all the fun of New Year's Eve, though I guess it was well and truly

New Year's Day now. The sun would be up in a couple of hours.

At reception a harried-looking nurse cast a professional eye over Lachie's still form.

"What happened?" she asked wearily.

"Oh!—nothing. He's fine. We're here about Ben Stevens. The ambulance brought him in a little while ago."

"You next of kin?"

I was about to say no, but I took in the crowded waiting room, and the exhaustion on the nurse's face, and thought better of it.

"I'm his sister."

"You'd better come in. You two can wait here."

"I have to bring my son," I said. "He'll be upset if he wakes and I'm not there." Not exactly true, but she didn't have to know that.

She looked about to make an issue of it, and I groped for my will, limp and exhausted as it was, wondering if I could even compel a kid to eat a chocolate at this point. But she must have decided she was too tired to bother, and led the way down a corridor depressingly similar to the last emergency room corridor I'd visited.

Only now, that remembered grief had no power to hurt me any more, for I could reach out and touch my son, sleeping in Garth's protective arms. The werewolf smiled at me as I stroked Lachie's head, as if he could tell what I was thinking.

There was some confusion finding Ben. It turned out he'd already left Emergency for the operating theatre, and an orderly had to be found to guide us through the echoing halls to the recovery room lounge.

We collapsed into the hard plastic chairs to wait. Garth looked exhausted. If he was anything like me he was probably aching all over, but he made no complaint. It was five o'clock in the morning and I'd flipped through every ancient magazine in the place before a nurse came out and told us Ben had recovered sufficiently to have a visitor. I picked up Lachie, who was awake and asking sleepily when we were going to have breakfast.

"No children," said the nurse.

"He'll be fine." I pinned her with a serious glare. I don't know if it was a compulsion or I just scared her, but she led the way through the swinging double doors.

Beeping machines lurked along the walls of the recovery room. Each bay had a hospital bed parked in it, with the occupant wired up to the machines, and nurses hurried between the beds. Someone got the all-clear to be released to the wards as we entered, and we stood aside to let the orderly wheel the bed past.

Ben lay in the far corner, propped up on pillows, his face nearly as pale as the bandages that swathed his whole right arm and stretched across his bare chest and shoulder. His free arm was hooked up to an IV drip, but he held it out to me all the same.

"You look like shit," I said, leaning in to kiss his cheek, now rough with stubble. His familiar woodsy scent was long gone, drowned out by blood and sweat and horrible antiseptic hospital smells. But he still felt like home. "How do you feel?"

"Like shit. Better now, though." His eyes rested on Lachie, suspiciously bright. "He's safe. You're both safe. Thank God."

"You missed all the excitement," I said, my own eyes welling up. It had been a rollercoaster of a day.

"I heard." He shifted uncomfortably, wincing as he moved his arm. "Someone said there were dragons fighting over the harbour. Or did I dream that part?"

"It's true." I looked round to see if anyone could hear us.

"She was really scary-looking," Lachie said, his dark eyes huge.

"She was?" Ben gave me an uncertain look. "Umm—how did you—?"

"Let's talk about it later."

"Okay." The drugs in his system made him more biddable than usual. Also a little spacey. He gave me a beatific smile. "I bet she made a beautiful dragon."

"What happened to your arm, Uncle Ben?"

"Aaah …" Daddy tried to kill Mummy and Uncle Ben got in the way? Stumped for an answer, Ben looked at me.

"We might save that for later too, when Uncle Ben's not so tired."

"Okay." He laid his head back on my shoulder.

Ben caught my hand in his. "It's good to see you. Both of you." His eyes searched my face. "I'm so sorry."

I squeezed his hand. "I know. I'm sorry too." For the things I'd called him, for the way I'd reacted. For the separate hells we'd both gone through in the past seven months.

"Are we … okay?"

There was a strange lightness in my heart, something I hadn't felt in so long I'd forgotten what it was like. I had my son back, I had a guy prepared to throw himself in front of a killing blow to save me—a guy who, even as beat up as he was, still looked pretty damn good with his shirt off.

The strange feeling was happiness. I reckoned I could get used to it.

"Oh, I think we're a little better than okay." I set Lachie gently on his feet, then leaned in and kissed Ben thoroughly, deep and long. Everyone said dragons had strong sexual appetites. As soon as those bandages came off, Mr Stevens would be finding out just how strong.

He grinned up at me. "Okaaay!"

THE END

Kate's story continues in *The Twiceborn Queen*. For updates on new releases, plus special deals and other book news, sign up for my newsletter by visiting my website, www.marinafinlayson.com.

Reviews and word of mouth are vital for any author's success. If you enjoyed *Twiceborn*, please take a moment to leave a short review where you bought it. Just a few words sharing your thoughts on the book would be extremely helpful in spreading the word to other readers (and this author would be immensely grateful!).

ALSO BY MARINA FINLAYSON

MAGIC'S RETURN SERIES
The Fairytale Curse
The Cauldron's Gift

THE PROVING SERIES
Moonborn
Twiceborn
The Twiceborn Queen
Twiceborn Endgame

SHADOWS OF THE IMMORTALS SERIES
Stolen Magic
Murdered Gods
Rivers of Hell
Hidden Goddess

For a full listing of books by Marina Finlayson, please visit the Books page on her website, www.marinafinlayson.com/books.

ACKNOWLEDGEMENTS

Thanks to my trusty team of beta readers: Mal, Peter, Geoff and Chris. Your help and encouragement was invaluable. Thanks also to my editor, Eliza Dee, and to my family for putting up with being ignored for long stretches of time.

ABOUT THE AUTHOR

Marina Finlayson is a reformed wedding organist who now writes fantasy. She is married and shares her Sydney home with three kids, a large collection of dragon statues and one very stupid dog with a death wish.

Her idea of heaven is lying in the bath with a cup of tea and a good book until she goes wrinkly.